D0407043

A VOICE FROM
THE FIELD

BY NEAL GRIFFIN

Benefit of the Doubt
A Voice from the Field

A VOICE FROM THE FIELD

NEAL GRIFFIN

A TOM DOHERTY ASSOCIATES BOOK
New York

This is a work of fiction. All of the characters, organizations, and events portrayed in this novel are either products of the author's imagination or are used fictitiously.

A VOICE FROM THE FIELD

A Forge Book
Published by Tom Doherty Associates, LLC
175 Fifth Avenue
New York, NY 10010

www.tor-forge.com

Forge® is a registered trademark of Tom Doherty Associates, LLC.

Library of Congress Cataloging-in-Publication Data

Names: Griffin, Neal C., author.
Title: A voice from the field / Neal Griffin.
Description: First Edition. | New York : Forge Books, 2016. | "A Tom Doherty Associates book."
Identifiers: LCCN 2015033359| ISBN 9780765338518 (hardcover) | ISBN 9781466839038 (e-book)
Subjects: LCSH: Human trafficking—Fiction. | Missing persons—Investigation—Fiction. | BISAC: FICTION / Thrillers. | GSAFD: Mystery fiction. | Suspense fiction.
Classification: LCC PS3607.R54845 V65 2016 | DDC 813/.6—dc23
LC record available at http://lccn.loc.gov/2015033359

Our books may be purchased in bulk for promotional, educational, or business use. Please contact your local bookseller or the Macmillan Corporate and Premium Sales Department at 1-800-221-7945, extension 5442, or by e-mail at MacmillanSpecialMarkets@macmillan.com.

First Edition: February 2016

Printed in the United States of America

0 9 8 7 6 5 4 3 2 1

To Olga Diaz

My wife and partner in life

ACKNOWLEDGMENTS

In my twenty-seventh year of police work, it's bittersweet to realize I'm much closer to the end of my watch than the beginning. With that in mind, I'd like to recognize the thousands of men and women I've had the honor to work with during my law enforcement career. Men who had much in common with Ben Sawyer; and women not unlike Tia Suarez. Cops who possess those attributes that can't be handed out by a department supply clerk or standardized in an academy exam: heart and desire to do the job the right way. Hopefully America realizes these cops are the overwhelming majority of the men and women who protect and serve the towns and cities of this country. It has been my honor to serve alongside them all these years.

As a writer, I'm just getting started and I want to acknowledge those who continue to help me along. Thanks to my friends at the Wednesday night San Diego Writers, Ink group led by Tammy Greenwood. Your feedback every week kept me on track and your fingerprints are all over this book. Thanks for the tough love.

Thanks to my agent, Jill Marr, and everyone at the Sandra

Dijkstra Literary Agency. We've come a long way together and we're still going strong.

My editor, Melissa Ann Singer, has once again stood by me all the way from first draft to the book you now hold in your hands. Thank you, Melissa, and the incredible team at Forge Books: Tom, Linda, Patty, Emily, Christopher, and everyone else. No writer could ask for a more supportive and capable group of professionals than the one assembled around me.

A special thanks to Seth Lerner, who once again created a book cover that demands to be opened.

And to my family. We've managed to spread ourselves all across the country but somehow we grow closer every year. Your love and support mean the world to me.

ACT I

ONE

Gangsters call it the blade. The track. The *ho stroll*. Back in
the day it was the red-light district, but by whatever name,
the area of downtown Milwaukee hadn't changed much in twenty-
five years. Pimped-out sleds loaded four deep with young men,
brown or black but never both, patrolled the dark streets with
windows down, bass-heavy music thumping out a steady urban
pulse. The latest generation of crack whores wandered the streets
or sat listless on the stoops of boarded-up brick apartment buildings, waiting for men who sought bargain rates.

One young woman stood out from the rest as confident, even
willing. Damn sure worth the money. She leaned against the shot-
out lamppost, listening as the nearby Allen-Bradley Clock Tower
chimed out the midnight hour, knowing the corner belonged to her.

A sleek late-model Volvo pulled to the curb and stopped. The
midnight blue metallic paint shimmered in the low light and the cus-
tom alloy wheels would pay her bills for a couple of months. *Nice
ride,* she thought, shrugging herself off the lamppost, stepping to
the edge of the curb. A skintight skirt and tighter T-shirt hugged

her slight but chiseled body, leaving little to the imagination. Thick black hair seductively framed her eyes and mouth and curled down her back, stopping just above the silver chain belt wrapped around her slender waist. The night air was heavy with humidity and even at this hour a thin layer of sticky sweat coated her deep brown skin.

She caught the driver's eye through the windshield and her instincts kicked in. Thirtysomething white boy with a hundred-dollar haircut, manicured hands poised on the steering wheel, and a smug expression of confident superiority stuck on his face. She flashed a grin and sauntered closer, clicking four long, acrylic nails against the window. The driver touched his finger to the center console and the dark tinted glass lowered without a sound. Leather scent mixed with cologne floated out in a blast of cool recirculated air. She leaned in and gave him her best *come fuck me* look.

"Lookin' for a date, boss?" She communicated the essentials in a thick accent that said she wasn't long removed from south of the border.

His hard look moved across her body and the set of his jaw told her he was out to satisfy a desire a typical wife would not abide. "Maybe. You a cop?"

"*Shiiiit*. . . . Hell no. Just lookin' to hook up." She let her eyes drift down, then back up. Her tone was meant to tease. "Party a bit."

The driver leaned over and opened the passenger door. "Okay, get in, but hurry up. I want to get out of here."

She stood up straight. "Do you one better, boss. Room twenty-two. Meet me in the parking lot. We'll walk up together. You got a fine ride and all, but come on now. . . ." Her fingers glided down her stomach and past her thigh. "How 'bout we get comfortable?"

She turned toward the motel half a block away. Its neon sign flashed a room rate of thirty dollars for three hours. The car door slammed shut behind her and she cast a glance back over her shoulder, catching the man's wry smile. "No thanks. Have a nice evening, Officer."

"Eat shit, asshole!" She stepped off the curb and thrust her middle finger high in the air as the car sped away. A familiar voice came through her earpiece, laced with just a hint of impatience.

"Come on, Suarez. Get nasty with these guys. Try flashing a little up top."

Maybe that would help, Detective Tia Suarez thought, shaking her head. It had been a while since she'd been out on a vice detail and there was no denying that she was a little uptight. She gave a nervous laugh. The put-on accent vanished as she responded, doing her best to keep the tremor out of her voice, "Yeah, Sarge? Well, if I did, it'd be the closest you ever got to second base."

"I never stop at second. Always head straight for home." The corner of Tia's mouth quirked up at this reply from her assigned cover officer and boss, Sergeant Travis "TJ" Jackson. He was monitoring Tia's position from the alley across the street, inside a box truck marked "Leno's Panadería." The two cops were assisting in a regional vice operation, on loan to Milwaukee PD from nearby Newberg.

Tia stood where she was sure the pole cam would have a good view and threw out her arms in invitation. "Well, feel free to come on out here. Just because the rules say U/Cs can't get in the car don't mean a stud like you couldn't close the deal, right?"

TJ's voice took on a challenging tone. "I don't know, Suarez. That gal Shelia from Milwaukee PD, she didn't have any problems working the corner. She bagged three. Maybe we ought to put her back out."

"Bullshit." There was no way Tia was getting shut out, not to mention shown up, by a rookie MPD cop working her first undercover detail. "Just keep your eye on the screen and tell the Milwaukee PD boys to be ready to roll in."

Tia's reputation was that of not only a first-rate detective but also a talented undercover operative who could slip into the role of "wet hooker" pretty quick. The average john figured she'd just recently

crossed the border and never suspected she might be a cop. But tonight the fish just weren't biting. Or was it something else? After
all she had been through, Tia couldn't help but wonder. *Is it me? Is
it too soon?* Again the buzz in her ear.

"All right, but remember. You're representing Newberg PD." His
voice was firm and Tia knew the chiding was only partially light-
hearted. "Gotta show these city cops we can hang with the big boys."

She made sure she sounded unconcerned. "You know, maybe
you should come out here, Jackson. I'm starting to think you'd
make a better queen-whore than I do a straight-up hooker."

"Bullshit, girl. You make a great hooker. Hell, if I was driving
by I'd be all over your tight little–"

In mid-sentence, TJ went from somewhere beyond flirtatious to
dead serious. "Okay. Get in character. You got one slowing down.
He's looking at you from the parking lot on your six." Tia picked
up on the tension as well as the excitement in TJ's voice. "He drove
off camera, but he's back there somewhere."

She turned and saw a man standing just outside an idling panel
van, taking a hard look at her. She set her hands on her hips, putting out the attitude of a working girl who was all business. Looking her up and down, the man kept his distance. Tia sauntered
half a dozen steps toward him and the earpiece crackled. TJ's voice
was no-nonsense. "Okay, I got no visual on him and you're right at
the edge of the window. Bring him to you, Tia."

The john took a few steps in her direction and Tia looked him
over, glad she wouldn't have to actually touch the guy. Bald and
pasty white, he was wearing a sweat-soaked flannel shirt with cut-
off sleeves. Tia guessed he was way north of three hundred pounds.
His thick red beard could use a good combing. He didn't strike her
as a guy who showered with any frequency and just the thought of
physical contact caused a shudder of revulsion that was hard to hide.

He stopped and called out, "Slide on over here, girlie. Let me
talk to you."

Tia walked forward a few paces but kept her distance. With her fake accent back in place, she put out the standard bullshit line that would tell anyone listening she had made contact with a john and was trying to reel him in. "What up, big man? You lookin' for a date?"

The voice in her ear was edged with frustration. "You've gone offscreen, Suarez. Move back into the op area."

The john closed in. "More than a date, honey. You work for somebody or you out here on your own?"

Tia ignored TJ's warning and edged closer to her intended target, making sure she maintained the attitude of a girl ready to get on her back. "I don't peddle this ass for nobody. Now, you wanna get with me or not?"

Her ear buzzed with an angry whisper. "Damn it, Suarez. Get back on camera, *now*."

She knew she'd hear about this later, but she also knew TJ wanted the score as much as she did. After a pause, he continued, this time addressing the rest of the team. "Okay, guys, stand by. Suarez is working the john. I've got no visual but good audio. Sounds like he took the bait."

The big man walked toward her, taking a hard look around the parking lot. He didn't show the typical apprehension of a john, more the menacing disposition of a seasoned crook. Tia decided she was out far enough—she'd reel him in from here or cut him loose. He stopped about five feet in front of her. The heavy odor of his perspiration wafted through the air and his gaze darted over her body, sizing her up.

"Where you come from, darlin'? You just get in from Mexico or further south than that?"

"Just tell me what you want, boss man. You're lookin' for something special, I think."

Without taking his eyes off her, he flashed a yellowed grin, raised one arm above his head, and waggled his fingers. Tia heard the van drop into gear and looked up to see it driving forward. The van stopped just behind the john and the driver, a skinny, pale-faced loser with a scraggly ponytail, stepped out. The deep red speed bumps of a hard-core tweak coated his face. *Forget this. Game over.*

"No go, man. I'm not doing two guys." She ran both hands through her wig to signal distress, then remembered she was a good ten feet off camera. She managed one step toward the safety zone, but that was as far as she got.

One vise-like hand circled the back of her neck and another clamped down over her mouth. Meaty fingers pinched off her nostrils and the sudden lack of oxygen filled her with a drowning panic. The big man pulled her by the head, nearly lifting her off the ground, pushing and dragging her toward the van. Her four-inch stilettos put her at a distinct disadvantage and he was able to get her within two feet of the vehicle despite her struggles. His partner flung the side door open and stood by, wearing a shit-eating grin that made Tia wonder exactly what they had planned. The fat man spoke up. "In you go, girlie."

Another shove and Tia stumbled toward the open door that now looked like a gaping mouth ready to swallow her whole. Yellow light from the streetlamps framed a shadowed image inside the vehicle. A face. A young girl. Dark brown skin. Brown eyes. A six-inch piece of heavy cloth duct tape covered her mouth from cheek to cheek. Long wisps of gray thread hung off each end, rising and falling in rhythm with her rapid breathing. Tia got her wits about her and pushed back, pulling hard at the hand across her mouth.

The john tightened his grip around her neck and called out to his partner, "Get over here. This bitch is strong."

Her wig slid down the side of her head and the earpiece dangled loose around her neck. Tia did her best to scream. TJ's frantic voice could be heard by everyone.

"Officer under assault. All units, code three response. *Move, move, move!*"

Engines and sirens fired to life, splitting the silence of the night. *Fifteen seconds*, she thought. *Twenty seconds, max. That's all I need.*

Tia pulled her arm back and turned her body, delivering a full-strength elbow strike against her attacker's windpipe, sending him to his knees. She sucked in a desperate breath and turned her attention to the second man, who came at her in a rush. She aimed a kick at his crotch and felt the stiletto heel pierce deep into the skin of his groin. He screamed in pain and joined his partner on the ground. The fat one clutched his throat but managed to speak. "She's a cop. Let's get the hell out of here."

Staring into the van, Tia kicked off her shoes. Her plan was simple. Grab the girl, hunker down, and wait for the cavalry. But Tia couldn't see the captive anymore. She reached into the van, fumbling until, *there*. She grabbed hold of what felt like a foot. The skin was young but weathered and Tia could feel the years of work under the sun.

"Come to me, *mija*. Get out!"

Tia pulled until a massive weight knocked her to the asphalt. The fat man was on his feet, slamming the door shut. His partner, already back in the driver's seat, dropped the engine into gear. The would-be john staggered for the passenger door as Tia pulled herself up off the ground. She spoke in perfect English, the accent gone. "Not so fast, fat boy."

She launched herself onto his back, landing as if he were a plow horse. She encircled his neck in the crook of her arm and clamped down with a perfect carotid restraint. He threw his body backward, slamming her flush against the side of the van, but she maintained her hold. He called out in a weak voice, "God damn it, Jessup, get this bitch off me. Don't leave me here."

The tires chirped loud against the pavement as the van sped from the parking lot. Still riding his back, Tia watched as the van turned a corner, and the taillights winked good-bye. Her backup closed in, sirens wailing. She heard the final acceleration of sixteen cylinders and the scraping sound of the undercarriage against pavement as the cop cars sped into the parking lot from all directions, ignoring the marked exits and entrances. Red and blue light bathed the air.

She looked up to signal her exact location and in that moment of distraction the suspect flipped her off his back. Tia landed hard and the big man dropped on top of her, all three hundred plus pounds pushing her flat against the asphalt still warm from the day's heat. His mouth was right up against her ear. "Out here playing cops and robbers, bitch? That's gonna cost ya."

The sound of opening car doors was followed by pounding boots. The first baton struck him near the head, barely missing Tia. More strikes began to rain down on his arms and legs and Tia was caught with a few glancing blows. "Watch out, guys. I'm right here." Tia's voice was now in command. "Get him off me and then you can beat his ass."

A Milwaukee PD officer who looked like he could play linebacker for the Packers rolled the suspect away from Tia and the tune-up continued for considerably longer than necessary. TJ, who didn't have the luxury of lights, siren, and 310 horsepower, arrived last. He worked to establish control over the chaos. "All right, guys, that's enough. Get him cuffed."

Still a little breathless from the thirty-second battle, Tia got to her feet. She grabbed Travis's patrol radio, her voice steadying as she spoke. "Dispatch, this is Newberg Unit David-Fourteen. One in custody. Second subject fled in a white panel van. No visible plate. Last seen westbound on Lincoln Avenue. Possible kidnapping victim in the rear of vehicle."

TJ took Tia by the shoulders and looked hard into her eyes. Tia saw the relief flood across his face, but his tone seemed almost condescending when he said, "Calm down, Tia. We're here. Are you all right?"

Tia kept looking in the direction the van had gone. "There was a second guy. He took off. There was a girl in the back of that van.

A teenager. Tied up and gagged. She . . . Damn, Travis. We need to find her."

"Take it easy, Tia. We got this. Just take it easy."

The suspect was now handcuffed and on his feet. Tia strode forward and delivered a full-force palm strike to his solar plexus. The air ran from his body as he dropped back to his knees. Tia followed up with a hard slap across his face with an open hand.

"Where's your partner headed in that van? Who's the girl?"

The man ignored Tia and looked at TJ. "This chick is crazy. I don't know what she's talking about."

Tia drew back her fist to deliver a more meaningful blow that she figured might loosen his tongue. A hand grabbed her wrist. She turned, her face hot with adrenaline.

"He's had enough, Tia," TJ said.

Tia pulled her hand away and stepped back. She stared down the empty road, then closed her eyes. Tia knew where this was going. She knew what was in store. *But it was real,* she thought. *Damn it, she was real.*

TWO

Tia walked across the marbled mezzanine of the Milwaukee County Courthouse and approached the long line of civilians waiting to shuttle through the metal detector. Three young, dark-skinned men received ample attention from guards who were damn near giddy at the rare opportunity to flex their cop-like muscle. The homeboys stood humbled in stocking feet, holding up their baggy pants, waiting to reclaim belts, oversized athletic shoes, ball caps, hair picks, and other proud symbols of their ghetto life. Tia side-stepped the group and went to the front of the line, where a rotund County Deputy, near despondent with boredom, watched over entry into the main lobby.

Overflowing his barstool chair, twiddling two pudgy thumbs in his lap, he maintained an air of indifference that implied he was of loftier rank than his peon co-workers, who were busy handling the heavy lifting of searches and property inspections. Tia held out her detective shield with photo ID. She watched as the deputy's startled expression took on a familiar look of disbelief and he leaned in to scrutinize her credentials. When it took longer than it should, Tia shoved the badge within an inch or two of his round face. The deputy jerked back and the furrows of his moist brow grew a little deeper. Tia met the man's stare and made it clear she was looking for a one-word answer.

"What do you say, Dep? Am I good to go?"

The deputy gave Tia's police ID card one last look, as if he studied it long enough he'd find some evidence of fraud. Several more seconds passed before he gave a reluctant jerk of his head.

At just a bit over five foot four, with a rich brown complexion and a lean build, Tia was accustomed to the long stares of the fat-ass courthouse cops of the world. No one could believe the petite little brown girl who looked all of nineteen was actually a sworn cop. Considering the circles she moved in, she understood. She didn't fit the profile. She was an outlier. An aberration. In most cases, the men she worked with didn't know what to make of her. And it wasn't just the cops. Tia had been dealing with this sort of bullshit her entire life and it never took her long to convince doubters she was the real deal.

Tia tucked her shield back inside her jacket pocket, making sure the uniformed hall monitor got a look at the grip of the forty caliber hanging from her shoulder holster. She gave a wink as she walked away. "Don't overdo it, Deputy. Pace yourself."

Tia ignored the wandering, sheep-like people and headed straight for the bay of elevators. Once she was alone in an empty car, her mind turned to the man named Gunther Kane. She had thought of little else since the hooker detail less than forty-eight hours ago.

State and federal records didn't have much on Kane, an ex-con with priors for dope and felony assault, who'd been out of the joint for less than three years. The current charge of assault against an officer, along with a possible kidnapping, meant Kane was looking at serious time. Tia figured with any luck he'd be willing to make a deal and provide a location on the girl.

Tia wished they could forego the formalities of a court hearing.

Just let me get it out of him like I should have at the start, she thought, *on the street.* Yet she'd relived the brawl a dozen times. Even now she felt the weight of him pressing down on her and she knew there was no denying it—if the other cops hadn't shown up, it could have gone the wrong way. *Again.*

Tia's mind jerked to life as if she'd changed the channel on a TV set. Her heart jumped at the sound of gunfire and panicked screams. Somewhere behind her a half-dozen plates crashed to the floor. She spun around but saw nothing other than the empty elevator car. The air took on the odor of frying walleye and the familiar burrow of a high-velocity intrusion burned against her skin. Tia's free hand went to her chest and she gulped for air. She closed her eyes, slowly blew out a breath, and let the moment pass. The sounds and images began to fade.

Gage—the shrink—called it a panic attack: a normal reaction to a traumatic near-death experience. *Whatever.* Tia knew she couldn't afford another setback. The whole post-traumatic stress bullshit was wearing thin and another relapse in a courtroom might very well spell the end of her career. Crazy shit going on inside her head was one thing, but Tia knew that's where it had to stay. She reached into the pocket of her blazer and fingered the smooth pills, half-convincing herself if she just took one it would calm her nerves. She pulled back her hand, chastising herself for even having the pills with her in court. She knew damn well the meds were for off-duty emergencies only . . . but courtrooms were an especially tough gig.

Tia shook her head, dismissing the idea that she had some sort of problem. "Jesus, Suarez," she said out loud, "forget about the meds. Calm your own damn nerves."

The elevator stopped and the doors opened. Stepping out, Tia bumped into a well-dressed man who seemed annoyed having to step aside for a woman with somewhere to go.

"Slow down, girl," he said, his voice dripping with casual disrespect. "Whoever he is can wait, right?"

The puny, suit-wearing stiff no doubt figured Tia to be some *chica* with family issues, despite her carefully selected, courtroom-ready outfit. Making bail for a locked-up husband. Maybe getting Dad out of the drunk tank. Tia was tempted to flash her forty cal again but let it go. As the man disappeared into the elevator, she muttered to herself, "Arrogant prick."

Tia checked in with the receptionist, who ushered her into a well-appointed conference space. Travis Jackson, wearing a tie and dark sport coat, sat at the table, opposite a professionally attired woman who had the dark skin of a fellow Latina.

"Hey, Sarge. Must be a big case for you to be on time."

Travis shifted in the hard-back office chair but said nothing. The woman, busy scrawling notes in a file folder, stopped and looked Tia up and down over the top of her tortoiseshell half frames. Her hair was pulled back tight into a shiny black ball balanced on the back of her head. Perfectly applied blush gave her brown cheeks just a hint of rose. When she spoke, Tia heard authority in her voice. It wasn't the least bit welcoming.

"I take it you're Officer Suarez?"

"*Detective* Suarez, Newberg PD."

The woman looked back at her notes. "I'm Patricia Graham. I've been assigned as prosecutor."

Tia stood there thinking there might be more coming from the lawyer and feeling an ominous amount of tension in the room. When Graham said nothing more, Tia sat beside TJ, knowing when it came to cops and lawyers rigid relations were nothing new. She leaned in and elbowed her fellow cop. He seemed righteously pissed off about something and she decided to try to snap him out of it.

"Why didn't you call me? We could've ridden over together. Is anyone from MPD here? They get anything on the girl yet?"

Graham closed the file and started right in.

"Officer Suarez, as I was just explaining to Sergeant Jackson, we've reached a pretrial agreement with the accused. We won't be needing your testimony today. You're both free to return to Newberg."

Tia was put off by the officious tone. She narrowed her eyes and pushed back.

"Like I told you, it's 'Detective' Suarez, and what are you saying? He copped a plea? What's he getting? Did he give up his partner? What about a location on the girl?"

"The details of the agreement aren't up for discussion, but thank you for driving over. The clerk will validate your parking."

The woman stood to leave and Tia held up a hand to stop her. Tia gave Travis, who was already half out of his chair, a puzzled look, then turned to Graham. "Wait a minute; I'm not getting this. You took a plea deal on a felony assault and kidnapping case? What's the exposure? He must have given up the girl then, right?"

"Officer Suarez—"

"I told you, it's *Detective*."

Travis fell back into his seat and shot the attorney a look that struck Tia as some sort of warning. Graham kicked out one hip and crossed her arms over her chest, her lips pressed tight together. "Yes, of course. I apologize. I won't be needing your testimony today, *Detective*."

A silence hung in the room until Tia spoke up.

"Okay, hang on a second." She looked back and forth between the cop and the lawyer, then hooked her thumb toward the door and forced herself to smile. "Did I shit the carpet coming in or something?"

When there was no answer, Tia shook her head in confusion. "How about somebody just explains to me what's going on."

Graham returned to her seat and drew a deep breath that Tia knew was meant to signal her annoyance.

"This case?" the attorney said. "It has some very significant problems. I don't see any chance for a successful prosecution for the charges listed in the arrest report. I've cut the best deal for everyone involved and we'll plead it out today."

"And that best deal is?" Tia asked. After several seconds of Graham staring at her, she got an answer.

"Disorderly conduct. Ten days' confinement. Considering time served and credit for good behavior, Kane will be released day after tomorrow."

Tia blurted out a laugh that was loud enough to be out of place. "Yeah, right." Travis sighed and stared straight ahead, not looking at Tia. Opposite her, Graham's expression remained impassive, detached. "You're kidding, right?" Tia pressed.

The lawyer's face seemed carved in stone; Tia realized the woman wasn't kidding. Tia turned to her sergeant, any hint of humor gone from her voice.

"Yo, TJ." Her tone was challenging. "Are you going to say something here or what?"

Travis shrugged, turning to send a thousand-yard stare out the nearby window. Tia tried to shake Graham one more time.

"You can't possibly be serious?"

"I don't joke about such things. It's the best I can do, considering all the circumstances."

Tia put her hands flat on the table to hide the fact that they were shaking. Her pulse pounded and she felt her face flush.

"Disorderly conduct? Ten days? This is a felony assault on a cop, not to mention Kane's involvement in what was obviously some sort of abduction."

The woman removed her glasses, withdrew a cloth from one pocket of her jacket, and began polishing the lenses, sending the message that this conversation was a waste of her valuable time.

"Officer Suarez, this case—"

Tia's voice approached a shout and she stood from her seat. "Damn it, lady. It's *Detective*."

Graham rocked back in her chair; Travis straightened up and seemed ready to step in if need be. Tia could see the prosecutor realizing she had miscalculated Tia's response and needed to regroup. The attorney conceded with a slight nod of her head and for the first time her voice held no attitude. "Again, I apologize. Detective."

Tia lowered herself back into her seat and waited. Graham took a deep breath, then held up the case file for display. "Like I said, Detective. This case has got serious issues."

"Like what?" Tia gave her boss a sideways glance to let him know she was doing his job. She was ready to fight for their case. "Name one."

"Okay. For starters, Kane says he didn't even know you were a cop and in your report you make no mention of identifying yourself. Do you realize how that affects my ability to prosecute an officer-assault case?"

Tia fired back, making no attempt to hide her frustration. "I was a little busy trying not to get thrown into the back of his van, but if you want I can go back and—"

"No, you won't. I'm not going to add 'amended police reports' to an already long list of problems."

"Okay, so what? He thinks I'm a hooker. That gives him the right to try and kidnap me?"

"That's not how he tells it."

"And how's that?"

"The defendant claims all he wanted was to get with a prostitute, then you jumped him. He figured he'd been set up for a robbery and any second your badass pimp would show up with a knife or a gun or whatever. Common occurrence and it makes for a good defense."

"Yes, but—"

"One moment, *Detective*. I'm not finished." Graham was back in control and all business. "Forget about the fact you don't ID yourself. It would appear you just so happened to have led the defendant out of camera range and that while he was out of view he sustained significant injuries. Word is, you joined in."

Graham pulled Kane's booking photo from the file and set it on the table in front of Tia. Kane's eye was swollen shut and a deep purple bruise ran across his throat. His lips were puffy and red with what looked to be dried blood. Tia also saw that behind the injuries was the face of an unrepentant, hard-core crook. She was about to say she'd seen worse, but Graham cut her off.

"I realize this sort of cowboy tactic is pretty much how you do business over in Newberg, but it won't sit well with a Milwaukee jury. I have no doubt Kane would show up in court with a neck brace."

Tia leaned against the table, incredulous. "He *attacked* me."

"Well, once again, the accused has a different story."

Tia scoffed, pushing the picture back toward Graham. "Is that how it works in Milwaukee County? Ass-bag defendants get more say than cops? This guy would have killed me given the chance."

"He *says* you jumped him. He thought you were going to rob him. He has a right to defend himself. Why didn't you identify yourself as a cop?"

"Oh for Christ sake, fine. In the heat of the moment, I forgot." Tia conceded the point to get to the bigger issue. "What about the girl in the van?"

"What girl, Detective?" Graham's voice was low, her words clipped. Tia heard the doubt in it.

There it is, she thought. She laced her fingers together on the table in front of her, working hard to control the anger building inside. Her answer came out slowly, each word measured.

"There was a girl tied up in the back of the van. She had duct tape over her mouth. She was trying to scream for help. *That* girl."

Graham shot a knowing glance at TJ. When she looked back at Tia, the sympathy was gone, replaced by a condescending attitude.

"Kane says he doesn't know what you're talking about. He says the only other person in the van was a man who was going to split the cost of the hooker. Some guy he met at a bus stop. Add to that the fact we never found the van and there's been no corroborating missing person report."

Tia opened her mouth, but Graham raised a hand. "Sorry, Detective. The deal has been struck and the offer accepted. The case is closed."

Desperate now, thinking of the missing girl, Tia said, "I'm telling you I can sell this. We'll get the guy bound over for trial. Then when he's looking at real time, maybe he'll talk. Just let me testify. Show him we mean business."

Graham shook her head as if she'd heard enough.

"Okay, Tia, let's just go ahead and deal with the elephant in the room, shall we?" the prosecutor said, her voice cold.

Tia lied, "I don't know what you're talking about."

"I know what you've been through—the episode in your county courthouse."

Humiliation grew inside her as the lawyer went on. "What was that? Eight weeks ago? If we go to trial today, there's no way that doesn't come out. All of it. Do you really want to go through that?"

"It's been three months and I can handle it." Tia held firm and her voice became indignant. "For Christ sake, I got shot to hell less than a year ago. I had a problem with the medication. They can ask me whatever they want. We'll let a jury decide."

"Forget about the jury. I don't think we could get this past a judge at the preliminary hearing."

"What are you saying, Counselor?"

The two women stared at each other silently for a long moment. Graham spoke first. "What I'm saying is, when you compare what happened in the Waukesha courtroom to what you say you saw in the van, it just doesn't ring true."

"What I *say* I saw?" *There it is,* Tia thought, turning to TJ, who had gone back to staring out the window. *Damn, him, too? They all think I imagined it.* Had TJ sold her out or did her reputation as a nut job now extend all the way to Milwaukee? *No matter.* She turned back to the lawyer.

"I don't need you or anyone else worrying about how I'll hold up in a courtroom. You put this in front of a judge or a jury and I guarantee you, I'll sell it."

Graham shook her head. There was pity in her voice. "Sorry. Considering all the circumstances, there's no way we can move forward on this case. We've got nothing."

"And the girl? What about her?"

"The girl?" Graham smiled thinly. "*If* there was a girl; whoever she was . . . I wish I could help her. Next time bring me a real case and maybe it'll be different."

"Next time, huh? Lot of good that does her." Tia stood in a huff and moved to the door. With her hand on the knob, she decided she wasn't done and turned back to look at Graham and the sergeant.

"Graham, is it?" Tia said, then effortlessly switched languages. "*Cuál es su apellido, amiga?*"

"I don't speak Spanish."

Tia thought it sounded like the woman took pride in her ignorance.

"I just asked your maiden name." Tia flicked her eyes toward the rock on the woman's finger. "Back before there was a Mr. Graham."

The lawyer returned Tia's stare with a hard glare of her own. After several seconds she responded. "Rodriguez. Jiménez-Rodriguez to be more ethnically accurate, but I was born in Sacramento if that's where this is going."

"Really. And your parents? Mr. and Mrs. Rodriguez? How about them?"

After a moment's hesitation, Graham answered as if confessing some shameful fact. "They came from Guatemala. Two years before I was born. They worked the fields in the California Central Valley."

"Wow. And look at you. College. Law school. They must be really proud. I'm glad it worked out for you."

The lawyer sounded exasperated. "Look, Tia. It's nothing against you. I get it. You thought you saw something, but it was dark, right? No one else saw anything. Maybe in the stress of the moment—"

Tia cut her off, not wanting to hear it. "What is it they say about six degrees of separation? That's all there is between you, me, and a girl like her. Think about that when you get home and crawl into bed tonight." Tia took two steps toward the table, pointing a finger directly toward the woman's face. She continued, her voice venomous, shaking with anger. "Just a couple of minor twists and turns in your life and maybe somebody slaps duct tape over your mouth and chains your ass up in the back of a van."

The lawyer stared at Tia. Her lips were pressed together in fury. Tia knew she had crossed a line in her world of cops, crooks, and lawyers. She'd made it personal. Something that just wasn't done. If she apologized right away . . .

But she didn't. The moment came and went. The weight of her offense pressed down on everyone in the room.

She yanked the door open and lurched into the hall, slamming the door behind her and bolting past the startled clerk. Her heartbeat pushed against the collar of her shirt; her hand fumbled in her pocket. Tia pulled out both capsules and tossed them into her dry mouth. She bent over and took a long drink at the fountain. As the water swirled down the chrome drain, the young girl's brown face stared back and a small familiar voice began to call out.

THREE

G ood morning, sir. You wanted to see me?"
    Chief Ben Sawyer turned to face Travis Jackson, who was
standing in the doorway of Ben's office, looking like a cowed dog
with no fight left in him. Ben figured his newly appointed detective
sergeant was still in recovery from the fallout over the blown hooker
detail in Milwaukee. Ben didn't see any reason to set the younger
cop's mind at ease just yet. He did his best to come off as officious.
Without standing, Ben waved the man inside.

"Have a seat, Sergeant."

Jackson made his way around a few moving boxes and pointed
to the only chair not covered with books. "Here okay, sir?"

Ben nodded. "Sit down."

Ben stared ahead and forced himself to remember he was as
much at fault as Jackson, but *Jesus*. When Ben had signed off on the
prostitution detail outside Newberg jurisdiction, the operation plan
showed that Tia Suarez was assigned to report writing. When Ben
learned Jackson had allowed Tia to work undercover as john bait,
he nearly blew a gasket. Ben made a special nighttime visit to the

department and the chewing out that followed was epic on any scale.

On top of the assignment issue, the Milwaukee PD cover units had been way out of position. Ben had listened to the tapes and, by his estimate, the response to Tia's call for help had taken nearly thirty seconds. If Ben had run the op, the units would have been positioned to respond in less than half that time. But, just as Ben had reminded himself a dozen times since taking over as chief, his opinion on tactics was no longer sought.

Ben Sawyer had the luxury of experience beyond Newberg PD. When his thirteen-year career with Oakland came to an abrupt if not well-deserved conclusion, fate and family allowed him to land on his feet back in his hometown, thirty-five miles due west of Milwaukee. Just a few years later, circumstances landed him in the position of police chief of the small but active department.

In his heart, he was the same young officer who had once patrolled the streets of deep east Oakland. When Ben looked at Jackson, he saw a cop who had spent his entire eight years in law enforcement working for Newberg PD. A man who had never really been tested. Suarez, on the other hand, had been to hell and back so many times, even Ben had to hold the woman in awe. He knew she'd been having a tough time of it lately, but he knew she still had to do her job.

Ben gestured toward Jackson's coat and tie. "You coming from court? Gunther Kane's hearing was today, right? How did it go?"

"It didn't go at all, Chief. The prosecutor pled it out. We didn't have to testify."

Ben mulled that over. "Well, I guess that could be a good thing. What was the deal?"

Jackson looked at the wall, telegraphing his dread. "You're not going to like it, sir."

"Why? What's the problem?"

Jackson took a deep breath and dove in. "The lawyer kicked it

all the way down to disorderly conduct. The guy got ten days. He's
going to walk by the end of the week."

Ben felt his heart jump in his chest and he swallowed hard. He
let the silence settle for a good ten seconds before he spoke, making
a conscious effort to keep his voice down.

"I thought you said we had him dead to rights on felony assault?
Aside from all the other stuff, I mean." His words slowed to a crawl.
"You said, Travis, the assault on an officer case was rock solid."

Jackson dropped his head and Ben could sense the man's
frustration. "I know, Chief. I thought it was, but this damn attorney. As soon as we sat down, she started talking about how Tia
didn't ID herself, how the guy had some built-in defense. She even
got all caught up in the force. Said it was excessive."

"You buying that?" Ben fired back. "Is that the real reason?"

"I doubt it. Seemed to me her mind was made up before we even
sat down." Jackson looked up to catch Ben's eye. "She even made
some crack about Newberg PD. How we got a bunch of cowboys
running the show."

"Is that right?" Ben felt his jaw tighten even more. He'd been
Newberg Chief of Police for less than two months, but already
plenty had been written about his appointment. A few of the larger
media outlets had rehashed his exploits in California, not to mention
the rather unorthodox investigation he'd conducted into a series
of murders. That had led directly to the resignation of his prede-
cessor.

"She also brought up the stuff with Tia," Jackson added.

Ben focused on his sergeant instantly. "What do you mean?"

"Before Tia even showed up, the lawyer, a woman named
Graham, hit me pretty hard with questions about Tia's history.
She knew all about it. Had all the ugly details."

"And? What else?" Ben noticed his fingers bouncing on the desk,
so he balled his hand into a fist.

"She wanted to know about the van. If anyone else saw the girl

Tia mentioned." Jackson shrugged. "Asked me what I thought of the whole thing."

"And what did you tell her?" Ben meant it as a challenge and he was glad when the man seemed to take it that way.

"What do you think, Chief? I told her I didn't see anything, but whatever Tia said she saw was good enough for me."

Jackson stared back and Ben reminded himself this was a good man. What he lacked in experience he more than made up for with heart. He was a good cop and Ben knew Jackson cared for Tia almost as much as Ben himself did.

"Where is she?"

"I don't know. She left there pretty worked up. She really had it out with the attorney."

"How so?" Ben closed his eyes. "Please tell me it didn't get physical."

"Everything but." Jackson shrugged and Ben could see the man was trying not to smile. "Tia gave her hell, Chief. I figure you'll be getting a phone call."

So what, Ben thought. Pissed-off attorneys were part of the landscape and the least of his worries. But Tia was another matter. His worst fears were coming true. A girl in the back of a van needing to be rescued. No one but Tia saw anything. Right off, it had struck Ben as a familiar—and unlikely—story. As chief of police, Ben was well aware of Tia's struggles since she'd returned to work. It had been an uphill battle with major setbacks.

"You think that's why the lawyer kicked the case?" Ben asked the sergeant. "Because of Tia's history?"

Jackson shook his head as if he wanted to avoid the whole subject of a cop who might be losing it. Ben couldn't blame him, but he knew that as chief he didn't have the same luxury. For Ben, dealing with Tia these days was like dancing on the head of pin. A grenade pin.

"So, should I go out here, Chief? To the farmhouse?" Jackson's voice was full of uncertainty. "I tried to catch up to her at the court-house, but I had to calm the attorney down. By the time I got out of the office, Tia was gone."

"No. It's okay. Don't intrude on her personal space. I'll send someone by to check on her."

"Okay, Chief." Jackson stood, ready to walk away, then stopped. He looked squarely at his boss and dove in. "This is all on me, sir. I should never have put Tia in that situation. But I swear, once she heard we were going over to Milwaukee for hooker detail she just wouldn't let it go. Told me she needed to get back out there. That she was ready. She seemed so . . . I don't know. So much like her old self, you know?

"I really blew it, sir. I'm sorry."

On his feet now, Ben closed the distance between them and clasped Jackson by one shoulder. He saw it now. The man had been tortured enough and it was time to put the operation behind them. "It's over and done with, Travis. We'll learn from it. Now let's just worry about Tia."

Jackson nodded. Ben gave the sergeant a friendly nudge toward the door. "Get back to work. I'll smooth things over with the at-torney and I'll make sure someone looks in on Tia."

When he was alone again in his office, Ben's thoughts went to Tia and what she might be going through. He wondered if he could go to her himself. Were they still that close? The answer was obvi-ous. *Hell no.* He would be the last person she wanted to see. The fallout from Tia's shooting had caused a rift between them that showed no signs of closing.

"Excuse me, Chief?"

Ben looked up to see his secretary, Caroline Gunderson, in the doorway. He was still getting to know the young woman, who had recently replaced Bernice Erickson, a fixture in the chief's office for many years. Bernice had retired from the PD to become the full-time nanny for the new baby in the Sawyer household.

"Yes, Caroline?"

"Ms. Patricia Graham is on the phone. She's an attorney." Caroline's voice carried just a hint of intrigue. "Says she needs to speak with you about Detective Suarez."

"Yeah, I'll bet she does."

"Shall I put her through?"

"Take a number, Caroline. Tell her I'll call her back in a few minutes." Ben knew the call would take some time, and there was something he wanted to do before placating Graham.

"She says it's important, Chief. She sounds upset."

Ben sighed and repeated himself. "Tell her I'll call her in ten minutes. I need to take care of something else first."

Caroline raised her eyebrows and walked back to her desk. Ben heard her pick up the phone and was pleased that her conversation with Graham was nothing less than a picture of professionalism. Ben grabbed his cell phone off his desk and scrolled through his contacts until he found what he was looking for. Ben couldn't go to Tia, but he knew someone who could. After a few rings, the familiar voice came on the line.

"Hey, Connor. Ben Sawyer. I need you to do me a favor."

FOUR

The sun overwhelmed her wraparound Ray-Bans. Tia closed her eyes and tugged down on the bill of her straw Stetson, which had turned dark with years of sweat. She sat slung low in the pinewood Adirondack chair, one bare foot kicked up over the wide armrest. Her sleeveless cotton shirt was mostly unbuttoned and tied off across her ribs in a knot her mother would have insisted was far too high. Tia traced the cold bottle of Montejo over the jagged, raised patches of still-pink scar tissue that ran across her stomach. The sweat of the bottle mixed with her own caused a sting that told her she still wasn't anywhere near drunk enough.

Tia opened her eyes and turned her head at the sound of a soft whine. Ringo, her eight-year-old yellow Lab–mastiff mix, lay nearby, his massive head flush against the wood deck of the porch like it had been poured there, his sad brown eyes full of disapproval. Tia had picked the 140-pound dog out of a rescue lineup at the Waukesha County humane society shelter just hours before his appointment with the needle. It had been only a few days after her discharge from the Marines and the idea of living completely alone scared the hell out of her. Nowadays, the neutered animal was the closest thing she could manage to a sustained relationship with a male and most times that was fine with her.

When their eyes met, Ringo gave a single hard thump with his tail against the wood of the porch. Tia couldn't help but smile and her voice was gentle. "Come on, Ringo. Nobody likes to be judged by their dog. Knock it off."

As if to show the old dog she meant business, Tia lifted the bottle of tequila from the nearby table and poured two ounces of the clear liquid into a shot glass. She tossed the drink back without the slightest grimace and chased it with another long swallow of beer. Settling her head against the wooden chair back, she took in the countryside spread out like a canvas before her.

The field of wild green grasses blew in the hot breeze and the Wisconsin landscape wavered in the heat. Chickadees darted in and out of her vision as if engaged in aerial military maneuvers. Tia did her best to ignore the line of prefab homes that sat a half mile away on her property line. She lifted her gaze to the cloudless sky.

The effects of the hot sun, perfectly aged silver tequila, and cold beer allowed her to stay in a place of thoughtful reflection. Between that and the lingering effects of the benzos she had popped a few hours earlier, her morning in the lawyer's office had finally begun to fade. She was under control and properly anesthetized.

What the hell am I doing? This isn't the way to deal with it.

In a brief moment of clarity she imagined herself dead on the porch, OD'd on booze and meds. She could practically read the headline:

FORMER MARINE AND NEWBERG POLICE OFFICER
DIES FROM OVERDOSE AT 29

She could almost hear the whispered conversations at her wake. "She was never the same after the shooting." Or, more likely, "That Suarez was one crazy cop."

What would Sawyer think? And her parents? Then again, worrying about other people was what got her into this mess. Tia pushed back on the images as well as the feelings of guilt.

It had been almost a year since her near-death experience, served up by an ex-con in a café in Danville, Illinois. Two rounds to the gut had left her on the brink, but she had battled back, at least physically. The long road to recovery had revealed truths that still left her struggling. Truths that terrified her and that she knew she could never share. Not with anyone.

She gave her head a vigorous shake, a conscious effort to not walk through certain mental doors. *Keep it safe,* she thought. *Stay in the moment. Here and now.* She forced her mind to return to what sat in front of her.

Home. The one place I can really step away, she thought. *Disconnect. Put away all the masks and disguises needed to survive every day.* The old two-story clapboard farmhouse and the land it sat on were literally the world Tia had grown up in. She'd bought the property, which sat just outside the city limits of Newberg, three years ago, after she'd learned the land was being parceled out to make way for six hundred tract homes that would house the insatiable horde of young thirtysomethings commuting to Madison or Milwaukee.

The landowner, the same farmer who'd hired Tia's father as general laborer almost twenty-five years earlier, was pushing ninety. After several years of poor crops, low prices, and a series of bad financial decisions, the bank was set to foreclose—and make a fortune from exploiting the land in a way that would never occur to the farmer. Tia couldn't save the whole spread, but she pulled a fast one on the developers and managed to buy the farmhouse and the surrounding four acres for half the market value. She made a promise to the old man that the last remnant of his homestead, land that had been in his family for three generations, would remain on the earth for at least one more.

To Tia the land was her stand against the world. An outpost

surrounded on all sides by the state's version of Levittown. Tia liked to think she was standing guard over a piece of Wisconsin history, but she knew it wasn't the land or even the house that really mattered. She gazed down the worn dirt path and gave some thought to taking "the walk," but before she could make up her mind she heard a familiar sound.

At the thrum of the truck engine, Ringo gave a deep, quick bark of approval. He pulled himself to his feet and rumbled down the steps, no doubt happy someone had come along who could talk sense into his human. The pickup drove fast over the hard dirt surface, navigating past the boulders and white birch trees with confident familiarity.

Connor Anderson locked the four wheels just shy of the grass, sending out a shower of pebbles and rocks. He stared at Tia from the driver's seat for several seconds, his large hands casually draped across the top of the steering wheel. The door whined on its hinges and he stepped out, walking halfway up the six porch steps before stopping and leaning against the rail. Watching closely, Tia saw only the barest trace of a limp. Connor dug his hands into the pockets of his jeans and studied the scene before him.

Surrounded by a bucket of cold beer and a parade of empties, a bottle of tequila on the table and a refilled shot glass in her hand, Tia returned his stare with a hard look of her own. Connor folded his arms across his chest and Tia knew what was coming. Ringo sat beside Connor's feet and grinned at his human with an expression that said, *Now you're gonna get it*. Tia stared back at the dog to remind him where his food came from. She downed the shot, then turned away to set the empty glass on the table, projecting nothing but indifference.

Connor's voice was patient but aggravating as hell. "You know it's not even supper time. You think maybe you should go easy on that stuff?"

Tia spoke cautiously to avoid slurring her words. "It's almost five."

He gave a light laugh, making her feel judged even though she knew he didn't intend it. "It's three o'clock, girl. Let's go inside. The Brewers are on TV. They're in New York playing the Mets. I'll throw something on the grill."

"You go on in. I'm good right here." Tia hoped he'd take the hint, then felt the warmth of connection when he climbed the remaining steps and moved toward the neighboring chair. *There's no denying it,* she thought. *It's always good to see him.*

Tia watched Connor fold his tall, slender frame into the seat, his right leg thrust straight out in front of him. He didn't look her way, just stared out across the open field, his blue eyes radiant in the sunlight, his jawline a near-perfect right angle, stubbled with a day's growth. The John Deere ball cap she had bought him at last year's state fair was pulled low over his brow, covering his thick blond hair.

"All right then, fine. Go on and sit there if you want, but don't ruin this for me." She leaned her head back against the chair and closed her eyes. "I'm just about right where I want to be."

Tia and Connor had gone to high school together. Well, not really together—Tia was a sophomore at Newberg High when Connor was a senior. He'd been making plenty of noise on the local sports scene as a star pitcher on the school's baseball team, but to Tia he was just one of five hundred students. He liked to take long looks at her . . . but after he passed she usually glanced back over her shoulder, taking a good look of her own.

After graduating, Connor had signed with the Brewers' Single-A team, the Appleton Timber Rattlers. He'd soon realized that an 83 mph fastball might mean something in high school, but it was a pitch made for batting practice in the pros, even if you could dress it up with a pretty good curve. After a single season, Connor returned to Newberg to work the family farm.

They hadn't really been in contact then—there was no connection between them, after all. So Tia had been quite surprised when she'd joined the Marines and climbed aboard a bus for a twenty-two-hour trip to Parris Island—and found Connor Anderson sitting by a window, with an open seat beside him. Tia was just eighteen and Connor was a month shy of his twenty-first birthday and it was during that long journey that they really got to know each other. Thinking about the bus ride still made her want to smile and cry at the same time.

Connor had spoken of his love of farming and his dream of owning land of his own. He'd talked about the secret of aging cheese and about the government conspiracy that was behind milk prices. He'd decided to join up to do his part in the fight against terror. He really believed in it. To him, the Marines were his way of paying back his country. Tia had just wanted to get the hell out of Newberg.

By the time they arrived at the recruit depot in South Carolina, Tia was thinking it was too bad they hadn't met before signing their lives away. Five minutes after the bus pulled in, Connor headed for the male side of the island and Tia went the other way. She didn't see him again until three years later, on the medevac chopper that carried them both out of Helmond Province. Tia with a flesh wound from a nasty fall that took a dozen sutures to close; Connor with his right leg shredded from the hip down and his left gone at the knee. What was left of him was in shock and near death. Looking at him now, she was impressed as hell with how far he had come.

Connor scratched at his hip socket—Tia knew that on hot days like this his skin became raw from rubbing against the hard plastic—but when he spoke his voice was lazy and laconic as ever, betraying no discomfort. "Hand me one of those?" He flapped one hand toward the ice bucket.

Tia passed over a cold bottle of beer.

"Shot of Patrón?" She figured she had to offer.

He gave her an easy smile that Tia thought had some pity laced in. "Nah. I'll stick with the beer."

"Suit yourself."

Tia poured another healthy shot into her glass and tossed it back. Connor shook his head like he had already seen enough. "I heard about this morning. I know you're angry but—"

Tia cut him off. "Don't start, Connie. Really. I just want to sit here and be free of all that bullshit. I don't want to talk about it. I don't want to think about it. So just do me a solid and sit there and drink your beer, go inside to watch the damn ball game, or get back in your truck and leave." Tia pointed an unsteady hand down the driveway to emphasize her point. "And by the way, next time Jackson calls to fill you in on everyone's favorite little pity project? Tell him to mind his own damn business."

"Wasn't Travis who called me," Connor said flatly. "Sawyer did."

Great, Tia thought, shaking her head. *That's all I need.* "Well, the same goes for him."

"Sure." Connor nodded. "I'll tell the chief of police you said he can–"

"Oh, knock it off, Connor." Tia took a healthy hit off her beer. She loved Connor more than anyone, but at this point she was pretty sure he was out to ruin her afternoon. She shook her head in frustration. "What is it about men? Why can't a woman just kick back once in a while? Can't we just take a six-pack and relax? You guys sure as hell do."

"Come on, Tia. You just told me a few days ago, you hadn't had a drink in two weeks." He looked at the empties. "You making up for lost time or what?"

Tia poured another healthy shot and blew an air kiss Connor's way before she tossed the tequila back.

Ringo whined, turning his head back and forth in conflict over the only two people he cared about it. They sat staring at each other until, after a long moment, Tia gave in and looked away. An instant later, she felt Connor's strong grip on her arm.

The gentle squeeze of his warm hand set off a cascade of memories. His familiar touch: strong when it needed to be but usually gentle. The way he could effortlessly get inside her skin, understand her moods like nobody ever had. The way he used ten words to say what took most people a thousand. She knew he wanted to help, but her temptation was to tell him to stuff it. *He's not a cop. What does he know?*

That was unkind, she knew. He had more experience of life and death than most of the people on the force in Newberg.

Sergeant Connor Anderson had been a team leader on a marine sniper unit, tasked with performing missions cleared at the highest levels of government. Connor had a dozen confirmed kills, the closest from seven hundred meters out. While on reconnaissance of an identified target, Connor had been less than three feet away from a marine who stepped on a massively powerful IED. That man was vaporized before his eyes and Connor's legs were shredded in the blast. His team came under immediate assault. Connor assisted in his own emergency first aid, then directed his team to repel the attack. Because of his skills, not only did the marines suffer no further loss of life, but the confirmed enemy body count was thirteen Taliban KIA.

After being evacuated, Connor spent ten weeks confined to a bed in the Landstuhl Regional Medical Center, undergoing seventeen surgical procedures. There were another half-dozen operations during his four months attached to the Wounded Warrior Battalion at the Naval Medical Center San Diego. Eventually the navy hooked him up with state-of-the-art prosthetic legs. Before being medically discharged, Connor was awarded the Bronze Star with a combat V. Tia had flown out for the ceremony, which had been attended by a thousand marines including the assistant commandant, along with both California senators and the lieutenant governor.

Three years later, Connor had reached the point where a stranger wouldn't even know his right leg was man-made starting at the hip joint and the left was fake below the knee. His superhuman recovery was a testament to his determination, but it had gradually become clear his new body couldn't hold up under the rigors of farming. Even doing the work of a hired hand had proven to be too much.

Tia knew the man well enough to know he'd never give up on his dream, but for now Connor Anderson was stocking shelves in the freezer section of the Piggly Wiggly grocery store, earning a buck over minimum wage. That, combined with his disability checks, left him eligible for food stamps, but to her knowledge he had never cashed in. If he felt like he had gotten cheated, she'd never heard him say it. Not once.

"You need to take a step back," Connor said. "Just regroup a bit."

Tia shook her head. "You sound like Sawyer." She knew her words were thick from the alcohol. "If it was up to you two, I'd still be sitting on the damn sidelines. How long, Connie, huh? How long am I supposed to sit around the office? I'm a cop, not a clerk. Both of you need to let me be."

"I'm not saying you can't work, but didn't the doc say go easy? You know, light duty and admin stuff. You shouldn't have been out there."

Tia didn't want to hear about what some shrink might think. "Being out there wasn't a problem. It was all the stuff afterward."

"Whatever. It doesn't matter. You were doing great. Now look where we're at."

"We?" Her voice was too loud. "*We* aren't anywhere. This is *me*. Me being alone with myself."

Alone wasn't the right word, Tia thought. *Abandoned. Forgotten. Deserted.* That's how it felt.

In the months before she'd been shot, Tia and Connor had begun a relationship that seemed to have limitless possibilities. It had started with Tia helping Connor in the gym with his rehab. Some days he'd stop by and do light work around the farmhouse. Their friendship progressed to ball games and a few dinners for two. Long walks and hours spent talking. They both knew what was coming, but neither knew what to expect. They were tentative at first, even awkward. But together they soon established that what the Taliban had done to the man's legs didn't affect the rest of him.

Then came the shooting, Tia's long recovery in Mexico, and a series of life-shattering revelations that she was still figuring out how to handle. Her ridiculous breakdown in the courtroom. A long period of therapy that she found so humiliating and confusing that she didn't know what to do other than lock herself away and drink. It all got to be too much.

There had been many opportunities for her to sit down with Connor and tell him the truth. To tell him just what it was that scared the hell out of her and pushed her to the bottle. To the pills. Instead, she pushed him away.

"Look, Tia. You've had a hell of a shitty year. Now this? That was a nasty fight out there. Maybe you should take a step back again. Take some time. Hell, why not you and me? We could just get away. Just for a couple of days. Nobody is going to think anything of it. I know Chief Sawyer will approve the time off."

Tia flared up. "I told you. Leave Sawyer out of this. If you talk to him, I swear, Connor Anderson, I'll—"

"I'm just saying I know he cares about you. I mean you and he are tight, right?"

"Tight? You bet, Connie. I'm crazy about him. The guy who pulled me off the front line and labeled me fifty-one-fifty. We're best buds."

"That's not fair. Sawyer's got your back. Any other chief, you'd be gone already, and you know it."

"Then why does he send you out here? Can't he come himself?"

"It's not easy, Tia. You guys . . . you and Sawyer. Hell, you've been through a lot, but he's the chief now. He can't be getting in-volved in this stuff without—well, without having to do some chief shit."

Tia looked at Connie. "Chief shit?"

"You know what I mean. He sent me to check on you so it can be unofficial. Make sure you're okay, without having to get formally involved," Connor said. "I know he just wants to help you get back to your old self."

"Well, neither of you needs to worry about me. And what's this 'old self' stuff?" She thumped the open palm of her hand against her chest and spoke with defiance. "This is me right here. Take it or leave it. People change, Connie."

Connor shook his head. "I'm not buying that. Drunk and stoned on your porch? This isn't you, Tia."

The truth hurt and she turned her face away.

Connor stood as if to leave. Tia knew she wanted him to stay. He leaned in and kissed her lightly on top of her head. She sensed another movement and reached out, clamping her fist over his where it was wrapped around the neck of the tequila bottle.

Her voice deadly serious, Tia said, "Leave it."

Connor pulled his hand back. "Fine, but I'm going to stick around, all right? I'll be inside watching the game. You should join me."

Tia had been terrified by the thought of being alone at the farmhouse, but she couldn't bring herself to show any gratitude toward Connor. She shrugged. "Do whatever you want. I'll be in after a while."

Tia watched him enter her house until the screen door shut behind him. *Get back to my old self*, she thought. *What if he knew? What if he knew exactly what that would mean?*

She shook it off, grabbing the bottle of tequila. She had bought it on the way home from the courthouse and had already powered through half of it. Tia knew if she put her mind to it she could muster the willpower to stop. It would have been harder alone, but Connie was here now. They could watch the ball game. Throw steaks on the grill. He would expect nothing in return. All she had to do was stand up and walk inside. It would be a smart decision. He'd stay the night and she knew that would help.

What happens if she shows up anyway? Tia asked herself. *Calling out to me. Trying to pull me back in.* At this level of intoxication, Tia knew the voice would be weaker, as if coming from underwater. But she could still hear her, calling out.

She needs you, Tia. Go to her.

Tia shut off her mind. Ignoring the shot glass, she raised the bottle to her lips and swallowed hard, twice. Her chest burned. Her thoughts looped in crazy circles and she laid her head back against the chair. Her friendship with Sawyer was a distant memory. And it didn't make any sense that a man like Connor Anderson could ever really care for her. There was no one to turn to. No one to confide in. Tia closed her eyes, consumed by the feeling she was utterly and completely alone.

FIVE

She woke in darkness. The humid air had grown cool and come alive with Wisconsin night sounds. Connor's truck still sat parked in the same spot. She heard Ringo's steady breath and saw his outline in the darkness. The dog had picked her after all. At first Tia couldn't move; it felt like her body had fused to the wood of the chair. She finally pulled herself to her feet with some effort, repeated explosions detonating just under the surface of her skull and growing louder when the empty tequila bottle fell from her lap and clattered on the porch. Ringo, no doubt fighting his own aches and pains, jumped halfway to his feet with a low growl.

Without warning her stomach did a complete 360. Tia grabbed the wooden bannister with both hands and leaned out just in time to retch up a gallon of tequila, beer, and prescription meds, all of it clearing the porch railing by a foot. The smell, along with the putrid taste in her mouth, nearly brought on round two. She turned her head away, drew a deep breath of clean air through her nostrils, and closed her eyes, concentrating on not vomiting again. The moment passed. She straightened up a bit, still swaying, and stared into the darkened field. In her present condition she could barely see the outline.

Three hundred and seventy-two steps, she thought. *Give or take a few, depending on how messed up I really am.*

Tia looked down at the porch steps as if staring into the abyss. Her first step landed with the wobbly thump of a drunk. Eventually she made it to the driveway, where she paused to gather strength, bending over and resting her forehead on the cool metal of the hood of Connor's truck. After a moment, she headed down the worn path, the grass soft and cool against her bare feet, homing in on the silver shell reflecting the moonlight. Even in her current state she walked along the path with a growing confidence brought on by childhood familiarity. She arrived at the thin metal door and pushed it open. She stepped inside and didn't fight the sense of being transported back in time.

The space was cramped but comfortable. She breathed in the familiar smell of refried beans mixed with her father's pipe tobacco. A worn couch and chair were turned toward a floor-model RCA console television that she remembered was heavy enough to double as the anchor for a naval ship. The black-and-white television took up a third of the room and the rabbit-ear antenna was still perfectly positioned to pick up the Univision broadcast out of Chicago.

Tia headed down the short hall, passing the closet-sized room that had served for twenty years as her parents' master suite. She walked into her bedroom, even smaller than the other. Brad Paisley stared down from one wall and the Dixie Chicks, still together, from another. She collapsed onto the single bed, amazed that somehow the sheets, which had spent hundreds of collective hours on the clothesline, still smelled of sunlight.

She lay there in a semi-conscious stupor, remembering. This place. This room. Looking back, she had grown to realize just how poor her family had been, but it didn't matter. As a child, Tia figured she had it all. After spending the first five years of her life traveling from one migrant camp to the next, her family had landed here. They had lived on this farm for nearly fifteen years in a tin trailer that was less than four hundred square feet. To Tia, it had been a palace. A home filled with the unconditional love of her parents, not to mention running water and electricity.

Right now, she wanted desperately to feel connected to that life. The simplicity and warmth. The *sanity* of it. Tia lay still, closing her eyes, trying to conjure up that love, those old feelings and images. Anything to help restore the life she had known.

A light weight settled onto the mattress alongside her. A small body nuzzled in close. Tia's mind screamed at her to ignore it, that it wasn't real, but it was too late. Reluctantly, Tia turned to look, knowing who was there. As expected, she saw a childish face, brown eyes filled with love and affection. The little girl's hair smelled like lavender. When she spoke, her voice was lyrical.

Hola, Tia.

Try as she might to resist, Tia found herself pouring her soul into the moment, into this bond with another person like nothing she'd experienced with anyone else. Not with Connor, not with Ben, not with her own parents. She tried to hold back, reminding herself that crazy people hear voices and see people who aren't there, not cops.

"No," Tia said out loud, shaking her head, fighting the hallucination. Fear crept over her, making her feel sluggish, her limbs weighted down. She knew the vividness of the moment caused the terror. Staring at the girl lying next to her, Tia rejected the evidence of her own eyes.

"I am alone," she told herself. "You're not real. You can't stay here. You need to leave me alone."

The child's reply seemed to be coming from outside her mind, as if a real person were whispering in Tia's ear. *Usted no está solo, Tia. Alguna vez.*

Tia shook her head, refusing the magic. The young face faded and grew older. The eyes went from joyful and innocent to terrified, the lashes caked in red mascara. Disembodied hands swam out of the darkness to slap duct tape over the now-mature mouth. An unseen force jerked the girl off the bed and she disappeared into a swirl of black. Tia heard the teenager's body thud against the floor, heard her muffled screams. Unable to move, pinned in place by fear and alcohol, Tia felt her mind was filled with the child's voice, shouting, *Ándale, Tia. Ándale!*

Tia buried her head in the pillow. She could still hear the sound of a body being dragged down the hall, the front door swinging open and banging against the aluminum siding. Finally the young woman's desperate cries faded into the distance. Tia had her hands clamped over her ears, but she still heard every strangled shout.

Is she real now? Do I go after her? What if none of it is real?

All the liquor and prescription dope in Wisconsin wasn't going to drown out the most terrifying thought: *What if I really am losing my mind?*

SIX

In the Milwaukee County Jail interrogation room, Tia sat, drumming her fingers on the wood tabletop as her knee bounced out a nervous cadence underneath. Her head throbbed and her tongue was thick in her mouth, like a crumpled sheet of 80 grit sandpaper. She felt like hell, but she pushed all that aside. Someone had to do something. For her, it was a simple fact: the girl in the van was real. She was part of this world, not a ghost, a memory, or some nether-world image.

The girl in the van needed help. She needed a cop.

The cube-like room where Tia waited was nothing more than four gray cement walls with a matching floor and twelve-foot ceiling. Two handle-less doors were cut flush into opposite sides of the room and could only be opened from the outside. A swaying lamp hung from a cable overhead, caught up in the draft of a wall fan that did nothing to lower the stifling heat. The light was intense and the furnishing sparse. It was a place that left Tia feeling exposed.

That's the whole idea, she thought. *Makes the lies easier to see.* Tia wondered what else might be visible: The paralyzing fear that followed her everywhere these days? Her desperation?

A warning light flashed in some hazy but still-sensible part of her alcohol-sodden brain. *Leave. No one would ever know. Just bang on the exit door and get the hell out of here. Chalk the trip up as the ultimate boneheaded idea, a narrowly averted disaster.*

She heard the sound of heavy footsteps accompanied by the jangle of chain. Her adrenaline kicked into high gear. Tia got to her feet at the exact moment the door leading to the cells swung open and a massive figure filled the doorway. *Too late.*

Game on.

Tia stretched to her entire five feet four inches and did her best to don the mask of power and authority. She tried to make it seem as if she had stood up to establish control, reminding him that she was a cop. A glance at the newcomer told her she had failed. *This guy reads fear for a living,* she thought. He was a cheetah to her tommy gazelle, and as he looked at her his expression went from stoic to predatorily amused.

"Well, I'll be damned. Lookie here. We gonna finish our little business transaction?"

Tia kept her response short and simple, hoping to keep the quiver from her voice. "Sit down, Kane."

She hadn't seen Gunther Kane since the night he'd been arrested, and he was even bigger and more repulsive than she remembered. The tight-fitting, triple-XL orange jailhouse jumpsuit, soaked in sweat, was open across his chest, the short sleeves hiding almost nothing of his massive arms, which were covered in tattoos. The mere sight of him reminded her of his weight on her, pressing her into the pavement. *He owned you,* she thought. *If the other cops hadn't arrived when they did, you were done.* She felt the air run out of her body.

Kane stepped into the room, towing a jail guard a third his size.

His hands were cuffed in front of his body. A two-foot-long chain leash attached to a thick leather belt that dug in tight around his waist connected him to the guard, who held the leash with the confidence of a toddler walking a pit bull. With a glance, Kane communicated his intent to stand, and the little corrections officer looked away, avoiding eye contact. Kane turned back to Tia.

"We got nothing to talk to about. Maybe you ain't heard. My lawyer worked it out. I'm outta here as soon as these dumb-ass turn-keys figure out the paperwork."

"That's right," Tia said in a tone she knew lacked conviction. "Your case is settled, so we can talk. Now, I said, sit your ass down."

Kane looked down from his towering vantage point and took her all in. Tia was pretty sure that included her heart slamming against her sternum. Her knees went weak as Kane licked his lips. He grabbed at the leash and tugged to get some slack, then moved over to the wooden chair on his side of the table, pulling his guard along. He flipped the chair around backward, threw a leg over, and lowered himself onto the seat, never taking his eyes off Tia. The cracking sound of the wood as it took his weight echoed off the close walls, but somehow the chair remained in one piece. Kane leaned forward so the chair back covered his chest like a breastplate, his arms and cuffed hands hanging over the top.

It had been dark during their first encounter and she hadn't seen the details of his prison ink. The shamrock of the Aryan Brother-hood stood out on one fully tattooed forearm, and the words "Trust No Bitch" were stenciled in green on the other. Once again he flashed that shit-eating grin.

"Fine. I'll sit here with ya. Don't mind me if I gawk a bit. Still got a couple more lonely nights to get through before I walk outta here." He made it obvious he was running his eyes over her body. "This is gonna help."

Tia dropped into her chair and returned his stare. Somehow she managed to calm her nerves enough to hold his gaze and speak in a steady voice. "I got a deal for you, Kane. It might even be better than the one you must've made with the prosecutor."

"Is that right?" Kane leaned in close, his face less than two feet from hers, his breath smelling of jail food and pruno. A thousand beads of sweat glistened off his enormous head, where Tia could also see the red stubble of four days' growth. "Well, the part of me that ain't dreaming about ass fuckin' you right now is all ears. So let me hear it."

"The girl. Tell me where I can find her. I'll go pick her up. Then, you walk out of here in a few days and never have to deal with me again."

Kane stared ahead, the grin still plastered on his face. With just the slightest movement of his head, he turned his eyes to the corner of the ceiling. "I've already been over that with the lawyers. I don't know what girl you're talking about."

"Forget the camera. Just listen. You make it happen and I leave you alone. Otherwise, I'll be in your shit from now until the time I lock you away. And that'll be for a lot more than ten days."

He looked at the tabletop and laughed under his breath for several seconds.

"You're Suarez, right?" Kane sat back, shifted his manacled hands into his lap, and gave his crotch a long rub. "That's bold talk for a split-tail cop. Especially one who's been through as much bullshit as you have."

Tia stuck to her guns. "Like I said, Kane. Produce the girl and you walk away. Otherwise, we're just getting started."

"Fine by me. Like I said, we got unfinished business. I oughta be out in two days. You be sure to come find me."

Fear gave way to anger and Tia let it fuel her. "It won't go like that, Kane. First thing I'm going to do is plant a few seeds of doubt out there in Aryan Nation. Get your ass-bag associates to wondering just how it is you cut yourself such a good deal."

For the first time a look of uncertainty crossed Kane's face and his smile faltered. Tia let it sink in.

"Fact is, I've been wondering that myself. You attack a cop, you got a pretty good rap sheet with a prison prior, and you walk with a misdemeanor? Makes me wonder what you gave up for that?" Tia paused. "Or maybe it's *who* you gave up."

"Bullshit." For the first time Kane lost his cool. "I didn't give up nothin'. I got no problem doing time for kicking the shit out of cops. Even little dyke cops like you. That builds a lot of cred in my world."

"But you're not doing time. You're walking out."

"You'll have to ask that pretty little lawyer why she took such a shine to me." Kane shrugged. "My animal magnetism, maybe."

"I'm thinking there's more to it than that, Kane. I'm betting your cracker homeboys will, too."

Kane nodded and leaned in, closer than before. He put his hands flat on the table, the metal cuffs scraping loudly against the wood surface.

"Do what you want, I got no worries. My people know, Gunther Kane ain't gonna make a deal with cops."

"Listen, Kane—"

"No, you listen," he said, cutting her off. "I don't often make snap judgments about folks. Making assumptions is a bad habit. But you?" Kane tossed his head in a gesture of dismissal. "I'm pretty confident I've got you figured out."

"How's that, Kane?"

"My lawyer tells me you're damaged goods." Kane raised his cuffed hands and tapped his finger against the side of his head. "Maybe even a little off upstairs."

Tia stared back, feeling exposed, laid open before him. When she said nothing, he went on.

"From what he tells me, you've had some issues in courtrooms lately. You ever think maybe that's why I might be getting a walk?"

Tia's mind reeled with anger and embarrassment. Her chin quivered involuntarily, pissing her off all the more.

Again came Kane's grin of satisfaction. "Don't cry, honey. Just know, you're gonna want to think long and hard about any further associations with me. That could end bad for you. Real bad. My personal opinion? Cute little gal like you, with all you've been through lately? You ought not to be out playing cops and robbers. You could end up on the wrong end of some serious shit. Again."

The last word hit Tia hard. She remembered his hand over her mouth. The strength of his grip as he pushed her toward the van. The girl staring back at her. His weight on top of her. Tia's heart began to pound.

Kane stood, the chair groaning again as he moved. Tia half-expected it to snap into a half-dozen splintered pieces. The guard backed up three quick steps.

"I get it, Suarez. I'll bet you're taking a lot of shit from your cop buddies. You need to show everybody you still got it, right?" His voice deepened, growing even more firm. "Whatever it is you need to prove ain't gonna involve me. We're done. Go back to Newberg. Write some damn parking tickets or whatever, but leave this shit alone. You don't want any part of me."

Kane glared at her, waiting for a response. Tia sat in frozen silence, as if her throat had somehow been clamped shut. She knew Kane sensed victory. Even the jail guard was smirking as if enjoying a rare chance to feel superior. Somewhere in the distance the shrill sound of an alarm signaled the beginning or end of some jailhouse routine. The guard gave the door three sharp raps.

When the door opened, Kane raised an eyebrow, but Tia was still incapable of speech. His smile grew wider as he turned and walked out, followed by his obedient escort. The door slammed shut and Tia sat alone in the small room, staring at nothing. Her fingers took up a new beat, drumming against the table, and her knee bounced hard underneath.

SEVEN

From the doorway Tia stole a look inside. Lit from behind by the midday sun, Ben Sawyer was turned away from her, staring at a framed photograph of his family that he held in two hands. Tia knew the picture well. She had taken it a few days after her return from Mexico. Ben and Alex had insisted she come by the house to see the new baby, Isabella.

The photo showed the whole Sawyer clan in the backyard of their Newberg home, with a backdrop of a perfect Wisconsin sunset. It was the last time Tia had visited the family. There were too many secrets between them now. Tia gave the doorframe a soft rap; Ben jerked slightly, startled, then turned quickly to face her. She stepped into the office.

"Excuse me, Chief. You wanted to see me?"

He was a near-perfect picture of professionalism: uniform pants sharply creased, boots and basket-weave belt polished to a black sheen. Only the snowy white T-shirt he wore detracted from his image—but a crisply pressed uniform shirt bearing a metal badge and four gold stars on the collar hung from the back of a chair, ready to be put on at a moment's notice.

His close-cropped salt-and-pepper hair, his flat stomach, and the jagged scar that ran across his cheek gave Ben the appearance of a military commando more than a small-town police chief. Tia knew he was coming up on forty-five, but he looked like he could still outrun and outgun most of the cops on Newberg PD, though they averaged a little over half his age.

The first time Tia had seen Ben wearing the four stars of a chief, she'd jumped to her feet, given him a mock salute, and called him Patton. The half-dozen officers nearby had laughed and Tia had felt a pang of guilt at the sight of his embarrassed expression. But even now, as he offered her a tight but genuine-looking smile, she hoped some part of him was still happy to see her.

"Get in here." His voice was laced with friendly sarcasm as he set the framed photo down on his desk. "You been dodging me?"

Tia navigated past half a dozen still-unpacked boxes as she cautiously entered the room. The office was too large for its current furnishings, but Ben had stripped away all reminders of the previous occupant. The mahogany bureau, the Italian leather desk chair, the fancy rug, and other opulent accessories were gone, replaced by a gray metal desk, two worn swivel chairs, and a new, cloth-covered couch. Practical items that spoke of dedication to the work.

The lingering stench of stale cigar smoke and a dozen empty wall hooks were all that remained of the man who had recently been evicted from the office of the Newberg Chief of Police, courtesy of Tia Suarez and Ben Sawyer. The sparsely decorated office represented a healing wound, one not yet scabbed over.

"Damn right," Tia answered. "You're the chief now. I've got a reputation to look out for, you know? Rebel. Department rabble-rouser. That sort of thing."

"True enough. I never liked spending time in the chief's office either. But now that I got you in here, take a seat. How are things?"

Tia remained standing. They had been friends once, but he was her boss and that was a boss's question. "Yeah, right, Ben. Like your phone didn't blow up with calls. Was it Kane's lawyer or did one of those jailhouse guards dime me off?"

She had to give the chief credit. He didn't shout. His voice was controlled. "Forget about who called. Fact is, you know better. The guy is represented by counsel. He's in custody. How is it you think you can walk into a jailhouse, in another county no less, and interrogate him?"

Tia hoisted herself onto the edge of Ben's desk and let her feet hang six inches above the carpet.

"Hey, the DA wants to kick him loose, why shouldn't I talk to him? No court proceedings. No charges. What the hell. I figured I might as well try to get something out of the guy before he walks." She shrugged. "Somebody has to."

She managed to sound flippant, hiding her guilty conscience, but Ben didn't take well to her tone. His smile vanished and he became all business.

"And you figured that was your decision? A case from another jurisdiction? Now this Patricia Graham woman tells me you threatened a prisoner with retaliation. She was so fired up she practically jumped through the phone."

"*She* called?" Tia really hadn't expected that. "I swear. The nerve of that—" She looked down at her boots and stopped herself. Insulting the DA wouldn't help. "This should have been a prison case. She let the guy walk on a misdemeanor. After assaulting a cop. One of *your* cops. You telling me you're okay with that?"

It was Ben's turn to sound indignant. "Of course I'm not okay with it. But what you or I think doesn't matter. We don't file cases; lawyers do."

"Are you kidding me?" Tia fumed. Her voice became a near shout. "Hell, I could win this case. If that lawyer—"

"That's enough!" Ben cut her off. "Tone it down. You were out of line with the prosecutor and you sure as hell were out of line by going to the jail. I'll say it again. This guy is represented by counsel. He's locked up. That means hands-off and you damn well know it."

Tia stared at him as the silence became uncomfortable. She knew she had pushed past his limits and tried to regroup. "Jesus, Ben. This whole thing has been a mess from the beginning. I can't help but think if the operation had just gone better . . ."

When her voice trailed away, Ben answered, his tone a bit more reasonable, "I've been over all that with Jackson. It's over and done with."

"Don't go blaming Jackson. Hell, I'm the one who wandered off camera." Tia tried to shrug it off. "It was all good until it wasn't. You know how it is when you look back. Woulda, shoulda, coulda. We all came out okay, but I'm telling you, the case on Kane was solid. We had him on felony assault. There's no way he should be getting a pass."

"Well, he is," Ben said with a sigh. "You need to deal with it and that means no rogue visits to the jail to try to put a twist on the suspect. This case is *done*."

He rubbed his hand against the deep scar that ran from the corner of his eye to his upper lip, giving his face the look of ill-fitted puzzle pieces. *Damn, we got some history,* she thought, remembering when he'd gotten that wound. *But now, it's like we're strangers. How did that happen?* She picked up on his frustration, something beyond Kane. *There's more to come,* she thought.

"I know I'm not operational anymore, Tia, but I have to say there is no way you should have been working U/C. If I had known about it, I would have put the whole thing down."

"It wasn't a big deal," she said, striving for lightness.

"It was too soon. You shouldn't have been out there. Jackson claims you talked him into it against his better judgment. Says you really pushed for this."

"Yeah? What do you want, Ben? Cops who like sitting around, twiddling their thumbs, waiting for something to just fall into their laps?"

"You could've really gotten messed up." She heard the concern in his voice.

"But I wasn't. It was nobody's fault, Ben. It was a one-in-a-million kind of thing. One second I'm talking to a john, and the next thing I know there's two of them and they're trying to force me into a van. That's where they had the—"

Tia stopped in mid-sentence as her grip slipped away from the girl's ankle. She felt the moist sweat on her hand. The van door slammed shut and sped from the lot. The sights and sounds of the event were as fresh as ever.

"That's the other thing," Ben said. "About this girl you say was in the van. . . ."

The doubt in his voice made her strike back. "That I say was in the van? She was *there*, Ben. Tied up and gagged."

He said nothing, watching her. Tia went on. "You think I made that up? Or what? That I imagined it somehow?"

Ben blew out a long breath. "Tia, doesn't this sound, I don't know, pretty damn familiar?"

"What?" Tia pushed herself off the desk. She couldn't believe what she was hearing. "What are you saying, Ben?"

"Look," he said, sounding defensive and a little exasperated. "You've been through a lot, Tia. It's been a rough few months. I mean, think about what happened in the courtroom. Couldn't it be—"

Tia shook her head. She knew exactly what Ben was talking about—the experiences she'd had after being shot. But this wasn't the same. "Ben, there was a girl in the van. I know what I saw. Let me work on it. All we have to do is put a tail on Kane when he leaves the jail. I bet the dumb ass will take us right to her."

"No. Absolutely not." Ben gave Tia a look that said he knew who he was dealing with. "Listen to me on this, Detective. You're done nosing around this case. Newberg PD has zero jurisdiction here, not to mention the case is closed. This guy is walking and that's where it ends. From here on out, you stay away. Are we clear on that?"

Damn, this is frustrating, she thought. On top of her having to sit through the lecture, her head was pounding from long nights of no real sleep. She'd snatched a few minutes here and there, but the face of the girl in the van had haunted her dreams as much as her waking hours.

How much longer could she keep this up? Maybe it was time to check out, head back down to Mexico. Her disability retirement pay would go a long way in Jalisco. Hell, maybe she could talk Connor into going. *Just the two of us. A beach in Mexico.* Ben's voice brought her back.

"So will you do that for me, Tia?"

"What? Sorry, what did you say?" Her mouth was suddenly dry as cotton and she craved the meds that had become part of her daily routine.

"I said, I think you need to talk this thing through with somebody who can help you deal with it."

"I thought that's what we were doing right here," Tia replied.

"I mean someone from outside the department." Ben took a deep breath and went on, "I think you should go back to Dr. Gage."

Tia shook her head, insulted. "I don't need any more shrinks. Especially him. I'm fine. I'm pissed, but I'll get over it."

"Tia, you were attacked. It was a traumatic event. It may have triggered something from before.

"It was your first time out since coming back. Like I said, I blame myself. I shouldn't have let you go out this soon. But what's done is done. You need to debrief this with a professional. Someone who can help you deal with it."

Tia stood up. "Well, like I said, thanks, but I'm not interested in getting my head shrunk anymore. I'm good with where I'm at."

Ben took a deep breath and blew it out. "What makes you think I'm *asking,* Detective?"

Irritated now, Tia spoke more aggressively. "I thought this was all about our special connection, Ben. Now you're playing the chief card?"

Ben got up and came around his desk to stand near Tia. He put both hands on his hips like he didn't know what else to do with them. *He hates this,* she thought.

"I'll fill out a form two ten right now, ordering you into no-duty status until you get cleared by the county psych. Or you can go on your own and there doesn't have to be any paper trail. I wouldn't extend that offer to anyone else on the PD, Tia."

Tia gave Ben a harsh look. Her tone of voice didn't hide the fact that she felt betrayed. "That's mighty big of you, Chief. Save the paper—I'll go see the damn shrink. But remember, whatever goes on between me and Gage is privileged. If he signs off on me, I come back to work and that's the end of it. No questions asked."

Ben started to respond and Tia put up a hand.

"I'm done talking to you," she said, heading for the door. "That is, unless you're going to order me to stay."

Ben shook his head and said in a tightly controlled, low voice, "No, Tia, you can leave if that's what you want."

At the door, Tia turned back to her boss and friend.

"What *I* want?" Her voice cracked. "What I want is the next time you call me in for a friendly chat you stick to the weather and family stuff. I am not interested in being judged by a guy who committed half a dozen felonies when he decided the whole law-and-order route wasn't working. But if *that* guy comes back, that Ben Sawyer, hell, I'll talk to him anytime. And about anything."

The air grew thick with tension and disappointment. After a long silence, Ben took a step forward.

"Tia—"

She didn't want to hear any more. "Stop, Ben," she said sharply. "I get it. Things are different now. I respect that."

Ben shook his head in surrender.

"Talk to Dr. Gage, Tia. Let me know when you've worked through all this baggage so we can move on."

"*We?* There is no we, Ben." Tia headed for the door, leaving him alone in the office. "It's pretty obvious you moved on a long time ago."

EIGHT

The hell with this chief crap, Ben thought. There was a time he could just lean back and say exactly what was on his mind. Now every word had to be guarded, even when talking to someone like Tia. He thought back over the conversation he'd just had. *How had it gone so wrong?*

Ben didn't care about the lawyer getting all up in his grill about his insolent detective and her unauthorized jail visit. Tia was right about Graham: she came off as some kind of high-strung control freak. Still, Ben had done the chiefly thing and offered his apologies on behalf of Newberg PD.

Tia going off the reservation and doing her own thing was nothing new. The jail visit was just Tia being Tia. Hell, that's what he loved about her. But something else was going on; he was certain of it. Something was wrong with her. *Unsurprising, perhaps, given that she's been to hell and back. And whose fault is that?*

Almost a year earlier, Tia had come to the Sawyer home and basically told Ben to pull his head out of his ass. Ben's wife, Alex, had been locked up on a bogus murder charge, staring down the barrel of a conviction. Ben had been wallowing in despair and frustration. If not for Tia Suarez spurring him to take action, what would have happened? On top of that, it was Tia's trip to Danville, Illinois, that broke the case . . . and nearly got her killed.

There was no denying that Tia's trials and tribulations had begun when she'd reached out to save Alex.

Ben conceded that Tia was right about one thing. He had broken just about every department regulation, not to mention more than a few laws, to prove his wife's innocence. But without Tia's help, Alex might be dead or serving a life sentence for a murder she didn't commit. Ben owed Tia a debt he could never repay.

Not that he hadn't tried, but at the beginning there wasn't time. While Tia was convalescing in Mexico, Ben had had to put his family—and Newberg PD—back together. When she'd returned to Wisconsin, the entire community had rolled out the red carpet for their local hero; on her first day back on the job, there'd been a ceremony, attended by all the local big shots. Tia had been promoted to detective. It should have been a great moment for Tia, but Ben had known even then that something wasn't right.

At first, he'd written it off as a case of nerves—until the episode at the Waukesha County Courthouse. The call had been stunning. Tough-as-nails Tia Suarez had been reduced on the witness stand to a sobbing mess, screaming about the girl in her head.

He'd had no choice. Police Chief Ben Sawyer had ordered Tia into "no-duty" status pending a psychiatric examination. Everyone—Ben included—assumed Tia was suffering from post-traumatic stress as a result of the shooting incident. There was some talk about forcing her into early retirement—a suggestion Ben rejected absolutely. After two months of intensive therapy, Tia had been cleared to return to limited duty.

Back at work the second time, Tia had let Ben know she understood. She'd said all the right things, including that there were no hard feelings and that she didn't blame him, but Ben knew things would never be the same between them. Their relationship was now strictly professional and Ben missed their friendship.

And now he had to wonder, *Should she even be a cop anymore?*

There was gossip about Tia showing up for work in rough shape. Hitting the bottle, hard. Maybe misusing her meds.

Ben knew the time might soon come when he would be forced to make a tough decision about Tia's future.

He shook his head, wondering how he had ended up on the wrong side of this fight. He picked up the phone and punched out the number he had written on his notepad. The call was answered after two rings.

"This is Patricia Graham."

"Ms. Graham? Ben Sawyer calling from Newberg. We spoke earlier and I promised you a callback."

"Yes, Chief. Did you get everything worked out?"

Ben leaned back against his desk and looked out the window at the parking lot. He saw Tia walking toward her GTO with the short, jerky pace she used when she was really heated up.

"I spoke to my detective. We'll have no further contact with Kane."

"I'm glad to hear that." The voice was laced with the fake sincerity lawyers specialize in. "I'll smooth things over on this end. I don't want anything coming down on your officer."

"She's a detective, actually." He'd heard from Jackson about Graham's mischaracterization of Tia's rank; he wasn't going to let her get away with it either.

"Yes, of course. Just no more jailhouse visits, okay? And make sure she gives Mr. Kane a wide berth."

"Like I said, Ms. Graham, we're out," Ben answered, matching the woman's terseness. "But I have to say, this is a tough pill to swallow. You kicked this thing all the way down to disorderly? Seems like you settled pretty low. I guess we're just used to taking officer-assault charges a little more serious in Waukesha County. "

"I thought we agreed, based on Suarez's history, that it would be a good idea to avoid any court proceedings."

"Forget about what Suarez may or may not have seen. I get it. But that doesn't change the fact Kane assaulted her."

"I understand how you feel, Chief. But I've seen the surveillance footage. Your detective got her licks in as well."

Ben was confused. "What surveillance footage?"

Graham sounded flustered when she continued after a long pause. "Thanks for speaking with Suarez, Chief. I hope we get a chance to work together again soon."

"Hang on a second. What did you mean by—"

The phone line went dead. Ben was certain TJ had told him Tia had wandered off camera. Why was the lawyer talking about surveillance footage? He took another look out his window and saw the sleek white GTO still in the lot. Tia sat in the driver's seat, her head resting against the steering wheel.

A friend would go to her, he thought. *Instead, you sent her off to talk to the frickin' shrink. Again.* He pulled the string and the venetian blinds snapped shut. He moved to his desk and got busy being the chief.

NINE

Gunther Kane sat alone at the bar of the Roadhouse Score and took a drag on his cigarette, thinking that the gateway to hell probably looked a lot like a strip club at 8:00 A.M. on a Sunday. A few stools away sat the faithful gathering of a half-dozen or so hard-core drunks, hunched over a liquid breakfast served up by head bouncer, Buster Cobb. At this hour, Buster also served as bartender and grill cook. It saved money on overhead and who knows—maybe one of those pickled bastards would miraculously decide to eat an egg or some such shit.

The men conferred among themselves, bemoaning the sad state of national affairs and the hijacking of the American government by a foreign-born, mixed-race dictator. It was the same rant day after day, but not one of the grizzled sons of bitches could stand up long enough to do anything about it. Kane shook his head at the pathetic state of the rank and a file of the notorious North Aryan Front, also known as the NAF.

Kane knew he couldn't be too hard on the boys. They were, after all, a pretty damn good meal ticket for a solider of the Aryan

Brotherhood and full-patched member of the Hells Angels who happened to be looking for a new home. When Kane was discharged from Waupun Prison almost three years back, he'd fallen in with the NAF and found it served as a solid base camp for his criminal enterprise. As he was a man who always had an ear to the ground, it had come as no surprise to Kane to learn the NAF was now recognized by the FBI, the Department of Defense, and most civil rights watchdogs as an organized hate group that espoused white Aryan superiority. Looking over the men at the bar, Kane thought, *If these guys are a threat to national security the U.S. better not piss off Canada. Or Greenland for that matter. A well-organized Girl Scout troop would kick the shit out of the NAF.*

For the morning, Kane had nixed the Roadhouse Score's usual country dance music and cranked up the thrasher rock of Metallica, currently spewing out his own personal theme music from *Kill 'Em All*. The lights were turned up high, exposing the nicotine-yellowed popcorn ceiling and the cheap faux wood–paneled walls. Three silver poles rose up out of the nearby stage, abandoned and empty, of no current interest to anyone. The thick air was drenched with the lingering odor of last night's five hundred unwashed bodies, mixed with the sickening, sweet smells of beer, cheap wine, hard liquor, and a dozen or so pools of vomit that still needed to be located and hosed down the floor drains. Even with the nighttime veneer of sex appeal stripped away, leaving the joint with the energy of a moonscape, Kane knew the Roadhouse Score still beat the hell out of county jail.

No doubt about it. Kane had dodged a major bullet. When the lawyer put the offer of disorderly conduct on the table his first thought was, *They're fucking with me. Cop humor or some shit.* Right up until yesterday, when the jail doors opened and they let him walk out, Kane had been waiting for the other shoe to drop.

He gave himself a mental shake. He was out. It was time to get back to business.

The run-in with the cops and the week in custody had cost him. Without Kane on hand to oversee operations the Roadhouse had done a fraction of its typical $10–15K a night. Not to mention the major deal that remained on the table. *Gotta get back in the game.*

The strip club's door opened and a single figure sauntered in. Kane sat and watched as the newcomer got put through a shakedown by Jessup Tanner, Kane's right-hand man. Curtis Bell wasn't just any patron, and even from a distance Kane sensed danger in the man's cold stare. Even as Bell turned over his cell phone, wallet, and keys, then took a seat on a lap dance couch in a far corner of the club, he kept his gaze fixed on Kane, who finally looked away as if he had grown disinterested.

Kane had known Curtis Bell long enough to realize the man had an appreciation for smooth-running operations. Today's meeting might be rough.

It had been almost three years since Kane and Tanner had gone to Sturgis for the single weekend of the year when the town was overrun with one percenters. Tanner, who had never been to the famous gathering of outlaw bikers, had talked Kane into making the run. It was there that Kane met Curtis Bell, turning the trip into a most fortuitous venture. Kane, a Hells Angel, found he had much in common with Bell, who, back in the day, had ridden with the Mongols. Both had moved on since then, Kane to prison and Bell to the army.

When they first met in Sturgis, Kane was still under the control of the Wisconsin Parole Commission but had already begun his association with the North Aryan Front. The NAF was never about ideology to him; it was an opportunity to cash in, to use the quasi-organized militia group as a base of operations for low-level organized crime. Prostitution, drug sales, and as of late, illegal gun purchases. That was where Curtis Bell came in.

In Sturgis, the ex-con and the war hero struck up a friendship based mostly on excessive shots of Jack Daniel's chased with PBR. Kane was fascinated by Bell's stories of killing Arabs at close range during his two tours in Afghanistan and one in Iraq. Bell wanted to hear all about Kane's life on the inside under the protection of the Aryan Brotherhood.

At some point the conversation turned to Kane's frustration over his inability to buy a gun on the legitimate market. A few days later they arranged to meet at a rest stop in Minnesota, where Bell sold Kane a still-in-the-box, government-issue, SIG SAUER 229 forty cal with three extended magazines. Bell had even thrown in a half-dozen boxes of Hydra-Shok ammo.

That first deal had marked the beginning of a mutually beneficial partnership between Bell and Kane. Over the past few years, Kane had played middleman for other NAF members and associates who, like him, felt incomplete without a forty caliber or above some-where on their body. Bell always provided new stock and Kane moved it along quickly at a tidy profit. The NAF provided him never-ending access to men with an insatiable iron deficiency. Bottom line: there was money to be made. Now, two years after their first business transaction, the time had come to find out just exactly what Mr. Curtis "War-Hero-Gone-Bad" Bell was really capable of.

Finished with Bell, Tanner approached Kane at the bar. "He's all set, boss. Cell phone's off, battery out. He's clean of any other electronic shit. But . . ."—Tanner hesitated—"he knows about the deal in Milwaukee. Seems put off about it."

Kane looked past Tanner and studied the new arrival.

"Is that right? I hope you took full credit." Kane stood and hitched his jeans up so the waistline fit snug under the overhang of his fifty-four-inch gut. "Follow me over, but hold back ten feet. You're strapped, right?"

Tanner pulled back on the denim vest that exposed his boney white arms, showing the forty-five shoved in the waistband of his jeans. He spoke as if he didn't like it when his preparation was called into question. "Come on now, boss."

"Fine. Walk with me. But don't speak. I'll handle this." Kane's tone was harsh. The ill will from being left to fend for himself in the parking lot still grated on his nerves. A long conversation on the subject still needed to be had. Kane would see to it that Tanner never left him behind again.

Kane maintained eye contact as he crossed the open dance floor and closed to within three feet of Bell.

"Come on," he said evenly, motioning with his arm. "We'll talk in my office. More private."

"We'll talk here," Bell said without moving.

Kane let his annoyance show. "What the hell, Curtis? Didn't you hear me? It's more private."

"You should always be so concerned about privacy," Bell said.

"Meaning?"

"Your run-in with the cops. What the fuck, Gunther? We're in the middle of a major deal and you're out trying to score some brown strange on a street corner?"

Because of their history, Kane allowed Bell to take some liberties, but history or not, he wouldn't have Bell talking smack in front of a bunch of foot soldiers.

"That's been dealt with." Kane continued the stare-down. "And it'd be best if you limit your conversation to the business at hand."

"Dealt with?" The dry tone made Kane wonder if he was being mocked—and Bell's next words confirmed it. "'Dealt with' would imply you made a deal. You do seven days' custody after assaulting an undercover cop? Remind me to get the name of your lawyer."

Kane took one step closer, to narrow the gap between them. "It was nothing. Some dumb-ass flatfoot out of Newberg. Their case was shit and the DA knew it. And like I said, that's got nothing to do with this business here."

"Maybe that's the way you see it, but that kind of notoriety? You start pulling down deals like that with a prosecutor, people will wonder about the nature of your legal relationships."

"What the hell is that supposed to mean?"

"It means I got partners, Kane. Men still in uniform. People who don't care to become part of your legal deal making. So until we reestablish some trust, I'll say where and when we meet."

Kane glared ahead, his heart pounding in anger. He wondered if that Suarez bitch had made good on her threat to sow seeds of doubt about his reputation. Several seconds passed before he relented and took a seat on the opposite couch with a low cocktail table between them.

"Fine. But if you end up stuck to the furniture, don't blame me. It gets quite the nightly workout, if you know what I mean."

"We had a deal." Bell looked at Tanner, then at Kane. He kept his voice low. "A hundred pieces plus accessories. I've been sitting on this stuff for a week. Are you in or not?"

In his early thirties, with Nordic features, pale skin without a hint of pink, and white-blond hair clipped short, Curtis Bell had the look of the all-American male. The skin of his face fit tight to his skull. His plain, stark white T-shirt covered toned muscle that was not blemished with so much as a single drop of ink. His gray eyes never held any of the normal intimidation or fear that Kane was accustomed to seeing in the people he did business with.

Kane had also come to realize Curtis Bell could deliver. Whether a man needed an untraceable revolver scraped clean of serial numbers or a high-end semi-automatic forty cal still in the box, for the right price Bell would come through. They had made dozens of single weapon transactions, but this deal would take Kane's relationship with Bell to the next level. This was where the real money got made. He was determined to make it happen.

"Don't get all black ass on me, Bell. We're getting ready to take shipment."

"Getting ready isn't good enough. This shit was supposed to happen a week ago," Bell said. "Time to get it done or we're moving on. It's a seller's market."

"So you really pulled it off, huh?" Kane said. "That's a lot of iron."

"What the fuck? You ordered it. You thought I wouldn't deliver?"

"That ain't it. But like you said, I had that run-in with the local cops." Kane tossed his head, indicating the men who stood back from the table. "Can't trust these guys for dick. While I was locked up, I ordered a shutdown of everything other than legitimate operations. Our cash flow is down, but we'll bounce back."

"That's not my problem, Kane. I need to move the inventory. A hundred pieces. Factory direct. Fully automatic. Plus fifty thousand rounds."

"That's a hundred large to me," Kane said, confirming the agreed-upon price.

"Yeah, it is. Cash."

Kane cocked his head. "That's a lot of cash."

"Maybe to some folks, but you told me your people could handle it. That you were ready to step up. Now we need to close this out."

"Fine. I need a week. Maybe ten days."

Bell shook his head, expressionless. "Not going to happen. You got five days. Otherwise I'll unload this shit on some dinge gang down in Chicago. You can deal with the brothers once you scrape together your nickels and dimes."

Bell's voice turned smug. "But you might want to remember, those boys have a tendency to jack the price when dealing with folks who hold certain views on the subject of race relations."

"Five days then." Kane made sure his voice was filled with judgment. "Good to know where your heart lies."

"Save it, Kane. My heart is green. This is business. My partners and I don't need to get wrapped up in politics. If that race war all you Aryan types are worried about ever really comes, you can be sure we'll be happy to supply both sides." Bell winked. "You can't get any more American than that."

Couldn't agree more, Kane thought to himself. But if the man wanted to think Kane was all about the movement, all the better. "Fine. Five days. We'll take delivery on payment."

Bell gave a long stare as if mulling it over. "Good. In the meantime, stay out of police cars. And that cop from Newberg? You might want to stay particularly clear of her."

Kane huffed up at the thought. "Suarez? The hell with that bitch."

"Not so fast, Kane." A hint of condescension had snuck into Bell's tone and Kane didn't like it. "We checked her out. Before she was a cop, she did two tours in Afghanistan with a Marine sniper team. Last year she took down a pretty hard player on a tough case. Word on the street is she can be like a dog on the bite. Doesn't have much in the way of quit."

"Nothing to worry about," Kane said. "You might say she and I have come to an understanding. If she's a dog on the bite, she's one of them little Mexican pocket dogs, the ones them rich bitches out in Hollywood carry around in their purses."

Kane laughed at his joke and Tanner yucked it up from the perimeter. Bell remained stone-faced.

"I know all about your jailhouse conversation, Gunther. The report I got is you held up pretty well. Handled yourself like a real soldier. You should know, that's the only reason we're still doing business. But like I said, stay clear of her. She can be persistent."

Kane nodded his head, intrigued. "God damn, Curtis. Ain't you all hooked up? Even got yourself a man on the inside? You're like some international spy or some such shit, huh?"

With no show of effort Bell stood, towering over Kane, who began to pull himself to his feet with a good bit of huffing.

"Don't bother getting up." Bell looked down at him. "And remember . . . my people aren't interested in getting famous."

Bell leaned down until his face was inches from Kane's. "And they don't like to be inconvenienced. We went through a good deal of effort to get this shipment together. Don't disappoint."

Tanner scurried after Bell as the man walked toward the front of the bar. Bell reclaimed his property, tucked the items back into his pockets, and turned to leave. When he opened the door, sunlight suddenly flooded the room, a reminder that there was still a world waiting outside the club. Pausing in the doorway, Bell turned back to Kane. He held up five fingers, brought his chin down sharply, then walked out. The door swung shut and the room fell dark. Kane turned to Tanner.

"What the hell are you standing around for? We got five days to score a hundred g's. Get the bitches busy on the poles and pull out all the stops. Even then, it's gonna be tight."

TEN

At moments like this, walking the tree-lined streets of down-town Newberg, Ben couldn't help but be flooded with nos-talgia. Even now, with him in full uniform, preoccupied with worry over Tia Suarez, the scenery took him back to boyhood. This small Wisconsin town, with its steadfast Nordic heritage, was the only real home he had ever known. Despite all the years he and Alex had spent in California, he'd never felt settled there, felt more like a gun-toting mercenary than a lawman. Being a cop in Newberg connected him to something he had come perilously close to losing.

"Afternoon, Chief Sawyer. Beautiful day, isn't it?"

"Hello, Mrs. Peterson." Ben smiled at the passing woman, who had been teaching at Newberg Elementary since before Ben and Alex had entered first grade. "It is very nice, isn't it?"

Like the Norgaard and Sawyer families, most townspeople boasted of being second-generation Newbergens, if not third. The twenty thousand residents of Newberg remained predominantly of Norwegian stock and maintained some Scandinavian traditions. These people farmed or worked locally, making their money as artisans or small-business entrepreneurs. Some worked in one of the manufacturing plants that still flourished in a township able to offer affordable housing, a stalwart labor force, and a wholesome lifestyle.

Ben walked past a Victorian home converted into a mix of apartments and commercial space. The occasional vehicle drove slowly along cobbled streets still pristine after a hundred years of use. He preferred the old-world charm of the central district to the outer edges of town, where large swaths of tract homes had begun to pop up to fit the modern lifestyle of the young suburbanites who commuted to Milwaukee, forty-five minutes to the east.

The new planned developments reminded Ben of the sprawling community his family had lived in out west. In California, people thought nothing of taking a thousand acres of scrub desert, redirecting a river or two, and churning out a sea of homes with five staggered floor plans, arranged and landscaped in a way Ben found nauseatingly repetitive. That might work in the frantic ten-year turnover cycle of California, but Wisconsin was different. When Ben looked at row upon row of new houses on the outskirts of Newberg, he didn't see a transformed, arid wasteland.

He thought back to the nineteenth-century farms and the families who worked them. The tens of thousands of acres that fed millions of people around the country and beyond. Now the farms were mostly gone, the price of corn and barley unable to keep pace with the worth of a five-thousand-square-foot lot leveled and cleared for a four-bedroom, three-bath prefab. Ben recognized the weakness of his nostalgia, but he respected the heartiness of the old life and he hated to think of it passing from the earth.

As he walked, various citizens called for his attention, some wanting to stop and chat about the nighttime activity of a neighbor or to suggest a strategy for combatting the drag racing that went on every weekend out on State Highway 12. When Ben finally got close enough to smell the aroma of roasting coffee beans, he picked up his pace, nodding at passersby rather than speaking with them. After his contentious meeting with Tia, Ben had developed a sudden urge to see his wife. Over the past six months, during all her stages of setback and recovery, no one had been closer to Tia than Alex.

Books and Java, Alex's coffeehouse and bookstore, was empty except for Ben's wife, who was squatting down low, checking the temperature setting of the coffee roaster. He stood in the open doorway for a moment to admire the girl—now woman—he had known and loved since he was nine. All these years later, and just five months after the birth of their second child, Alex still had the body of a twenty-year-old. Her blond hair was pulled back in a tight ponytail and her skin glowed with its usual rich summertime tan. When he realized she hadn't heard the door open, he called out.

"Can I get one of those triple foamy caramel frappu things with whip cream and chocolate shavings?" Alex stood up and spun around, already smiling at the sound of her husband's voice. Ben winked. "Nonfat milk, though, okay?"

Alex turned back to the commercial-grade roaster, shaking her head. "Walk down the street to the stoplight. Ugly green mermaid sign on your left. They've got just what you want."

Ben walked over and gave his wife a peck on the cheek and slung an arm around her waist. She pushed him away, playing like she had better things to do.

"Not now, Ben. I'm getting ready to dump the seeds."

"Hey, sorry." Ben feigned offense. "I think you paid more attention to me when you drank Folgers."

"I never drank Folgers." Alex pulled on the large silver handle and the chute opened. Dark brown coffee beans, which Alex always liked to point out were actually seeds, cascaded out of the spinning drum and into the cooling bin. She switched on the metal paddle that began to slowly stir the warm beans, then flipped on the cooling fan, filling the air with the unmistakable aroma of fresh-roasted whole-bean coffee.

Soon after buying Books and Java, Alex began roasting coffee in the store. The eight-foot-tall, four-hundred-pound piece of machinery sat just a few feet inside the front door. When she was roasting, which was most mornings, Alex would leave the door open and the smell would bring customers from blocks away. In the winter months, when it was too cold to keep the door open, every patron's arrival and departure sent a blast of warm, aromatic love into the world. Business had doubled. Ben didn't know why he was surprised to add entrepreneurship to her list of skills.

"What's the blend?"

"Sumatra Peaberry. Sit down. I'll bring you a mug."

Alex scooped some still-warm beans into her hand and went to the grinder behind the counter. Ben made himself comfortable at a nearby table. Alex had switched out the artwork since the last time he had come by, he noticed. Used books were stacked on the cement floor, waiting to be shelved. Head tilted, Ben was reading titles when Alex glided over, setting two steaming mugs onto the table and taking a seat.

Ben held a cup high and gave his typical salute. "Fuck-Bucks."

Alex shook her head at his coarse language. "Cheers," she said, lifting her own mug.

Ben took a sip of what most people agreed was some of the finest coffee sold east of Seattle. "So," he said, doing his best to sound casual, "Tia come by this morning?"

"No," Alex said. "Why do you ask?"

"No reason. I know she is a regular customer, just wondered if she'd been in."

"So you walked down here to ask me? You can't keep track of your detectives?"

Ben said nothing.

"What aren't you telling me?"

"It's just . . ." He wasn't sure what he wanted to say. "I don't know. She's going through some stuff. I thought she might have come by. She and I don't really talk much. Not like we used to."

"Why is that? She's back to work right? Full duty?"

Ben had held off on telling Alex about the hooker detail, but he knew she would find out sooner or later, so he launched in. After fifteen years of being a cop's wife and a lifetime as a cop's daughter, Alex was more than familiar with all aspects of police work. Ben never had to dumb it down or sugarcoat it. In fact, if he ever tried Alex would call him on it. Ben gave Alex a complete rundown of the operation and how the wheels fell off with the prosecutor. Alex listened intently, without interruption.

"Disorderly conduct?" Alex said when Ben finished. "She has every right to be upset. Can't you do something?"

"Apparently the deal's been struck. Can't unring the bell."

"Should she have even been working a U/C detail? I mean, I thought you were going to start her off slow?"

"Yeah, that was the plan, but I didn't make the call." Ben thought back to his conversations with Sergeant Jackson. "TJ gave her the assignment, but Tia twisted the hell out of his arm. You know how she can be."

"So she saw a girl in the back of the van?" Alex asked. "What now?"

Ben sipped his coffee and looked over the top of the cup. "What do you mean?"

"I mean, what are you doing about it? So what if the DA kicks it. Get back in there and build a stronger case, right?"

"That's not going to happen." Ben shook his head and began to question the wisdom of having brought it up at all. "I got a call from the prosecutor. She was all worked up about Tia going to see the suspect in county lockup. If we go sniffing around the case now, it'll get really ugly."

"So what then? Milwaukee PD?"

Ben shrugged. "That's up to them."

Alex sat back in her chair and shook her head. "Well, if I were Tia, I'd be pretty mad, too."

"Come on, Alex. Really?" Ben's voice reflected his disbelief. "A girl in the back of a van? Does that make any sense? When you consider all the circumstances—"

"Don't tell Tia you feel that way. She might bite your head off." Alex grimaced.

Ben thought about stopping there, but again, the woman was going to find out one way or another. "Too late. And you're right. She wasn't happy."

"I can imagine." Alex looked hard at her husband and Ben knew she suspected that there was more. "So now what? Back to business as usual?"

"Not exactly." Ben looked into his cup. "I told Tia she needed to get cleared by Dr. Gage."

Alex set her cup down. Her voice was pained. "Oh, Ben. Really? Gage? Do you realize how awful he has been to Tia?"

"I don't have a choice, Alex. She was in a major fight. She says they tried to kidnap her. An event like that is considered traumatic and requires a fitness for duty eval."

"But Gage?"

"Can't be helped. He's got the county contract. Tia just needs to answer the man's questions and she'll be back to work. That's how it is."

The couple sat quietly and Ben knew that Alex was pained by what he had done. He also knew she was wise enough to understand that he hadn't had a lot of choice in the matter.

He sighed. This was as good a time as any to bring up the real issue.

"You know, Tia never really bounced all the way back. She's not the same."

"How so?" Alex said in a voice that told Ben she had her own misgivings.

"Drinking. Maybe script meds. I've heard rumors she shows up to work late. Kind of disheveled. She hasn't closed a major case in over a month."

"Did you talk to her about it?" Alex looked at him and Ben saw the hint of anger on her face. "Or are you just going to let Gage deal with that, too?"

Ben's first thought was that the low blow was unfair, but then he thought, *Not so much. I kind of deserved that.* He blew out a deep breath. "I want to talk to her, but it isn't like it used to be between us. I don't even know her anymore."

Alex reached out and took her husband's hand. "Yes, you do. You know her better than anyone and you know right now she needs *you*. Not some damned shrink."

"I'm the chief of police, Alex. She doesn't talk to me."

"Then stop being the chief for a while. Just talk to her." She squeezed his hand. "You two were friends long before you became chief. If I remember right, you were pretty good friends."

"Good morning, Alex," said a new voice. "That smells wonderful. What in the world is it?"

Ben looked up to see a group of women in the doorway. He watched as Alex switched gears from concerned wife and friend to coffeehouse barista. She stood to greet her customers. "Fresh roasted, ladies. All the way from Indonesia."

Ben watched and listened as his wife engaged the group in the finer points of coffee roasting. Before she finished with them, three more customers walked in. Alex looked between her patrons at her husband and it was as though she were whispering in his ear.

You know what to do, Benny. Be Tia's friend.

Ben stood from the table and mouthed, *See you tonight.* Alex smiled and waved. He left the coffeehouse, heading back to Newberg City Hall. He wished things with Tia were really that simple.

Their friendship was one of the cornerstones of his life. But lately his relationship with Tia had faded, becoming a pleasant but disconnected part of his past. Like the scent of the fresh-roasted coffee, with every step he took the memories that he and Tia shared seemed to slip away on the breeze.

ELEVEN

Tia hustled along the sidewalk leading to the upscale office building, which was tucked back on a grassy hill of white-barked birch trees. She bolted the stairs two at a time to the second floor, then quickstepped down the open-air breezeway, mentally ticking off the familiar nameplates as she rushed by each door. Three CPAs. Two law offices. A dentist, a podiatrist, and finally her destination. Tia stopped and took a deep breath. She took one last look back toward the greenbelt landscape, dotted with parking lots and sidewalks that were empty of people. She opened the door and slipped into the small waiting room that had been designed for a single occupant.

She assumed that the muted tones of the room, the bubbling fish tank built into the wall, and the quiet jazz music were intended to be soothing, but she always found herself on edge in this space. Large tropical fish stared at her, their expressions seeming to say, *What, you again?* There was only one chair in the room, a fabulous leather recliner-and-a-half that Tia figured put the good doctor back a couple of grand. She perched on the arm, knowing she wouldn't be there long. One thing about Doctor Elliot Gage, he was always on time. Expected patients to be, too. No sooner had the exterior door closed than the door leading to the inner office swung open. The shrink glided in.

"Tia." It was amazing, how much judgmental crap he could communicate with a single word.

Dr. Elliot Gage was the contract psychiatrist for a dozen law enforcement agencies throughout the region. When cops got involved in a shooting or other critical life-and-death event, they had to take a mandatory three days of administrative leave. Gage was the one who evaluated the officers and signed off on their clean bill of health, allowing a return to regular duty. A post-crisis psych eval was an industry formality that for cops amounted to a game of hide the ball. Avoid discussing anything too personal. Reveal nothing. Give the right answers—that is, the answers the shrink wanted to hear.

"Hey, Doc." Tia did her best to appear nonchalant but suspected Gage wouldn't be fooled again. Tia knew Gage looked at her with equal parts of resentment and intrigue. He'd sent her back to work, months ago, only to have her suffer a major, on-duty relapse. He'd blown the call. That had to have him fuming, but Tia knew her case was too interesting to ignore or write off. She figured by the time he got done with her he'd publish an entire series of articles in *Psychology Today*. Maybe a book: *How I Fixed a Broken Cop*.

Most cops who survived an encounter like Tia's shooting happily accepted a high-dollar payout, a tax-free medical retirement, and a hero's exit. Tia had discovered her fellow officers didn't appreciate a daily hallway reminder that sometimes things go wrong, that cops die on the job. In fact, in the unforgiving, eat-their-own-young world of law enforcement there would always be one or two who figured Tia had screwed up and gotten a cop killed. That she walked away and a good man went in the ground. None of that had mattered to

Tia. As soon as she'd been physically able, she'd met with Gage and given him all the right answers and gotten back to work. And now here they were again.

"Good to see you, Tia. Come in."

"Thanks, Doc."

Gage offered his large mitt of a hand and Tia took it. His firm grip and calculated stare let her know he was conducting his initial assessment right then. Gage specialized in the treatment of PTSD, and to him words were the least significant form of human communication. Tia did her best not to lock eyes with him, instead moving quickly past him and into the office. She went straight for the stiff-backed upholstered armchair she knew was meant for her. In contrast to the recliner, this chair was solid and rigid—a chair that forced the occupant to pay attention. Tia hated "the chair."

Gage was only a few inches taller than Tia but twice as thick, with a muscular frame that reflected a dedicated workout regime. His skin was deeply tan from regular trips to Fiji, where Tia knew he kept a second home. Gage preferred crew-neck, short-sleeved knit shirts that Tia figured served the purpose of not only avoiding a necktie but also allowing a fortysomething man like Gage that one last opportunity to show off his physique. He kept his hair short enough for the military, but Tia had checked and knew he had never bothered to enlist.

She sat down and crossed her legs at the knees. She put her elbows on the armrests, laced her fingers together, level with her stomach, and stared straight ahead. *Hold this position,* she thought. *Avoid external movement.* She waited for the games to begin.

Dr. Gage took his seat directly in front of Tia, his chair set right at the edge of her personal space. He stared back, notepad and pen at the ready. "It's been a while, Tia. How are things going for you?"

"Great, Doc. Never better." She was pleased that her voice was steady.

"My records show you recently renewed your prescription for Librium. Went through the last batch kind of quick?"

Tia pursed her lips and shrugged. "I talked with your receptionist, explained that I accidentally dropped a bunch of the pills, probably half of them, in the toilet. I would have fished them out but it seemed kind of silly to go through all that. I hardly ever take one."

Gage nodded. "I read the arrest report from your undercover detail. Chief Sawyer sent it over." He paused as if he wanted to be sure Tia picked up on the alliance that existed between her shrink and her boss. She shrugged again. "I was surprised. I thought we agreed you would take it easy. A gradual return to full duty."

"The shooting was seven months ago, Doc. That's pretty gradual."

"I'm not talking about the shooting, Tia."

More traps, she thought. She let the insinuation hang in the air, and after a few moments of silence Gage changed tactics and threw a new line into the water.

"I see you had another hallucination."

Reflexively, Tia took the bait. "You got that from my police report?"

Gage began the slow process of setting the hook and reeling her in. "From the report and about a hundred hours of our therapy sessions."

"Funny, because in that police report I don't mention hallucinating anything. I witnessed an abduction."

Gage studied her face for several seconds, then looked down to scribble on the notepad he kept in his lap. Like always, he kept his knee at just enough of an angle to prevent Tia from seeing what he wrote. After several seconds of writing, Gage looked up. His expression showed concern mixed with pity and draped over insincerity.

"I thought we had worked through all this, Tia. I thought we both understood that because of your shooting, you would probably have episodes. Recurrences of a sort, especially when you're under a lot of stress. Doesn't this sound very much like the episode you experienced in the courtroom?" Reaching to his desk, the doctor retrieved a manila folder that was nearly two inches thick. He opened it and turned several pages. "That was just three months ago."

"That was a reaction to the meds. You told me that yourself."

His smile exposed a small, neat row of whitened teeth. "What I told you was that you experienced a significant psychological breakdown manifested through visual and auditory hallucinations and that the episode was likely to have stemmed from *abuse* of the medications I prescribed for you. I believe we determined you were mixing the pills with alcohol." Gage made sure he had eye contact before saying, "Is that something we need to talk about again?"

Tia looked away and immediately regretted it. She tried to re-establish eye contact but knew Gage had picked up on the sign of avoidance. He made a note while she chastised herself for the rookie mistake.

Squaring her shoulders, Tia decided to ignore the question and get back to the issue at hand.

"There was a girl tied up in the back of the van Gunther Kane was trying to force me into. I didn't hallucinate anything."

Gage gave a condescending nod. "And why do you think it is that no one else saw any of this? That there are no missing person reports? No evidence of any sort? Not to mention that this Mr. . ." Gage made an issue of pulling the Milwaukee PD arrest report from his file and Tia knew he wanted her to react. This time she was like a rock and gave him nothing.

"Ah, yes, Mr. Kane. He tells a much different story. Something about you attacking him while he was trying to—well, when he was trying to complete the transaction, so to speak."

"Got some news for you, Doc." Tia nodded toward Gage's

notepad. "You might want to write this down. When it comes to the truth, crooks make like rugs."

Gage's pen stopped and he looked up, confused. Tia smiled, amused that the man with three diplomas on his wall couldn't follow the simple humor. She helped him out. "They lie."

The psychiatrist smiled thinly, then pressed harder. "Tell me why this is different, Tia. Why is this girl so real to you?"

She noted the "to you" but replied honestly anyway.

"Because I know. I was there. I saw her. I touched her, for God's sake."

"You touched her?" Gage leaned forward and his interest seemed to peak. "That wasn't in your report. Tell me about that."

"I tried to pull her out. I grabbed her by the ankle, but then . . ." Tia paused, hearing the van door slam shut in her mind. She shook the image away, knowing Gage was watching every breath she took. "Kane got back in the fight. Slammed the door shut. You can read the rest."

"What did she feel like?"

Tia couldn't hide her frustration anymore. "Excuse me?"

"The girl. You said you touched her. What did she feel like?"

Tia wasn't going to let him drag her in. "Like a human being. A real, live human being."

"Describe the texture of her skin. Was she wet? Dry? Hot? Cold? Describe it."

"Rough. Her skin was rough."

"I see. Fascinating."

Gage began a furious scribble and Tia shook her head. She'd reached her limit and didn't care if the doctor knew it. "There you go. You push and push until I give you an answer, trying to satisfy you; then you act like there's been a big revelation."

"Indeed, there has been, Tia."

"I can't wait to hear it," she said dryly.

Gage leaned in. "Tia, you had actual contact. Physical contact that involved tactile stimulation. You're even able to describe the sensation. This is very serious."

Tia looked to the ceiling, shaking her head. She didn't try to hide her irritation. "No, it's not. I touched a person, like I might touch anyone else I happened to come in contact with."

Gage shook his head dismissively and Tia knew he wouldn't stop until he made his point.

"What did she look like? This girl you saw in the van?"

A face flashed across her mind as if Tia were driving at high speed past a billboard: there for a few seconds, then gone. But in that flash of a moment, the terrified image of desperation was seared into her mind. Tia shrugged and did her best to sound unaffected. "Teenager. Dark hair. Probably Latina."

"So, an older version of the girl we both agree wasn't really in the courtroom?"

Tia shot back, "Yeah, Doc. Exactly. All us brown folks look alike."

"That is not what I'm saying, Tia, and I think you know that. Let's go back."

Tia rolled her eyes. The last thing in the world she wanted was to go back. She just wanted to go.

"When you were shot in the café that day, bleeding on the floor, you saw a girl. She came to you, protected you. You described that girl as very young. Dark skinned. Isn't that what you told me?"

And I've regretted it ever since, she thought to herself. She flashed back to that day in the Danville café. "Yes. I know, but that has nothing to do with this."

"Oh, but it does, Tia," Gage said. "We both agreed that the little girl was a hallucination . . . and that your breakdown in the court-room was directly related to that hallucination. Remember? You and I decided that the girl in the courtroom was the same as the girl in the café."

Tia's pulse began to pick up and she knew her chest was rising and falling more than it should. It didn't matter how many times she had been through it; whenever she thought of that day in the courtroom the same mixture of anxiety and humiliation descended on her.

It had been a child abuse case. The victim, a five-year-old girl who only spoke Spanish, had been molested over a period of months by her thirty-five-year-old stepfather. Tia, who had interviewed the child at length, knew all the hideous details. To avoid making the child testify, Tia relayed the story to the jury. An ugly story for sure, but one that had to be told.

At some point—Tia couldn't say when—she stopped talking about the events and began experiencing them. Stopped reporting and started to live it. To see it. She was in the room, night after night, when the stepfather would come in. When he touched the girl. When he pushed himself inside her and put the pillow over the child's face to stifle her cries. Tia listened to the monster whisper that bad girls who let such things happen to them didn't get to keep their families. She saw his hulking figure, hunched over a little girl who whimpered and cried, begging for someone to make it stop.

It wasn't until Tia stood up from the witness chair, her hand going to her gun, that the prosecutor finally broke in. When he said, "Detective Suarez?" in a voice that sounded both frightened and angry, the images disappeared and Tia found herself standing up, her hand on her weapon and tears streaming down her face. Twelve confused jurors stared at her, terrified but captivated by what they had witnessed.

Tia had told herself that no matter what she carried inside, she would never allow such a public display to occur again.

She had to be careful, now, not to let Gage take her down that road. "Yes, we worked through it, Doc. And that was an isolated event. I'd been back on duty for less than two weeks when it happened. It's over and done with."

"Are you sure of that, Tia? There haven't been other occasions where you imagined something? Heard something?" He looked directly at her. "Are you sure there is nothing else you and I need to work through?"

"No." The lies were becoming complicated and Tia grew flustered.

"No, you're not sure?"

"I mean, yes." Her frustration turned to anger. "I'm sure there isn't."

Gage smiled. "Well, which is it?"

Tia clamped down hard on herself. There was no way she was ever going to let Gage drag *that* out of her.

No one knew that since she had returned from Mexico she had had almost nightly visits from . . . something. That in some way she welcomed the contact. That she somehow needed the feelings of warmth and affection that accompanied the strange experiences. Tia knew if she ever spoke of it her days as a cop were over.

"Look, Doc," she said, leaning forward and smiling, trying to project competence and sanity. "I'm here on Chief Sawyer's orders. I got into a pretty dicey situation with a crook; we tussled a bit.

"I know what I saw, but if the DA and everyone else want to blow it off, then so be it." She shrugged as casually as possible. "It's not the first time I've had a case I thought should be prosecuted get kicked to the curb. I say we all just move on."

"Yes. I heard about your problem with the prosecuting attorney. It sounds like the conversation got pretty heated. Again, doesn't that strike you as reminiscent of your earlier breakdown?"

Only Ben could have given up that detail—TJ would never throw another cop under the bus—and Tia felt the sting of disloyalty. She quashed it and managed to reply in a normal tone of voice.

"I argued my case. I lost. That's all. Now I just need you to sign off on my fitness for duty."

Dr. Gage put his pad of paper and fountain pen on the desk and folded his hands in his lap. "I think we are going to have to put that idea on the shelf for the time being."

Tia's heart dropped to her stomach. "What does that mean? Put it on the shelf?"

"Tia, it's evident you're still suffering from significant post-traumatic stress. The only question at this point is, are the symptoms related to your actual shooting or due to something else altogether? But whatever the case, I'm sorry, I can't approve you for a return to full duty."

Tia felt the simmering anger roil up inside her. She lashed out without any consideration of the consequences, "Are you kidding me? You're going to put me back on light duty? What's your problem, Gage?"

For a moment Tia saw a flash of satisfaction cross his face. She cursed herself—she'd finally given Gage just the reaction he wanted. The headshrinker tilted his head and spoke in a tone of paternalistic admonishment. "Tia. Please. Let's not make this any more complicated than it needs to be."

"Fine. Keep it simple," Tia almost shouted. "Mind your own damn business and let me get back to work."

"You can work, Tia. On restricted duty. I want thirty days free of any episodes. And . . ."—Gage paused—"I'd like to start you on a regular urinalysis screening. Every seventy-two hours should suffice."

Tia braced herself on the arms of the chair, about to leap to her feet, then controlled herself. She couldn't keep the incredulity out of her voice. "You're going to piss test me?"

"I'm going to confirm that you're taking the proper dosage of your medication, Tia." Another look over the top of his glasses. "And get a sense of your alcohol intake as well."

"Jesus." Tia fell back against the chair and turned her head. Even she could hear the sound of her own indignant guilt. "I can't believe this bullshit."

"I'm sorry, Tia, but I'll be recommending a period of desk duty. No fieldwork. No assignments requiring the carrying of firearms. No off-duty police authority." Gage pulled his iPad off the desk. "How about we schedule a two-hour session for early next week?"

"Forget it." Tia stood and headed for the door. "You aren't the only shrink on the list, Gage. We're done. Find yourself another lab rat."

"This isn't a car dealership, Tia. You don't get to shop around. Any other therapist you approach will consult with me before beginning treatment."

"I'll take my chances on that, but we're done talking. I don't want you in my head anymore."

Gage gave Tia a long look. He hadn't moved even when she'd finally exploded out of her seat. "As you wish, Tia. You can continue therapy with another psychiatrist, but with regard to your employment, I still hold certain professional responsibilities."

"What's that supposed to mean?"

Now Gage stood and moved behind his desk. He scribbled on his prescription pad, tore the page off, and held it out to her. "This is the address of the laboratory. You have twenty-four hours to submit a urine test. While you're there, set up a screening schedule for the next four weeks."

"And if I don't?"

"I'll recommend you be placed on *no*-duty status indefinitely." He spoke with such a casual air it seemed as though the conversation were about the weather, not her life. "Of course I can't be certain, legal appeals and all, but I assume my report would lead to your eventual dismissal."

"I'd get fired?" Tia's voice cracked.

"Well, not fired," Gage said coolly. "You'd receive a psychological retirement. But, yes. Your police career would be over."

Tia was panting. She took two steps back toward the doctor and snatched the paper from his hand. She kept her mouth shut, finally realizing every time she spoke she dug her grave deeper. A moment later she was on the breezeway, pretty sure the truckers on the highway heard the slam of the door.

TWELVE

Settled at home on the couch, Tia closed her eyes, doing her best to just be in the moment. With Connor's arm around her neck, she rested her head against the deep pillow of muscle where his shoulder and upper chest came together. Connor had taken off his prosthetics and Tia's bare legs and feet were draped over where his legs used to be. The lights were low and her old AM/FM clock radio played a mellow jazz tune from a station out of Chicago. Ringo lay in a nearby chair, curled into a half-moon, breathing heavily, paws twitching.

Tia allowed herself to give in to the soothing sense of contentment and shelter that she knew in many ways she'd done her best to destroy. Even when he was like this, she thought, when someone else might look at him and see a cripple, Connor always struck her as larger than life. As so much more of a man than anyone else she'd ever known. Deep in her heart she couldn't help but be sad for him, but she knew he never looked for anyone's pity.

Then there's me, she thought. *Blubbering, crazy-ass me.*

Tia had called Connor, crying hysterically, after leaving Gage's office. When she got home, Connor was waiting for her at the farmhouse, still dressed in his white uniform from the market. Now, after dinner and with a glass of white wine in hand, she sat with him, clearheaded but desperate as hell.

"Thanks for coming over. I wouldn't have blamed you if you'd told me to just go piss up a rope," she said, tilting her head back so she could see his face.

He smiled. "You always say that."

"Always say what?"

" 'Piss up a rope.' I'll be damned if I even know what that's supposed to mean."

"I don't know." She shrugged. "Somebody in my old unit used to say it. Just stuck with me, I guess."

He buried his face against her neck and took a deep breath. His voice sounded playful despite being muffled by her short hair. He patted the stump of his leg. "Taking any kind of leak these days is hard enough without making a trick shot out of it. But anyway, Suarez, you know damn well I'm powerless to refuse you."

Tia reached up and stroked his hair, staring straight ahead. She had told him all about her session with Gage. Every detail. "You think I'm losing my mind, Connie? Have I gone over the edge or something?"

"Yeah, Suarez." He nuzzled in deeper and nipped at her neck. "You're looney tunes. Ready for lockdown."

She gave him a soft elbow. "Come on. I'm serious."

"Serious?" His voice went soft and he pulled his head back to look at her. "Okay then, seriously, it's hard to know what to think, when you spend so much time drunk and high on meds."

She felt a pang of insult that she tried to hide with a nervous laugh. She pulled away and sat up straight. "Damn. There you go again. Don't hold back. Tell me how you really feel."

Tia regretted breaking the lighter mood. Her eyes welled and she turned her head. *You've cried enough. Knock it off.*

"Remember, Tia. I went through the whole prescription med thing. I get it. They give you that shit like Skittles at a kid's birthday party. But at some point you've got to walk away or the pills will own you. It's no different than a hype on the street chipping heroin."

Tia sat up, defensive. "Come on, Connie. It's not like I'm a frickin' addict."

He looked at the wineglass she held. "You sure?"

"It's one glass of wine," she said, her voice incredulous. "How do you go from that to a dope fiend on the street?"

"It's just a different crutch, Tia."

Smart-ass, she thought. *Damn know-it-all.* But he'd nailed it.

Tia knew. She had known for a while. She didn't need to go to a meeting, sit in a church basement, and listen to a bunch of strangers pour their hearts out. She could care less about following the steps of some program. But she didn't need to hit rock bottom to know the truth. Even now she felt the desire to anesthetize herself. Just one pill, to put a protective balm over her fear of being discovered, over the guilt she carried every day.

Her mouth watered at the thought of a real drink, something that packed some power. She felt the cool cylinder of a shot glass against her lips. The magnificent burn in her throat. What had started as a way to quiet a haunting memory had become a full-blown addiction. She could practically see the bottle inside the kitchen cupboard. Top shelf on the right.

When did I buy that? Yesterday, right? There's still a couple of inches left. Maybe even a little more.

To fight the pull of it she took a gulp of her wine, finding it a completely unsatisfying, temporary fix. *Just like a hype chipping heroin.*

"I worry about you, Tia. The independence. That attitude you carry around. Telling everyone to go 'piss up a rope.'" He pulled her back to nestle against him once more, kissing her cheek and tapping his finger lightly against the top of her head. "But I know there's more going on in there. You don't want to talk Gage? Fine. Then pick someone else. Me. Ben. Alex. We all need somebody, Tia. Even you."

In the dim light Connor's blue eyes went gray, softening his face and making him seem open to the truth. She took a breath, ready to launch in. A breath away from telling him everything, the words got caught in her throat. She took another drink of wine; when he looked away, she knew that Connor realized she was holding back.

So I'm a private drunk, she thought. *What if I'm okay with that?* She ignored the internal dialogue, knowing it wasn't what people wanted to hear. *Time to appease. Make a few promises. Change the subject. Create some distance. Isn't that what addicts do?*

"I'll stop, Connie. I will. No more meds. I'll go easy on the booze. But just tell me something." She turned to look him right in the eyes. "You believe me, don't you? I don't care what Gage thinks. And Sawyer can believe what he wants. But Connie, I need you to believe me. There was a girl in that van. As sure as I'm sitting here. She looked right at me." Tia shook her head and her voice turned angry. "Tactile stimulation my ass. I *touched* her."

"If you say you saw it, Suarez, I believe you. But are you trying to convince me or yourself?"

"Gage says hallucinations are—"

He cut her off. "What did you just tell me? The hell with Gage, right?" Connie rubbed his hands over his face. "Look, I know how it is with shrinks. I had a whole team of them who wanted to tell me all about what it's like to lose half my body. To wake up every day scratching at a leg that isn't there. To remember watching a guy get blown to hell and winding up with his brains all over my uniform. They know all about that shit even though they never leave their offices.

"The hell with them. In the end we all have to find our own way. Figure life out for ourselves.

"Believe in yourself, Tia. Forget all those experts. Whatever it is you're carrying around inside you, find your own answers. The hell with the experts. They can just go piss up a rope, right?"

Tia closed her eyes, resting her head against his chest. "I know what I saw, Connie. Damn it. I know what I saw."

"I believe you, Suarez." His voice was tired but still reassuring. "Just believe in yourself."

That's the hard part, she thought. *It's hard to know what to believe. How to divide the real from the surreal. If you only knew what goes on in my head.* What if she told him?

She knew how he'd react. *Entire conversations, Suarez, sure. You're losing it.*

Now, as she sat here with Connie, sobriety felt good and oddly familiar. She wondered why she didn't let herself always feel like this. Why not just be this way?

As if on cue, somewhere in her heart a tiny voice called out. Small and quiet, lacking any of its usual joy. Nothing for Tia to take comfort from. Only anxiety and fear. Just like when it came to her that day in the courtroom. Once again, the voice was pleading for Tia to do something. *Ir a su, Tia. Go to her now. She needs you.*

It was the same voice. Tia was sure of it. When she had stood at death's door, it was this voice that had kept her in the living world. The same voice had been in the courtroom during the abuse case, overwhelmed with the sadness of Tia's testimony.

Hearing the voice is one thing, she thought. *Listening is another.* And hearing voices in your head was not a confession any cop would ever make. It wasn't the sort of thing Tia would share with anyone—not even Connie. Tia needed to keep her feet planted firmly in the real world. She put her wineglass on the table, then leaned in and kissed Connor on the lips. He began to respond and she backed away, teasing him.

He looked at her and she could hear affection along with feigned offense in his words. "Knock it off, you little shit."

"Knock it off?" She pushed him back on the couch, pinning his arms above his head. She lay across his chest and took a playful nip at his neck. "Make me."

She squealed as he easily flipped her onto the floor before purposely falling off the couch and landing on top of her. Their banter continued until it turned into something more. The small voice went quiet and Tia reminded herself how lucky she was to have Connor Anderson in her life. She closed her eyes as he kissed her neck and she worked hard to enjoy silence in her head and just be in the moment.

THIRTEEN

The third man in thirty minutes stood over her. Or was he the fourth? Angelica couldn't be sure, but like those before him he dropped his trousers to his ankles as he stared down, sizing her up. He hefted up the fat of his belly with one hand while dipping his other into the metal bucket set on the flipped-down tailgate of a pickup truck. Scooping thick, greasy lubricant into his palm, he reached below his waist to coat himself, his gaze never leaving her naked brown body. His face bore a familiar expression, one she'd often seen on men back home when they bartered over the value of livestock. In the moonlight she picked up on the squint of his eyes and the purse of his lips. He shook his head in the obvious belief he'd overpaid. Angelica cringed and turned her face away.

Not looking didn't make her unaware. The man above her tossed his worn hat to another who stood nearby, dropped to his knees, then lowered himself on top of her. His substantial weight forced the air from her lungs, filling her with panic. He bumbled and pushed his way inside her, huffing and cursing as if the awkwardness of the moment were somehow her doing. Once in, he began a steady pounding that allowed her only gulping breaths of air at the intervals when his weight was lightest. Brittle cornstalks poked through the coarse wool blanket that was like sandpaper on her already-bloodied back. A thousand fire ants joined in the vicious assault, welting her buttocks, thighs, and legs. The hot summer air trapped odors of sweat, dirt, and whiskey against her face.

While her latest rapist lost himself to some fantasy place, it seemed to Angelica the surrounding circle of tall corn bowed down over the scene like a sorrowfully compelled audience. Beyond the small clearing she heard *ranchero musica* blaring over a radio and voices of a dozen men she knew were waiting their turn. Some would have the decency to pass, but she had come to learn none would have the courage to intervene. The beat of the music kept time as the man continued to thrust against her.

She pulled her arms close to her body in a boxer's clutch and tears squeezed out as she screwed her eyes shut tight. He grew inside her, his hot breath wet against her cheek, his steady grunt in her ear. Overwhelmed by pain, she screamed, begging him to stop. Instead, his pounding intensified. She heard bargaining begin with the next man in line, who was asking for the acts she most despised. The man on top of her finished with a series of thrusts that left the lower half of her slender body numb and pushed deeper into the dirt.

Dry cornstalks crunched under familiar boots, filling her heart with bitter hate. The one called Tanner approached. The American *ratón* with the pale body of a sickly boy and the scraggly hair of an old woman. He was responsible for this nightmare that seemed to have no end. Sneering, he delivered a rough kick to the man's bare skin. Angelica saw that Tanner was shoving a wad of bills into the bulging pocket of his overalls.

"Time's up, amigo," Tanner said. "Get back in line if you wanna pay for another go."

As her attacker struggled to his feet, Angelica realized he was not much more than a husky boy around her own age of seventeen. He pulled his trousers up. As he slinked away, their eyes met for an instant. His judgment seemed to turn inward and Angelica saw he now shared her look of humiliation.

Tanner's voice called out, *"Vamonos, hombre."*

The next man stepped up, already fumbling with his belt. Swaying on his feet, he was glassy eyed with what seemed to be a look of drunken expectation. Angelica saw he was much older than the last man to take her. He could be an *abuelo,* she thought. Maybe even a *bisabuelo.* His small, black, rodent-like eyes stared out from a face with skin that had the plated look of an armadillo. Clothes hung loose on his boney frame, which took odd turns at the knees and waist. He stared down, slack jawed, and raised a gnarled, shaking finger toward her face. The fingers of his other hand hung at his side, wrapped loosely around the long glass neck of a half-empty bottle of mescal. His voice rattled like a snake.

"La boca."

Tanner pulled Angelica up to her knees. With his unshaven face just inches from her own, he took a fistful of her hair in one hand and cupped her chin with the other. He gave her head a harsh shake and said the simple foreign phrase that Angelica had come to understand. "Open up."

Angelica pulled free of his grip. She pushed her long black hair back from her face and spewed out a string of defiant words that said she wouldn't be rushed. Snatching the bottle of whiskey from the old man's hand, she took a long pull. The nearby crowd noticed the exchange, and a raucous chorus of jeers for her display of gumption rose into the night sky. Angelica ignored the crude comments she knew were directed at her. She had come to welcome the strange effect of the alcohol. It deadened not only her body but also her mind, allowing her to surrender and let go of any foolish hope for a different life.

Cuánto tiempo? Angelica wondered. *How long have I lived this life?*

It had not always been this way. Even now she could still imagine the beams of this very same moon dancing on the waters of Lake Pátzcuaro. She could picture the green hills surrounding the farm where her family worked the fields and lived in a small mud shack. She could recall their faces, but they faded a little more every day. How many brothers and sisters, cousins, aunts, and uncles? She could no longer be sure, but there had been many and they had been happy. Poor, but happy.

The promise of a life beyond the hard work of a dirt farm had lured Angelica away, but it had all been lies. Now this was her life and everything else was fading away.

Angelica thought back to the woman she thought of as "the bold one." The one who had fought. Who had resisted. That one would never find herself in such a place as this. Even now Angelica could see her eyes. She could feel the strength of the woman's grip on her foot, pulling her to safety. Angelica remembered the warmth of her hand. Even now, Angelica heard the bold one call out, *Come to me*. But then she was gone.

The hard smack of a man's hand against the side of Angelica's face brought her back to this place of dehumanization. His words were unintelligible to her, but she understood the threat they carried all too well.

The old man moved closer and Angelica reached out, taking him in her hand. She leaned in, closing her eyes in silent recognition of her station in life: a *puta* girl. *I coveted a world not intended for me,* she thought. *I disobeyed my Almighty Father. I shamed my family. I deserted my country. And now I must take my place in hell.*

ACT II

FOURTEEN

Inside Newberg PD, Tia tucked her head and took the stairs two at a time, holding a twenty-ounce Starbucks at arm's length. At the sound of laughter, she looked up just in time to try to avoid a collision with a group of uniformed officers headed the opposite way. Tia managed to maneuver past the first two but ran smack into the third. Despite her best efforts, a good amount of hot coffee sloshed over the top of the cup and onto the cop's black uniform trousers.

"Damn, Suarez. What the hell? I'm not even five minutes into my shift."

"Sorry, Jimmy." Tia bent down, swiping at the cop's pants with the back of her hand, just missing the crotch area.

"Damn, girl. Back off from my junk."

"There," Tia said, standing up. "Can't even see it. The coffee, that is. Put the dry-cleaning bill on my desk, all right? I'm really sorry."

Of course it had to be Jimmy Youngblood, a five-year patrol officer well known for his good ole boy ideology and his belief that women just don't belong in police work. Jimmy had been in the courtroom when Tia had her episode. In fact, he'd been the only other cop there, which made him the prime witness, a role he'd played to the hilt.

Not only had he provided all the ugly details for the official investigation; he also even came up with his own artistic re-creation that he practically turned into a stand-up routine. Rumor had it that Youngblood had taken the show on the locker-room circuit and he was a hit.

"Yeah, whatever." Jimmy grabbed his crotch as he walked away. The three male officers continued down the steps, probably headed for the day-shift briefing. Though they spoke quietly, Tia heard their hushed comments and a reference to "another major meltdown." She could only wonder what the latest rumor was; she knew a mangled version of the Milwaukee detail had gone around. She resisted the temptation to run down the steps, catch up with the group, and set straight any bullshit. *You'll only make it worse*, she thought. *It's all your own doing.*

Tia looked at her watch. *Twenty minutes late.* She rolled her eyes at the thought of the chewing out coming her way. Half-jogging down the short hallway, she blew a breath into her palm and breathed it back in. A pretty good whiff of burnt coffee was all she got, but she wondered if the patrol dogs had picked up anything else. She'd done pretty well all week, but last night Connor had had to work an overtime shift at the market and Tia had been home alone. *Well, not really alone,* she thought.

That's the damn problem. Spending entire days stuck at a desk on light-duty work was frustrating enough, but being cut off from meds and booze at home was more than she could take. When that tiny voice began to cry for her attention, Tia knew there was only one way to silence it. She ended up hitting the bottle pretty hard and now she was paying for it. She hadn't taken any pills but hadn't been able to resist swinging by the liquor store on the way home last night.

It's this damn light-duty bullshit, she thought to herself. Not to mention Gage and his testing schedule. Tia knew she had less than four hours to sweat out a fifth of tequila or there would be hell to pay.

She took a last sip of the rancid brew that had cost her four bucks at a drive-thru before dumping it in the hallway trash can in disgust. *How do people drink this shit?*

Tia's normal routine was to stop every morning at Books and Java, Newberg's one and only indie coffeehouse. But in addition to being a good friend, Alex was also the wife of the chief of police. No reason for Tia to put the woman in a tough spot by showing up in her store hungover and on her way to work.

Tia slipped into the bullpen she shared with three other detectives and was relieved to find it empty. *First break of the day,* she thought. She slid behind her desk, piled high with pawn slips and burglary reports. Her light-duty assignment had her acting as nothing more than a glorified file clerk, comparing the stolen property listed in local burgs to what was taken in by the half-dozen pawnshops in the area surrounding Newberg. The duty normally went to a senior citizen volunteer.

And here I sit, Tia thought. *This would drive any cop to drink.*

Tia rubbed hard on her temples, thinking she should have kept the lousy mermaid sludge. Her head throbbed and a tide of liquor rolled in her stomach. She rummaged through the desk, scrounging for an old energy bar or something she could munch on to soak up the booze. Nothing but a three-week-old banana that was more gray than black and in a gelatinous sort of state. She left the banana where it was and slammed the desk drawer in frustration, smashing her thumb in the process.

"God damn it!" she shouted, looking at her broken nail.

"Where you been, Suarez?" Tia looked up and saw Travis Jackson staring back at her with nothing short of contempt. "You missed the weekly crime update."

"Oh, hey, Sarge." Still shaking her hand in pain, Tia was in no mood to take a lot of grief from her boss. Her voice was way less than sincere. "Sorry. It won't happen again."

"Until it does."

Shit. He knows, she thought. Tia half-expected him to pull out a Breathalyzer, but she was angry enough to not really care. In Tia's mind, Jackson had caused a good amount of the bullshit she was dealing with. He could have stood up to the attorney. He could have done more to support Tia with Sawyer. He could have done his fricking job, but instead he took the easy way and left her twisting in the wind.

She pushed back. "Is it really a big deal, Travis?" She motioned to the pile on her desk and tried to downplay her offense. "You've got me going through pawn slips and patrol field interview cards. So I'm a few minutes late, so what? The last thing I need is to sit in on a crime update."

Travis stared back, stoic and quiet in a way that left Tia unnerved. He closed in and Tia picked up on that way cops looked at a drunk. He spoke in a low voice and Tia could hear frustration mixed with what she thought might be genuine concern.

"Look, Tia. This sucks for you. I get that, but if you want to get back on full duty, you've got to go with the program. If Chief Sawyer finds out you're coming in late, not to mention half in the bag, he's gonna have both our asses."

Tia took on a level of indignation normally reserved for guilty people. "Half in the bag? Come on, TJ. I had a couple of drinks last night. So what? I'm here, aren't I?"

"Oh yeah, you're here. Late for the third time this week and no doubt you plan on sliding out an hour early."

Tia knew he was right and had every right to jump her shit about it. "All right, I'm sorry I was late. Just cover me this one last time, okay? I'll get all these pawn slips filed today. I won't go home until it's done."

TJ shook his head. "Wish I could help you, but Sawyer's waiting for you in his office. Told me to send you over as soon as you got in. That was almost a half hour ago."

"Oh, shit." Tia felt the blood run from her face, thinking back to her blowout with Dr. Gage two days ago. "What's he want? Do you know?"

Travis shrugged. "I have no idea, but he looked serious. Better get over there."

Tia stared into space. If Ben had talked with Gage, anything was possible. Her mind reeled until TJ pulled her back in.

"And splash some water on your face." His voice was a mixture of disgust and pity. "Rinse your mouth with that Listerine you keep in your desk. You smell like a jail cell."

Tia stared back, embarrassed. "Yeah. Okay, Travis. Sorry if I put you in a bad spot."

Travis turned to leave shaking his head. "You need to pull your head out of your ass, Suarez."

Tia stared at the empty doorway, her head cluttered with shame, alcohol, and fear of what might be in store. She pulled herself to her feet and headed down the hall. Ducking into the women's locker room, she went to the sink and doused her face and the back of her neck in cold water, following TJ's advice. Her hands shook with a mixture of nervous tension and the effects of detoxing. The panic attack was sudden and quick. Thoughts of what might be coming gripped her mind.

I'm finished. This is it.

Her stomach began to heave. She turned from the sink and pushed into a stall. She felt a hard, blunt pain when her knees hit the cement and her chest thudded against the porcelain. She hung her head over the opening just in time to project pints of a chunky yellowish-brown concoction into the bowl. A good deal of splash-back struck her face and her throat burned with a mixture of tequila, bitter coffee, and bile. A second wave of nausea arched her back, not as violent as the first but still enough to make her eyes water. Her body shuddered in revulsion at the sour odor, but she found some comfort from the fact that her stomach was suddenly empty and quiet.

When she was certain it was over, Tia used her forearms to push off against the rim of the toilet and stood on quaking legs. She pulled off a length of toilet paper and swiped at the long strands of thick spit hanging from her lips, then tossed it into the bowl and wiped her hands on her jeans. She boot flushed the toilet and backed out, slowly turning to the mirror. An unfamiliar face stared back. Tia was disoriented, as if seeing someone she should know but whose name escaped her. Then it hit her.

Holy shit, Suarez.

Red glassy eyes rimmed in dark circles stared out from the mirror. Her pasty skin was specked by the vomit plastered against her cheeks and chin. A few chunks had gotten in her hair—which she suddenly realized hadn't been combed since she'd rolled out of bed not quite an hour ago. Nearly a minute passed as she stood frozen, returning her own stare. Then her chin began to quiver and heavy tears of shame rolled down her cheeks. She wanted to sob out loud. She wanted to curl up on the bathroom floor and wait for someone to find her. They'd probably throw her into a detox facility. Fine. At least it would be over. No more games. No more pretending. No more living a lie.

Is that really what you want? To quit? Give up?

This has got to stop, she told herself. *If I somehow survive today,* she vowed, *this shit has absolutely got to stop.*

Tia washed her face and rinsed her mouth in the sink. She lingered, fighting for her composure, then turned off the water and stepped back. She went to her locker, combed her hair, and put on some light makeup. She squeezed an inch of toothpaste onto her finger and rubbed it across her teeth.

Tia walked out of the locker room and headed down the hall. The liquor and vomit had sucked nearly all the moisture from her body, so she bent over the fountain for one last drink of cool water, doing all she could to calm her nerves. She finished the walk like a condemned woman headed to the gallows. *How did this happen?* she wondered. *How did I go from being on the top of the heap to, well,* being *the heap?*

Gage had to have talked to Sawyer; Tia was certain of it. No doubt Gage jazzed the story up pretty good, but thinking back on it, she knew he did not need to embellish very much. Tia figured the decision had already been made. With any luck, Sawyer would let her go out on physical disability. Make up some bullshit about complications from her not-so-old injuries. That would fool the people at a distance—civilians or maybe even a few prospective, non–law enforcement, employers. But the real story would be well known throughout the cop world. Tia Suarez went out "51-50."

Tia stopped and took in a deep breath through her nose. A cascade of proud moments flashed through her mind. The academy. Major arrests. Returning to work after the shooting. Making detective. Good times with the Sawyers. She forced herself back into the moment at hand, put her shoulders back, and walked into the chief's reception area. She did all she could to sound at ease. "Hey, Caroline. Sergeant Jackson tells me the Chief asked to see me."

Caroline, already picking up the phone, smiled, but Tia picked up on the pity in her voice when she said, "Have a seat, Tia. I'll let the chief know you're here."

Caroline no more than put the phone down when the office door swung open and there stood Ben Sawyer, his face somber but impossible to read.

"Hey, Suarez. Get in here."

FIFTEEN

Angelica moved her palm lightly across the dirt surface beneath her, back and forth, tiny pebbles rough against her skin. The feeling of the earth was familiar to her. It was the stuff of a farm, and in her seventeen years Angelica Mendez-Ruiz had memory of little else. Sure, there had been occasional celebrations in the local plaza, with her mother always nearby, monitoring Angelica's every breath. There was the pilgrimage to Mexico City when she was seven, an event heavy on suffering and piety by design. But save those few worldly adventures, most of Angelica's earthly experiences were drawn from the clay of the earth. Honest work. Hard work. Even God's work. She understood all of that, but it hadn't seemed wrong or evil to hope for something more.

She lay flat and unmoving so that the cool dirt of the floor could offer some minor relief to the pain in her breast and stomach, to the searing burn between her legs. Where her cheek was pressed against the ground, a thin line of light snuck down through the outline of the trapdoor above her head. Beyond that there was only black. There were stretches of time when even that strip of light was gone—Angelica assumed those were the nights. She had come to welcome the blackness, thinking that perhaps it meant death was near. But it never came and Angelica realized she wouldn't be allowed to die. That she would be kept alive in this place. This place that she had become convinced was hell.

She was in an underground pit of some sort, with dirt walls supported by thick wooden beams. Far above her head was a wooden door that led to the world outside. There was nothing like this place on the farm in Michoacán where she had lived her entire life, not even the graves where her ancestors had been buried for almost three hundred years. Graves didn't have doors.

She thought again how wonderful it would be to just die, to have a grave, but she knew this was not death. This was hell and people didn't die in hell. They suffered. Suffered for their sins. Hell was a grave without the benefit of death.

Angelica was certain she was no longer near the place of her crossing. How long had it been since she'd made that trip? She had started her journey on foot, heading for the train called La Bestia. She and hundreds, even thousands, of others from all over Mexico and Central America, clinging to all parts of the train, had ridden for days until the tall fences of El Norte could be seen on the horizon. From there, the long walk began. Always at night, hiding during the day. No food and almost nothing to drink. Every day more people would fall from thirst and exhaustion, left behind to die in the desert sun. The coyotes led the survivors to a house that stood alone in an arid wasteland that left Angelica regretting her decision to come to this godforsaken country. There they stayed for many nights. She slept in a room with a dozen other women and children, locked inside as if they were prisoners. Every night the coyotes would come and take away another woman, sometimes even a child. Some returned. Others did not.

Then he came. The one called Tanner. And the other. The man with the terrible smell and a long beard that was the red color of

Mexican dirt. Angelica had seen them standing in the doorway, pointing at her. She saw the exchange of money. Even now, she cursed her foolishness. To have gone with them. To believe that men who reeked of evil would want her for anything other than their own devilish pleasure.

The days after that fell into a miserable pattern. They would drive for hours, then stop and take her into a dingy *posada*. There would be a bed and little else. Men would come. One after another. She could hear them outside the door, waiting, even while one was on top of her. Then it was back to the van, hours of driving, another room. After many days—she didn't know how many—the rooms vanished. Now they took her in the fields. Day after day. Field after field.

If only she had listened to Antonio. Her oldest brother had been to America and he thanked God every day he had been able to return safely home. He had warned her. He had refused to even consider allowing her to take the journey that had killed their father. That had nearly killed him. Antonio spoke of a wall that rose up from the ground. Of helicopters and soldiers. Government agents along with vigilantes, all of them armed and eager to use their guns. Full of hate for the people of Mexico. He spoke of a crossing that covered hundreds of miles of arid wasteland. A desert riddled with the bones of people from all over Mexico and beyond. People who, like their father, had believed in the lies up until the time they lay down in the sand to die.

Antonio chastised her, calling it a sin to have such a *pasión de viajar*. Angelica preferred the English translation. Her *wanderlust*. It was a lust. She had inherited it from her father, who, like her, had felt a desire he could not ignore, to see the world beyond their farm. But she had not intended to desert her family. She had heard the stories of girls who disappeared and were never heard from again, but she knew it would be different for her. She would be smarter.

"I'll be careful, Mama. You'll see. I'll send money and before too long I'll come home."

She had been a fool. Why had she allowed them to take her away? Why hadn't she fought harder? Screamed? Did anyone even notice that she was gone? Did she even matter?

It was quiet now. No noises came from outside. She knew the rattle of keys would eventually break the silence. The heavy footsteps. The opening of the door. The cackling call. But for now it was silent and she lay still, her body numb, her mind dull. She closed her eyes and tried to picture her home and family, but instead a voice called out from somewhere in the blackness. A voice of hope.

Come to me, mija.

SIXTEEN

Tia walked into the office and took the chief's extended hand, making sure to hold her breath. "Good morning, Chief."

"I was starting to worry." Sawyer shook her hand slowly and gave her a hard look. "Figured you got caught in all that Newberg early-morning traffic."

Tia understood the not-so-subtle message but let it go without any comeback. The episode in the locker room remained fresh in her mind, not to mention in her throat, and her voice was genuinely humble. "Sorry, sir."

Ben turned to the other man in the room, who got up from the couch as Tia walked toward him. "Detective Suarez, I'm sure you recognize Sheriff John Solo. He tells me you two have never met."

Tia offered her hand to the man, whose face and public image were well known. Solo was in his third term as sheriff of Waukesha County and Tia thought he was holding up pretty well. The rugged good looks of his campaign posters were apparently not the work of Photoshop. His thick, wiry hair was more white than gray, and styled in a crew cut that sat well on his angular face. His muscular physique was wrapped in deep ebony skin, smooth and un-blemished, giving the impression of a healthy lifestyle. His crisp khaki uniform shirt was tailored to his V-shaped torso and the four stars on the lapels were polished silver. A Western-style hat bear-ing the emblem of Waukesha County sat on the coffee table.

Still uneasy about the nature of the meeting, Tia offered the eas-iest greeting. "Nice to meet you, Sheriff."

Solo smiled and a map of deep, ancient laugh lines appeared around his brown eyes. He looked down from his six-and-a-half-foot vantage point and Tia felt swallowed whole by his personality. He pumped her hand and said, in a booming voice, "Call me John. Good to meet you, Tia. How's the gut?"

"I'm, uh . . . I mean, it's great. Never better." Tia patted her mid-section with an open palm. The story of her near-death encounter had stayed in the local headlines for several weeks. All the atten-tion had gotten old, but if the sheriff wanted to remind her boss of all the shit she'd been through for this department, who was she to stop him?

"Have a seat, detective," the chief said, leaning back against the edge of his desk. Tia dropped into the visitor's chair, doing her best to appear at ease, though her skin was clammy and her stomach had roiled back to life.

Tia hoped whatever the chief and sheriff needed to talk about would take less than fifteen minutes. Any longer and round two might be all over the chief's carpet. The sheriff resumed his seat on the couch.

Watching her carefully and speaking coolly, Ben said, "Sheriff Solo came by to talk about your run-in with Gunther Kane."

Tia swallowed hard. "Well, chief, like you and I have talked about, that was a pretty messed-up operation and I know we made some mistakes. But I get it. Kane is off-limits. I was out of line before, so—"

"Suarez?"

Tia looked at her boss. "Yes, Chief?"

"Can I finish before you mea culpa yourself right out the door?" One of Ben's eyebrows was arched, an expression Tia knew well.

"Sorry, sir." From the corner of her eye Tia saw the sheriff look down at his boots and stifle a laugh.

Ben took a breath and started again. "Sheriff Solo, maybe it would be better if you explained why you're here."

The sheriff leaned his tall frame forward on the couch that took on the look of doll furniture. He put his forearms on his knees. "Tia, are you familiar with the North Aryan Front?"

"The militia group?" He nodded. "Yeah, I've heard about them in various intel briefings and training seminars. White suprema-cists, right? Preach all that 'hate the government, love the land' bullshit?"

"Those are the ones. They've been a minor pain in my ass ever since I took office, mostly low-level stuff. Demonstrations at public events. Membership drives out in front of the county office build-ing. Every once in a while they'll hold a public meeting to try to drum up support for their cause."

"Which is what exactly?" Tia asked.

He shrugged. "Nothing too specific. It's not like they work off a manifesto or anything. Mostly a bunch of pissed-off, down-on-their-luck farmers. Lately they've been recruiting a few younger guys, vets coming back from overseas. They're pretty much con-vinced the federal government is conspiring to take away their guns and turn them all into vegetarian socialists. Most of their get-togethers are glorified bitch sessions. I've written them off as ped-dlers of harmless nonsensical bullshit."

"Okay, sir." Tia smiled at the sheriff's colorful description and shrugged. "What's that got to do with Kane?"

"Gunther Kane came onto the local scene about two years ago. In his younger days, going back ten or twelve years, he rode with the Hells Angels chapter out of Milwaukee. Full-patched member.

A one percenter all the way. He got busted for felony assault and did three years in Waupun. While he was locked up, he parlayed with the Aryan Brotherhood."

"Yes, sir." Tia wanted to move the conversation along. Her stomach was at a full churn. "We got all that off his rap sheet when we arrested him. Didn't mean much to the prosecutor in Milwaukee."

"Yeah, so I've heard," Solo said.

Her stomach gurgled loud enough that she was pretty sure both men heard it. "Again, sir, no disrespect, but what do you need from me?"

"Kane discharged parole two years ago. He's been free and clear of the law ever since. He stumbled onto a job at the Roadhouse Score out on Highway 53. Started off as a bouncer and worked his way into management."

"That's the old strip joint, right?" Tia asked. "Can't say I spend a lot time there, but it sounds like just the place for him."

"A bunch of the regulars are some of the more hard-core element of North Aryan Front," Solo said. "That's where they hold their get-togethers. Look out for new members. That's where Kane comes in."

Tia thought it over. "So the guy goes from riding with HA and being a soldier in the Aryan Brotherhood to hanging out with a bunch of yahoos who like to run around in the woods dressed in camouflage? Pretty big step down, wouldn't you say?"

"You'd think so, but it seems Kane may have found his niche. When he was running with Hells Angels and the Brotherhood, he was a face in the crowd. With the NAF, he can run the show."

Tia and Ben exchanged a glance. Tia knew she wasn't the only one who was starting to get interested. The sheriff went on.

"Kane helped the boys of the North Aryan Front set up an LLC and take ownership of the Roadhouse. It's a strategy he learned from his days with HA. Those bastards own enough legit businesses to have their own Chamber of Commerce."

Tia found herself warming to the distinguished sheriff, beginning to understand why, in a county that was 90 percent white, he
kept getting reelected.

"Kane avoids the spotlight," Solo said. "He lets the old guard
bang the drum with all the philosophical bullshit. He seems more
interested in raising capital. We think he's doing pretty well."

"So they make their money through the club?"

He shrugged. "Some of it, yeah. Probably running dope and
I'm sure they've got some special hanky-panky going on with the
dancers—the usual strip joint stuff. But it looks like they've got
another income stream, outside the club."

Tia cocked her head. At this sign of interest, Solo cleared his
throat and leaned in.

"Now, this is where it gets a bit dicey. We've had to keep a few
things off the books. I'm going to ask that you do the same."

Tia nodded. "Of course, sir."

"Chief Sawyer told me about your run-in with Kane. He says
there was a second man. The fella who drove off in the van?"

Tia nodded and spoke matter-of-factly. "Yep. Kane called him
Jessup."

The Sheriff picked up a file folder off the couch and pulled out
a black-and-white eight-by-ten photo. He held it up so Ben and Tia
could both see it. It looked like a surveillance photo and showed a
group of men in a dusty parking lot. "That was taken two days ago
outside the Roadhouse Score. Recognize anyone?"

Tia didn't hesitate in pointing to a man in the crowd. "That's
him right there. The skinny, tweaker-looking prick. I landed a
pretty good shot right in his nut sac. Any chance he's walking with
a limp?"

Both men cringed. Solo said, "That's Jessup Tanner."

"So who is he?" Tia asked. "Another outlaw biker turned busi-
nessman?"

"Not hardly. Tanner's NAF, but he's no Johnny-come-lately like Kane. Tanner's a true believer, drank the Kool-Aid a long time ago. Hard-core racist politics. Separatist ideology. Lives off the grid. Hunkered down on a few acres here in Waukesha County. It's been in his family for a hundred years. Used to be a lot more, but the dumb son of a bitch refuses to pay property taxes, so the state has taken most of it. In a few years he'll be nothing more than a white-trash squatter.

"Kane and Tanner are thick as thieves. The brain trust of the NAF, if you can imagine such a thing. In the past three months, they've taken two major road trips that we know of. Both times they hauled ass to California in less than twenty-four hours. Then they took about three weeks to get back to Wisconsin."

"How do you know this?" Tia asked. "You got them on a tracker?"

The Sheriff looked down to his boots again. "Yeah, that's one of the things we need to keep kind of quiet."

"So that's a yes on the tracker, but a no on the warrant to go along with it?"

"Exactly. My deputies were just trying to get a quick sneak peak. Turns out they got an eyeful."

It made sense. Tia had used the same strategy on a few cases. Any cop can follow a crook around public places without a warrant, but if the bad guys start covering any kind of distance local agencies are hard-pressed to keep up. It takes resources to run that kind of surveillance. A good solution was to throw an electronic GPS tracker onto the crook's car and follow him by computer, but that requires a warrant. On occasion, cops would ignore the legal requirement and take a quick "sneak peak." If things got interesting, then the cop would formally request a warrant. In the world of cop rule bending, Tia knew, a "black tracker" was pretty low-level stuff.

"Once my guys realized what was at stake," Solo said, "they fell on the sword and told me what they were up to. I chewed their asses appropriately and we've moved on."

Tia forgot about her stomach. She wanted to hear more. "What did they tell you?"

His voice sounded grim. "From the intel we got off the tracker, we know Kane and Tanner spent some time in LA and Vegas. After that, they hit a bunch of truck stops, low-rent hotels, some farms. We figured they were running dope, buying some pretty good weight on the West Coast, then doing nickel-and-dime deals all the way home. Course we can't use any of that because it's ill-gotten off the unwarranted tracker, but it all made pretty good sense. That is, until you arrested Kane in Milwaukee."

Tia was confused. It didn't help that she had killed off a pretty good portion of her frontal lobe the night before, but she was still staggered by the picture forming in her mind. She refused to accept it. "I'm not following you, Sheriff."

Solo stared at Tia; his voice seemed almost sorrowful when he said, "We can't be sure, but when we put together what we already knew, along with your run-in with Kane, we got to thinking maybe the dope angle might be all wrong."

Ben added, "I told the Sheriff about Kane's assault on you. How he tried to pull you into the van. I told him about the girl you saw."

Tia's head was spinning. Ben had said "the girl you saw," not "the girl you thought you saw."

"What? What are you saying?" She knew she sounded confused. She couldn't help that.

"It all makes sense now," Solo said.

Ben spoke patiently. "Think about it, Tia."

Tia shook her head. She couldn't think, didn't want to think. Her head was still pounding. Angry, she said, "Think about what?"

The sheriff answered, "We think Kane might be involved in trafficking."

"Yeah, I heard you," Tia said, desperate for some other truth. "Meth? Grass? What?"

"No, Tia," Solo said. "*Human* trafficking."

There it was. The thing she hadn't even acknowledged to herself.

Jesus Christ. And you let them drive away.

The office disappeared and everything went dark. Tia stared into the back of the van as if staring down a long tunnel. The face. The screams. The heat of the night. TJ's voice buzzing in her ear. Sirens wailing. The van door slammed shut and it all disappeared. Tia was back in Ben's office.

The chief was talking. "You said Kane figured you to be a wet, right? Just across the border?"

"Yeah." Tia's mouth had gone dry and it was difficult to speak. "He asked me . . . if I'd just come up from Mexico. Something like that."

"Like maybe he could snatch you up and not worry too much about anyone taking notice?" Ben asked. "You said the girl looked Latina, right? And she was pretty young?"

"Yeah. Fifteen, sixteen." Tia's voice was a whisper. "Seventeen tops."

Ben rounded out his explanation. "Well, what if they—Kane and Tanner, that is—what if they snatched her up just like they tried to do to you? Maybe out in California. Arizona. Somewhere down by the border, anyway. Then drove across country with her. Pimping her out all the way back."

The sheriff said, "If they played it right, if they snatched up a streetwalker, somebody who was undocumented, nobody would notice. And even if she was reported as a missing person, it wouldn't garner much attention." He shrugged. "Course just as likely, she didn't get reported at all. She just . . . went away."

Tia stared out the window behind Ben's desk, the girl's muffled cry for help filling her head. Her brown terrified eyes. The duct tape across her mouth. Tia's stomach heaved and she almost reached for the trash can. She swallowed and willed the bile to stay down. She spoke to no one in particular, her voice barely audible. "So she was there."

The sheriff confirmed what everyone was already thinking. "They haven't been tripping out west for dope. They've been tripping for people."

The words hung over all three cops in the room. The gravity of the discovery wasn't lost on any of them. Tia asked the obvious question. "Now what?"

"That's why I'm here." Solo leaned back, signaling the end of his tale. "Seems like somebody needs to make a project out of Mr. Gunther Kane and his dimwit partner, Tanner."

"I absolutely agree, Sheriff," Ben said. "What do you have in mind?"

"Seeing that Kane and Tanner operate out of that shit-hole strip club right smack in the middle of my county and five miles outside Newberg, I think a joint operation between our two agencies would be a good next step. I'd like to get things started with surveillance tonight, if you can spare Suarez."

"It sounds like a lot to bite off," Ben said. Tia noticed that he avoided the issue of surveillance and her availability. "Any thought to giving the feds a call? Maybe they'll throw some money and people your way."

The sheriff waved a dismissive hand in the air. "Yeah, I called them. Got nothing but lip service. Bunch of excuses and double-talk, so the hell with them. If we make a human-trafficking case on Kane, we'll go with state charges for kidnapping. I don't doubt once all the work is done and the headlines are in the paper the feds will try to steal it away from us. Damn glory hounds. But that's a battle for down the road."

Ben turned to Tia and she picked up the reluctance in his voice.

"Well, what do you say, Detective? You clear to work a detail tonight?"

Tia was speechless. It was all too much, but she tried to push out an enthusiastic response. "Uh . . . yeah. I mean hell yeah, Chief. I'm all over it."

The sheriff stood and turned to Tia. "I've assigned a couple of U/C detectives to work surveillance at the Roadhouse tonight. We'll start slow. Just try to get the lay of the land. Zero in on the comings and goings of our two main players. Try to ID some of the lower-level guys. Maybe we'll get lucky and find somebody we can put a twist on. Get somebody on the inside to wire up for us. Sound good to you folks?"

Ben answered for them both. "Sounds like a plan, John. Let me talk it over with Suarez and my detective sergeant. We'll work out the details, but count us in."

The sheriff was headed for the door when Tia called out, "Excuse me, Sheriff?"

"Yes, Tia?"

"Uh, so where is she?"

Both men looked at her in confusion, so she tried again. "I mean the girl in the van. Where is she?"

The sheriff shook his head and his voice was solemn. "I can't answer that, Tia. I don't know."

Tia looked at both men and found herself wishing she were like them. Their suspicions of what was happening were still nebulous and nonspecific. For Tia, the whole thing came with a face. Ben's voice brought her back to the moment.

"Thanks again, Sheriff. We'll get things rolling on our end."

Solo nodded and left. The door closed and Ben and Tia were alone. The chief moved over to the couch, taking the Sheriff's place. He leaned forward and Tia wondered what form of an apology would come next. Finally he spoke.

"Before we go any further, Tia, you and I need to get something clear."

Tia began to feel the inkling of some sort of retribution. "What's that, Chief?"

"Tia, I know things have changed between you and me. I figure it's probably hard for you to . . ." Ben hesitated. "Well, I guess it might be hard for you to think you can trust me."

Ben paused, obviously waiting for Tia to say something. When she looked at him in silence, he went on. "But I want you to know something, Tia. You *can* trust me."

Elbows on his knees, Ben went on. "Before anything else, you're my friend. A friend who was there for me when no one else was. Someone who stuck by me during a pretty rough time. That kind of friendship doesn't come along very often. When it does . . ." Tia watched as Ben's eyes darted around like he was expecting to find just the right words written on a wall or hanging outside the window. Suddenly he did find them and his tone changed. "You *damn well cherish that*. You know what I'm saying?"

Struck by his emotion, Tia could only nod.

"That's why, as hard as it is, I need to say something to you. I'm only going to say this once and I want a two-word answer." He stopped as if to be sure she was listening. "Either 'yes, sir' or 'fuck off.' Your choice."

Tia tilted her head, perplexed. After a long pause that grew uncomfortable, she spoke. "Say what you have to say, Chief."

"Here's the deal." Suddenly Ben was all business. "You flush the pills and lay off the booze. Keep taking the piss tests, but I'll be the one getting the results, not Gage.

"Agree to that or I'll find someone else to go after Kane. And if you can't live with this arrangement, then I'd like your resignation." Ben put out his hands, palms up, and went on. "I want it to be your decision, Tia. Don't make me move forward on Gage's recommendation of a psychological retirement if you can't handle the job."

Tia looked into his eyes, her heart pounding. She gave some thought to going with the more colorful of the two choices. Where was his apology for not believing her about the girl in the van? Who did this guy think he was, dictating terms? She'd been right all along. Now instead of apologizing, he was going to get into shit that he didn't understand and that was none of his business. When Tia didn't respond, Ben went on.

"There will be no hard feelings, Tia. Not from me at least. It's your call, but I need your decision right now."

Tia stared at her boss. Her friend. She thought of their history, felt the pull of the affection that exists between people who have worked together to overcome insurmountable odds. She and Ben Sawyer once had that connection. She missed it. She wanted it back and this was certainly that chance. It might even be the last chance. She knew the right answer and her humble reply was barely audible. "Yes, sir."

She saw relief flood his face before he spoke. "*Your word*, Tia?"

She answered, her voice strong and clear, "Yeah, Ben. You've got my word. But I've got some terms of my own."

"Of course you do, Suarez. What are they?"

"I'm off light duty starting now and I'm on this case. No restrictions. We put together a team to go after Kane and Tanner. But the primary mission is finding that girl. If you can't give me that, then yeah, I'll walk. No hard feelings. But you should know, I'll just go all private-citizen vigilante and find her on my own."

"Great." He shook his head. "That's just what I need. Tia Suarez on the loose."

Tia watched his expression grow serious and still. She knew that when Ben Sawyer mulled a decision, the bigger the issue, the harder it was to get a read off the man. Thirty seconds went by with his face looking like it was carved in granite. She was about to break the silent stalemate when he spoke.

"Go find Sergeant Jackson and get him up to speed. Let him

know you're working a special detail tonight." Ben stood and stuck out his hand. "You're reinstated to full duty."

Tia stood as well and accepted the handshake. She was surprised when Ben pulled her in close and hugged her tight, clapping her on the back, his voice thick with emotion. "Don't make me regret this, Tia."

SEVENTEEN

Kane hunkered low in the seat of the rented sedan, doing his best to conceal his size. The slow-moving westbound afternoon traffic out of Milwaukee ebbed and flowed, heavy enough that if he stayed back a dozen or so cars he could maintain a good visual on his target. Driving the nondescript Chevy Lumina, with a ball cap pulled down over his head, he was confident his target up ahead had no idea the tables had been turned. A humid breeze blew across Kane's face through the open window, a hint that a summer storm wasn't too far in the future.

Settling in for what would probably be a long ride out of the city for who knows where, Kane found himself consumed by equal parts anger, betrayal, and relief. Reflecting, he had to admit to a trace of fear and uncertainty. If things turned out as he suspected, he needed to plan. It might not be too late.

Coming out of prison, Kane knew he had chosen a path fraught with risk. Stepping out from behind the protective cover of the Aryan Brotherhood, Kane had made the bold move of going independent. With his credentials, it would've been easy enough to rejoin the ranks of the HA and pick up a position as a chapter VP or at least a sergeant at arms. There was something to be said for that sort of job security, but Kane had other ideas. He'd spent years kicking money up to the bosses, and what had it gotten him? Women for sure. Plenty of booze and drugs. A new bike every other year and he always had a place to crash. But the time had come for Kane to look out for himself and cash in. The North Aryan Front offered just that opportunity.

Kane had come along just as the NAF was struggling to survive. Most of the ragtag membership thought white America was on the edge of extinction, suffocating under the jackboot of the federal government as it pressed down firmly against their throats. Most had failed to pay property taxes or had engaged in some form of fraudulent farm relief. A few had defaulted on government-subsidized farm loans—resulting in their property and assets being seized. More than a few had ended up on a government watch list. Their associations were monitored. In other words, they were ripe for recruitment into a criminal enterprise. Arriving on the scene, Kane had surveyed the situation and quickly realized he had found his opportunity. Three years later, Kane was finally hitting his stride. Earning serious capital. Now, just when the big payoff was coming, everything seemed to be slipping away.

No denying it. Something wasn't right. The ten-day deal out of Milwaukee was too good to be legit. He should have been looking at a return to Waupun. All the talk about the cop, Suarez, being a head case might have worked in his favor, but ten days? No way. Laying a hand on any cop, regardless of the circumstances, meant prison time. For a convict with a record like his? Kane knew he should have pulled a long stretch of hard time. But for some reason, he was back on the street.

Why? he wondered. *Who's pulling the strings?* He had a short list of suspects.

The traffic finally cleared and most vehicles sped up. Kane hung back a half mile, keeping the car in view. The miles clicked off, faster now, and his mind continue to wander. *Suarez.*

Kane had no idea what to make of the small-town cop. At best, she could be characterized as unpredictable yet formidable. A worthy adversary. The word in county jail was she was damaged goods. The package that crooks carry on any cop was always a lesson in embellishment, but the one on Suarez had an unusual twist. In the parking lot, Kane had smelled fear coming off her until she got a look at what was in the van. Then she had managed to dig deep and get back in the fight, though she'd still needed her partners to dig her out. When she turned up at the jail, Kane saw that her fear and desperation had returned.

That bitch is in over her head, he thought. *She's not the issue.* That much he was certain of.

Twenty miles south of Madison his target exited the freeway and Kane followed with a loose tail. The car pulled in to the lot of the roadside Best Western, but Kane passed the upscale extended-stay hotel and parked in a crowded lot across the street. He slipped lower in the seat, maintaining a line of sight to his target. From a good hundred yards away he watched the man step out of his car and start a slow 360. Kane dropped out of sight, lying down across the passenger seat. After counting to thirty, he raised his head to the level of the dashboard and scanned the motel parking lot. He reacquired his target, spotting the man outside a room on the ground floor. The subject tossed a last look over his shoulder—Kane didn't move, knowing that stillness was his best protection at that distance—then knocked on the door. A few seconds later it opened and he slipped quickly inside, but not before Kane glimpsed the slender arm of a woman in the doorway. A woman who no doubt had the answers to all his questions.

Kane leaned back in his seat, fighting the rage that always

accompanied the realization he was being played for a fool. But no matter. He'd been in tighter spots and worked himself free. The key was to stay a step ahead. The door shut. Kane spoke to himself in a low voice. "Now there's a little lady I'd like to get to know."

EIGHTEEN

Tia pushed the screen door open, her go bag slung over one shoulder. The cold steel in the small of her back felt odd, but she knew it wouldn't take long to readjust to carrying the weapon. Connor sat on the top step of the porch, his legs straight out in front of him. His back was turned, but she saw his shoulders tighten when the door slammed shut behind her. He didn't move or turn, though, and Tia assumed he was staring at the horizon where the sun would hang for another twenty minutes or so. The day had been hot and muggy, but a breeze now kicked up, offering some relief.

A bank of towering black thunderhead clouds had taken over most of the blue sky and begun to roll toward the farmhouse. The field of tall grass whipped in the light wind, a familiar sound along with the rustling leaves of oaks and hemlocks. The birds had gone silent, having either hunkered down or just up and left. All ominous warnings that gave the impression Mother Nature had thought about whipping up a tornado but instead dialed it back to what promised to be a late-night show of thunder and lightning. Tia dropped her bag and took a seat next to Connor, leaning over to drape one arm around his shoulders.

She put her lips right up to his ear. "I'll just be on perimeter surveillance. I'm sure I won't even be a player. It's no big deal."

"Until it is. Problem is, it's not like somebody is going to make an announcement: 'One minute till the shit hits the fan.' When it happens, it'll be on you before you know it." Connor turned to look her dead in the eye. His tone was humorless, even icy. Tia knew he was in no mood to joke around. "You sure you're ready?"

"It's a surveillance, Connie. We're not talking Taliban. It's a bunch of yahoos at a strip club."

"So you go from desk duty to U/C field ops, *again*?" Connie shook his head. "Think back, Tia. How did that work out for you last time?"

Tia shook her head, refusing to respond, so Connor went on and she could tell he was doing his best to contain real anger. "It's like you got some damn cowboys running this shit. I thought Sawyer was smarter than that."

Finally, losing patience and feeling more than a bit patronized, she pushed back. "It's a sheriff's operation, but yeah, Sawyer assigned me. He gets it, Connie. Why don't you?"

"Get what?" There it was. Real anger.

"That I need this." She stood and looked down on him. "I need to see this thing through."

"What are you talking about, Tia? What is it you're trying to prove?"

She looked out across the field. "For a week now, everyone's been treating me like damaged goods. Like I'm some kind of nut job. But guess what, Connor?"

Connor shrugged and Tia spoke with vindication. "Turns out I'm not so crazy after all. There *was* a girl in the back of that van. Kane and Tanner need to be dealt with and in a big way."

"Nobody's arguing about that. And who gives a shit what

people think? I told you. Just believe in yourself. That's how you get through stuff like this. Not by worrying about what other people think and not by joining some half-baked operation."

"Half-baked? I wonder if the victim would agree. Because to tell the truth, what she thinks is all I really care about right now."

"Come again?"

Tia could hear the frustration in his voice and saw the confusion in his eyes.

"Like I said, I let all these cops"—her voice turned spiteful—"all these *men,* convince me that maybe I was losing it. Got me to doubting myself. And when I did that? What happened to her? While I've been wallowing around here, feeling sorry for my damn self, what has she been going through?"

He stared back and Tia knew she'd given him pause. It was his turn to stop and think about a girl who had been abandoned and left to the likes of Jessup Tanner and Gunther Kane. She went on to paint an even clearer picture.

"She heard the sirens. The voices. There were cops all over the place. She knew that. And we didn't do anything. I'm ready to own that, but I'll be goddamned if I'm going to sit here, get drunk, and write her off as a lost cause."

Connor tried to reason with her. "Look, Tia, I understand all that. You were right all along. But you're talking about interstate travel. Kidnapping. You said yourself, they've gone all the way to the West Coast. Jesus. What are a handful of local cops going to do if these guys hit the road?"

Tia regretted filling him in on the details. She knew the information was safe, but she also knew that with his tactical knowledge Connor had figured out real quick the cops were in over their heads. She couldn't offer a good answer because she didn't have one, so instead she made excuses.

"It's surveillance. There's no reason to think anything will happen tonight. We just need to start figuring out who the players are.

Get the layout of the organization. Once we establish that, we can call in some more help."

"Yeah? Well, when is Sheriff Jack-Off going to call Uncle Sam? This case needs federal resources. You know it and so does he."

Tia knew better than to try to argue with a guy who had a thousand hours of real-world experience in urban surveillance. "We won't trip, Connie. I promise. If they hit the highway, I'll make sure we put the op down. All we're hoping for tonight is to ID some players. If we get really lucky, they might even lead us to where the girl is."

Connie stared at her, then shook his head and looked away. She knew he was done talking about it. Tia looked at her watch. Briefing was coming up soon.

"I gotta go, Connie. I'm meeting two sheriff dicks for the briefing. Like I said, I'll get parking lot duty. I mean, come on. Can you see me trying to blend in at a strip club? How's that going to work?"

Connie kept his head turned away, so she knelt on the step in front of him and pulled on his chin until he was forced to look at her. Looking into his eyes, she sensed his anger warring with his affection for her. Maybe he was right—was she really ready to get back in this fight? She hadn't been sober for even twenty-four hours yet.

"You're working tonight, right?" she asked, her voice soft. "I'll text you every hour or so, okay?"

Connor's voice was cold, dispassionate. "We got two trucks coming in and both have to be unloaded by end of shift. The boss catches me looking at a phone and I'm done." She saw shame rising on his face. "Sorry. Life of a working stiff, you know?"

Tia pushed off on his shoulder and stood. She could tell there was no way he was buying her line of bullshit. "Well, I'll text you anyway. Read 'em when you can. I'll meet you back here in the morning and we'll do the whole country breakfast thing."

Connie reached up and patted the small of her back where her forty cal rested inside the waist of her jeans. "I'm pissed at you, Suarez, don't forget. But be careful. Stay sharp."

Lightning flashed in the distance and Tia counted the seconds to thunder. Less than five; a strong but still-distant crack rumbled across the open land.

"See?" she said, heading for her GTO. She tossed her go bag through the open window. "It's going to be coming down like crazy in an hour. Probably put the whole op down. I'll meet you back here in the morning."

Yanking on the door, Tia gave Connor one last look, feeling the pull of affection. "Forget breakfast," she said, sliding into the seat. "With this weather, it's going to be a great day to just lie around in bed and do what comes natural."

Connie managed a half smile. "Be careful out there, Suarez. Even if you ain't looney tunes, it don't mean you all of a sudden turned into Superwoman."

Pulling out of the driveway, Tia gave one last look into the rearview mirror. Connor's smile was gone and the expression on his face was unfamiliar. How odd it was to see that man look afraid.

NINETEEN

The steady thump of bass music bounced off thin office walls and Kane looked at his watch. *Almost five. Right on time,* he thought to himself. *The joint's heating up.*

Kane stood in the doorway of his office, surveying the main floor of the Roadhouse Score. The lights had been dimmed and the past-their-prime girls, who took the less lucrative early-evening dance shifts, were onstage, working the moderate crowd. Kane was glad to see just about every barstool was occupied by the usual dinner-time clientele: mostly bankers, lawyers, and accountants headed home to the suburbs from downtown Milwaukee. The men sat at the bar in their eight-hundred-dollar suits, munching on burgers and fries that would end up written off on a company expense account, while the girls danced at eye level just a few feet away.

After finishing their meals, the younger jet-set types would, more often than not, slide a fifty to the bartender, who would shove the bill into the slot beside the cash register, then hand the patron a numbered magnetic keycard. The man would make his way to the back room with the matching number and swipe the card for entry.

Then a girl would help take the edge off his day before he headed home to the little missus. For an extra twenty-five bucks a guy could trade up for some serious action that made the frustrations of the office and home life drift away.

Kane knew that come eight o'clock or so, when the early crowd had long since gone home to the wife and kids, things would roughen up and it would be standing room only. By 9:00 P.M. a team of six bouncers would be on hand to maintain order. All three dance poles would be continually draped with a rotation of a half-dozen girls, each one with a body and the talent to pull in a thousand dollars a night. Waiting lines would form five deep for the private lounges that were really nothing more than walk-in closets with a couch and lava lamp. There lap dances would be performed at a price of fifty bucks a minute. Real action started at two hundred. Serious money . . . and Kane knew he needed every dime of it.

It had been four days since his rather contentious meeting with Curtis Bell. Tomorrow Kane was expected to take delivery of one hundred fully automatic M4 Colt machine guns along with fifty thousand rounds of armor-piercing ammunition. Kane would turn around and sell the hardware piecemeal and gross about five hundred K. But it wouldn't be easy to close the deal. Kane had come to realize Curtis Bell was not the sort of black-market arms dealer who would give a lot of second chances. Kane needed to move the deal along, all the while being particularly cautious in his dealings with Bell.

Kane walked the crowd, estimating the night's impending action. He worked his way past a table full of frat boys from Madison, chuckling to himself when he realized they were sitting next to a group of former frat boys who were now political staffers at the state capitol. Nearby, a dozen or so middle-aged men in cowboy hats and Western boots were starting to get a load on. A bouncer told Kane the men were part of a convention of Texas preachers, looking for private entertainment and ready to spend big. Kane slowed down long enough to let them know the VIP room and two dancers would be made available as long as there were at least ten men in attendance, and they averaged five hundred a head. The deal was struck, Kane stuck his fingers in his mouth and gave a loud whistle, catching the attention of Buster Cobb. He signaled Cobb over to take care of the details, then moved along.

Kane figured he was looking at a twenty-thousand-dollar crowd. Not bad, but not good enough. He was going to need at least another fifteen thousand to be able to pay Bell the hundred thousand the dealer was expecting.

Kane made his way to the corner table Jessup Tanner was sharing with Pepper Hill, one of the lead dancers in the Roadhouse's stable. Hill had been with the club for six months. A natural blonde with an authentic forty-two-inch rack, she had proven herself to be a real asset. Even in the low light of the club, her complexion was a perfect milk white, and her honey-colored hair fell into alluring curves, just long enough to brush the swell of her breasts that lay round and natural against her chest. The girl was by no means fat, but she had a healthy, robust set of curves—none of that anorexic hip bone protrusion on this gal. Best of all, she was genuine and free of any artificial enhancements. A rare, old-school commodity in the striptease industry.

Hill had come to the Roadhouse with solid credentials from an upscale gentleman's club in Chicago. A top-shelf dancer in every respect, she had developed a love of the nose candy. At first it had just been about controlling her weight. Then the dope started to get hold of her, so the high-end club, not wanting to draw any more attention than cops naturally paid to strip joints, turned her out. Hill had been forced to take a step down the career ladder and wound up at the Roadhouse, where addicted dancers were not just tolerated, but encouraged.

Kane looked to Tanner, who was supposed to be the man in charge of overall operations. Kane was well aware of Jessup's infatuation with Pepper Hill. Jessup spent hours fawning over the girl during the day and never missed her dance sets at night. Even now, Jessup stared at the young woman, who was dressed in a sheer robe that left little to the imagination, with the lovesick look of a teenage boy. A few weeks back, Kane had caught Jessup providing Hill with free dope. Kane had set the man straight on that. Only *he* doled out the drugs—and the first rule in the life of a Roadhouse stripper was: nothing's free.

After several seconds of going unnoticed beside their table, Kane shouted to be heard over the music, "What the hell, boy? You think this club will run itself?"

Tanner's head jerked up. Kane made sure Tanner saw his anger; the smaller man immediately tried to lessen his offense. "Just getting ready for the crowd, boss. Pepper's got a new routine. She's going to perform it tonight. Ain't that right, Pepper?"

"Yeah, Gunther." The stripper's voice was coy but full of spunk. "You should come see."

Kane looked Hill over, figuring her to be twenty-one or twenty-two years old. Twenty-three tops. She had a few good earning years still ahead of her. Kane had her up to about a gram and a half of cocaine a day, which meant she was well and truly hooked, but the physical effects were negligible so far.

Kane didn't have a problem with Hill's love of dope. It was her personal no-touch policy that he found irritating. He was pretty sure she wasn't even putting out for Tanner. Kane didn't care what Tanner might or might not be getting out of Hill, but that sort of uppity behavior with a customer really limited the earning potential of any dancer, even a hot number like her. If she was ever going to earn him top dollar she needed to loosen things up. Kane knew when a customer paid upward of five hundred dollars for a private show it came with the expectation that the house rules would be lifted. Although he'd grown to admire Hill's moxie, Kane had already decided that the time had come to train that shit out of her.

"Good. I got just the audience for you." Kane took hold of Hill's elbow and pulled the woman out of the booth. "Get on back to the VIP room. Tell Buster you'll be one of the dancers for the private show."

Pepper's eyes turned to Tanner. "I don't do private shows. I'm a stage dancer."

"Yeah, Gunther." Tanner's voice held a tremor. "I'll find another girl for that crowd."

"You forgetting something, Pepper?" Kane towered over her. "You're into me for two grand."

She said nothing and Gunther let his gaze drift to take in all of her there was to see. He reached out and squeezed one breast. Her body went tense and he bent down, putting his mouth next to her ear.

"You wanna pay me back another way? Just you and me?"

The stripper shook her head but knew better than to pull away. Gunther dropped his hand, letting it glide along her down-covered belly. He tilted his head to catch Tanner's jealous gaze and winked at the other man, still talking low in Hill's ear. "Then you get on back to the VIP room and you make those Texas preachers praise the Lord for their good fortune. You hear me?"

The young woman pulled her robe tight, wrapped her arms around her body, then double-timed it to the door that led to the VIP room. Tanner stared after her. His forlorn expression made Kane's blood boil. He smacked Tanner across the back of the head with an open hand. The other man looked up at his superior, terror in his eyes.

"You got anything to say?"

His voice shook. "No, boss."

"Good. I'm in no mood to put up with some schoolboy bullshit. We're running a business, not a dating service. Now, you got some numbers for me?"

Tanner knew the drill and started right in. "The joint's been off the hook the past three nights. We've been pushing the girls hard on the extracurriculars, just like you said. We did almost forty-five K."

"What about activities outside the club?"

"We've still just got the one dog in the pound for now, but we worked her hard. We hit three camps between here and Chippewa County. The wets really turned out. And of course it's growing season, so there's no shortage of the horny little bastards.

"In three nights, we did forty-five hundred. But I gotta say, boss, the product is about wore out. Maybe good for one or two more rotations. After that, we're going to need to head out west and re-up."

"That's it? Not even fifty grand? With what we already had on hand and tonight's take, we're still gonna be almost twelve grand short."

Tanner pushed back. "I got nothing to work with. We can only go to the well so many times. But we're good. I talked to my contact in California. New load just came in. We can get two for five grand apiece. One of 'em, he says, can't be a day over sixteen. Don't speak a word of English. Meek as hell."

"We ain't got time for that. We need the cash now."

Kane found himself wondering about every word that came out of Tanner's mouth. Getting left behind in the parking lot had been a turning point in their relationship. After Kane's enlightening road trip, he and Jessup had finally had their long overdue chat. And that had brought everything into focus for Kane. He realized he couldn't trust Jessup Tanner to do anything other than look out for himself. The little bastard would kiss whatever ass kept him out of jail.

Kane smiled as a thought struck him. Maybe it was time for Tanner to step up. Let him take the risk for a change. Make sure he stayed invested. Kane nodded toward the door that led back to the dressing room. "Might be time we have one of the girls step up. Earn some top dollar."

Nodding, Tanner flipped through the pages of his notepad. "Who you got in mind? Rachel's into us for almost five grand of product. I can run her down to Chicago. Set it up. She can pull in that much if we put her out there for twenty-four hours of high-end work. I figure if we threaten to cut her off, she'll be willing to step up."

"Nah, she can't bring in that kind of money anymore. We need somebody who can score big. And I'm thinking more along the lines of an auction. Forty-eight hours. No restrictions."

Tanner flipped through a few more pages, then looked up. "All right, boss. Make the call."

"I'm thinking Pepper. After the private gig, let's reach out to the high-dollar audience. Let 'em know we have a onetime offer. Special deal, winner takes all. That'll bring in some high-end money."

"Auction Pepper?" Tanner's voice was hollow; his eyes were black pits in his pale face.

"Yeah. Tonight. Work it right and that oughta bring in a good portion of what we need to close the deal with Bell."

"Yeah, but boss, she—"

Kane cut him off, "Yeah but nothing. We need to score big and score quick. Guys will pay top dollar to spend a couple of nights with a gal like that. Whatever you can't cover with Pepper, we'll turn that little brown bush-hoppin' bitch out for one more circuit."

Tanner shook his head. "Pepper ain't gonna go for anything like that, boss."

"Course she ain't going to go for it. You still gotta do it. " Kane stared hard at the man.

"I don't like it, boss. I'll get one of the bouncers to step up."

"You'll do what I tell you, Jessup. That's what you'll do." Kane closed in. "Or maybe you and I need to have another talk. Take another look at the nature of our relationship. Is that what we need to do?"

"No, boss. That ain't necessary."

"I didn't think so." Kane laughed. "In six months we'll have her working for a Happy Meal at Mickey Ds. Hell, maybe she'll even give you a little taste by then, right?"

"She ain't like that. Pepper is—"

"Pepper is part of the Roadhouse stable, Jessup. And that's all the hell she is. Time we introduce her to the reality of the life. Now, are you in or not?"

It took Tanner several seconds to answer, and when he spoke it was through a clenched jaw. His voice was flat and he gave a mock salute. "I'm on it, boss."

"Glad to hear it." Kane grinned, enjoying his power over Tanner. "Like I said, set it up for tonight. Go upscale. Be sure to get a security deposit. I don't want to be getting her back all beat to shit or marked up."

"Yeah, boss," Tanner said. He lowered his head, staring at his notepad.

Kane cuffed the man across the face. "I ain't feeling you, boy."

Tanner looked up. "I'll get you the money, boss."

"That's more like it, boy." Kane turned to walk away. "Set it up tonight. Get back here when it's done."

TWENTY

Tia pulled the GTO into the lot of the sheriff's substation and eyed two men leaning against a pickup truck, both dressed in jeans and flannel shirts. One sported a full beard; the other looked like he'd gone a week or so without a shave. Badges hung from around their necks and each carried a forty cal in a pancake holster. She pulled up close and parked, knowing both cops were giving her the same once-over. She pushed back on the sense of fear mixed with a bit of guilt. Uncertainty came over her and she thought back on her conversation with Connor. *What am I doing here? I don't need to prove anything to anyone.* Tia reminded herself she was trying to save a life. She got out of the car, doing her best impression of a cop who fit in.

"You Suarez?" the bearded one called out.

"Yeah. Looking for Detective Lonnie Jacobs."

"That's me," he answered, and nodded to the man next to him. "My partner, Grady Phelps."

Tia moved in and shook their offered hands. "This it? The three of us?"

"Yeah, 'fraid so. Our overtime budget sucks. Tonight we'll just try to get the lay of the place. Maybe see who the players are. Shot callers and such." Jacobs looked at his partner, then back at Tia. "Understand you've already had a run-in with two of them? Kane and Tanner."

"You could say that."

"Case went to shit on you?"

"No." Tia shook her head and held the man's eye. "Case was solid. DA dumped it."

"That happens," he said, nodding.

Tia didn't want to dwell on it. "So what's the plan then?"

"Well, being that it's a strip club, we figured you could go U/C again."

Tia was wondering if she'd heard him right and trying to come up with a response when Phelps gave Jacobs a shove.

"Shut up, Lonnie. Damn, man." Phelps looked to Tia. "Sorry. His shit is weak like that a lot. Thinks he's a real comedian."

Jacobs laughed, giving Tia a look that bordered on a leer. Tia ignored him and turned to Phelps. "I figured you guys would go inside. I can take the long eye outside. Watch the comings and goings."

"Yeah. That'll work," Jacobs said, drawing her attention. She detected a little chill in his tone—likely he was offended that his joke hadn't gone over. "Probably the further back the better. If they burn you, we'll be next."

"Or," Tia said, "if you guys get torched, they'll come looking for me?"

"Don't worry about us," Jacobs said. "Just stay put in the parking lot."

"What's your cell, Tia?" Phelps pulled out his phone. "We can stay in touch by text."

The three of them traded numbers quickly.

"How come the DA dumped your case on Kane?" Jacobs asked, returning to his earlier topic.

Tia shrugged as if the whole thing were no big deal. "You'd have to ask her."

"I'd rather hear it from you," Jacobs said, clearly unwilling to give up.

An uncomfortable silence hung until Tia broke it. "Graham said the assault was bad because I didn't ID myself as a cop. As far as the kidnapping charge, nobody saw the girl but me."

Phelps looked down, kicking his toe in the dirt. Jacobs nodded and looked thoughtful. "You get that a lot? DAs dumping your cases if you don't have a corroborating witness?"

Tia bit her lower lip and shook her head. "Not really. In fact, never."

Jacobs wasn't going to let it go. "You mean never until the last few months, right?"

"You got a real question, Jacobs, or you just going to keep up this gay-ass gentle bantering shit?"

Jacobs stood up straight. His brows lowered, his eyes narrowed, and he seemed ready to probe deeper until Phelps jumped in, saying, "Let's get moving. We'll go in separately. Tia, why don't you wait till it gets dark, then set up in a corner of the lot. Sound good?"

Tia stared at Jacobs but answered his partner's question. "That's fine by me."

Phelps reached into the pocket of his jeans and tossed Tia a set of keys. "Take the Chevy truck. You don't need to be burning your own gas on this. Nice goat, by the way."

Tia decided Phelps was all right and Jacobs could go jerk himself off for all she cared. "Thanks. It's a '64. My dad and I restored it ourselves. All original."

Phelps nodded. "Sweet."

Clearly unhappy with the casual conversation, Jacobs turned on his heel. He spoke as he walked away. "All right. We'll head out. Be in the lot after dark. If we get into any shit inside, don't worry. We'll call uniformed deputies for backup."

Shaking his head, Phelps took a deep breath, then followed his partner toward their four-wheel drives. He offered Tia a fist bump as he passed. "Ignore him, Tia. He's a prick. I'll try to text every half hour or so, give you an update."

After the deputies pulled out, Tia went to her car and grabbed her go bag from the backseat. As she ran her hand across the vinyl tuck-and-roll upholstery, a memory swept over her, suddenly vivid and clear. She and her dad pulling up in front of the house in Eau Claire.

They had driven almost two hundred miles, after reading an ad offering interior seats for a '64 GTO. When they met with the owner, Tia, who was about fifteen at the time, served as her dad's translator. They'd negotiated the man down to $175.00 for the mint-condition black vinyl seats. After carefully loading the bounty into the back of their battered pickup truck, they celebrated with root beer floats at the A&W drive-thru. She had dozens of similar memories covering their hunt for engine parts, light fixtures, and dashboard knobs. As she remembered the major score of the convertible roof assembly she gently caressed the fabric surface, feeling the ribs of metal underneath.

They had bought the car at an auction when Tia was thirteen years old. Her dad told her it was a classic American muscle car. All she saw was a rusted-out shell of metal that belched black smoke whenever you started it up. On her sixteenth birthday, her father had handed her the keys to a fully restored classic '64 GTO. She was the envy of Newberg High School.

Tia grabbed the bag and slammed the door shut, harder than she needed to. Memories and lies all folded into one. She thought back to the time spent with her family in Mexico. *Everything is different now. Jesus, what am I doing here?*

Tia threw her bag across the front seat of the pickup and hoisted herself inside. The Roadhouse was only about a fifteen-minute drive away and it wouldn't be dark for an hour. She would have too much time to sit and stew.

What a waste of time, she thought. *Sit my ass in a parking lot for what? For who? How does this help anyone?*

Tia thought about the bar, not far up the road. She could see the neon sign: Fireside Lounge. She'd been in many times, drawn to the place's dark, typically empty interior. She could slide in there, knock back a couple. That, plus a bottle to go, would make the boredom of a long stakeout much more tolerable.

Why not? Jacobs sure the hell wasn't going to know. Just the thought of a drink lifted her spirits and lightened her mood. She pulled out a mental barstool and ordered a tequila sunrise and a shot of Jose Cuervo. By the time she hit the highway, her imaginary drink glowed like an orange ball floating just beyond her reach. *It'll be real soon enough,* she thought. She pressed the accelerator to the floor, making sure not to look back at her goddamned car.

TWENTY-ONE

T here's at least a couple of 'em inside, boss," Buster Cobb reported. "Another one, a female, in a lay-off truck in the
parking lot."

Kane wasn't surprised. In the privacy of his office, he used the
closed-circuit surveillance cameras to zero in on a white dude sitting alone at a corner table. The black-and-white images on the
screen were grainy, but Kane could still make out the man's long,
clean hair and neatly trimmed beard. Throw in the healthy tan, the
fact that the guy didn't smoke, and he'd been nursing the same beer
all night, it all signaled "cop." Kane had sent over a dancer, who'd
pushed the envelope of what was legally allowed, and the man hadn't
so much as touched her tit.

Dumb ass might as well wear a badge pinned to his forehead. Kane
had sent Cobb to scour the rest of the club and the perimeter of
the parking lot. Hearing that the one outside was female, he already
knew who he was dealing with.

"Let me guess. The one in the parking lot. Brown bitch. Kinda
hot looking?"

"Bingo."

"Suarez."

"You want I should let 'em know we made 'em, tell 'em to shove off?"

"Nah. I like knowing where they're at. In fact, make sure we don't tip our hand. As long as they feel their cover ain't blown, they'll stick around."

"You got it, boss. You need anything else. A drink? Maybe I send one of the girls back?"

"Nah, but spread the word. Make sure security knows a no-touch policy is in effect. Bartenders shouldn't offer any special activities. You go through the girls' dressing room, check their shit for dope. Tonight we're nothing short of model fucking citizens."

"Right, boss."

Cobb sauntered out, leaving Kane alone in his office. So Suarez was following through.

He looked out the window of his second-floor office, getting a bird's-eye view of the Roadhouse Score. The place was packed and the bartenders were hustling to keep up. The cops on-scene would put a damper on the final score, but he'd give them nothing to react to. Just a legal strip club providing wholesome adult entertainment. Even without the extra income from the under-the-table stuff it was going to be a good night at the till. And his other plans would take care of what he needed for the deal with Bell.

Kane wondered if he should give Tanner a heads-up. He tapped his fingers on the desk, thinking about making a phone call, then let it go. Always risky to get on the phone and start talking specifics. Besides. Tanner sure as hell knew the score, could take care of his damn self. But Kane might need an insurance policy.

Cobb returned after checking the dancers' gear. Kane didn't ask what he'd found and Buster offered no specifics, just said, "Everything's clean now, boss."

"I got a mission for you, Buster. It's a road trip and it's damn important." Kane scribbled an address on a pad of paper, ripped off the sheet, and handed it to Buster. "You're going to have to haul down there and back. Don't dawdle. You hear me?"

Buster looked at the address. His face took on a look of childlike excitement at being given what was clearly an important assignment. "Don't dawdle. Got it, boss."

"All right, Buster. Listen close. This is what I need you to do."

TWENTY-TWO

Rain pummeled the roof and hood of the pickup truck hard enough to drown out the country music, but the voice had been persistent.

She needs you. Go to her.

From the far corner of the muddy parking lot she could smell the booze inside the Roadhouse Score. Tia had somehow mustered the will to resist a stop at the bar, but now she realized a liquor store was less than two miles up the road and would be open for another hour. She could be there and back in less than five minutes. *Just a couple of those little airline bottles,* she told herself. *Three of them ought to do it. Then again, what the hell. Get a fifth and call it a party. Who's going to know?*

A clap of thunder cleared her head and she wondered how much longer the deputies would want to stay on the surveillance. She picked up her phone. Almost 1:00 A.M. She had been slumped down in the seat of the pickup truck for over four hours. She punched out a quick text to Connor. "still quiet here. how r u?"

Tia set the phone back on the center console, assuming she'd get no response. She'd sent half a dozen text messages to Connor; all had gone unanswered. She pictured him on the back dock of the Piggly Wiggly, unloading two semi-trailers full of slabs of meat, cases of beer, canned goods, dairy, and whatever else ended up on the shelves of a grocery store. Heavy lifting for sure and taxing on his legs. But Connor wouldn't think of asking for special treatment. *And here I am,* she thought, *bitching about sitting on my ass in a parking lot, collecting overtime.*

The monotony didn't help. Tia had been assigned to the outer perimeter, which was about the same as being a security guard. From her vantage point at the farthest edge of the lot she could keep an eye on the front entrance to the Roadhouse Score and monitor any cars that were coming or going from the rear. So far she hadn't seen any of the players. Then again, there were only two she was really concerned about, and from what she had gathered from Jacobs and Phelps, only one of them was present. Gunther Kane had been in the club since the deputies had arrived, but Jessup Tanner was nowhere to be seen.

Tia thought back to the morning. *A little over twelve hours ago,* she thought to herself, *you were heaving your guts into a toilet, figuring your career was about to end. Now you're ready to get back in the mix? Yep. Sure am.*

Tia fought against the urge to drop the truck into drive, instead allowing herself the fantasy of picturing all the different bottles of tequila, vodka, and whiskey stored neatly in the imaginary liquor cabinet in her mind. Bottle after bottle in long beautiful rows.

Despite her boredom and her demons, Tia figured her low-level assignment beat the alternative of being inside the club. The parking lot had been packed when she first set up. Probably the place had been standing room only, and the last place she wanted to be was shoulder to shoulder with a bunch of Wisconsin rednecks in a strip bar. Over the past hour the lot had gradually cleared out, and now it was occupied by the last ten or fifteen pickups and beat-up Eldorados.

Tia's phone chimed and she grabbed it, hoping for a message from Connor. She was disappointed to see it was a group text from one of the deputies inside the Roadhouse.

"Putting operation down. S-One on-scene. No unusual activity. S-Two a no-show. Place emptying out."

Had they been made? She couldn't see how, but it seemed like a good idea to at least talk it over, try to figure out where Tanner had gone. She texted back: "where 2 4 debrief?"

The response was quick.

"No need 4 debrief. Try again 2mrrw night. Go ahead & secure."

Fine with me, she thought. If she left the goat at the sheriff's station and drove straight home in the truck, she'd get to the farmhouse about the same time as Connor. She banged out a text she knew he would be happy to get.

"no activity all night. told u so. headed home. see u there."

A moment later her phone rang; she looked at the number and was again disappointed. Still not Connor.

"What's up, Phelps?" she said, answering. She spotted him leaving the Roadhouse Score and heading for his vehicle, phone at his ear.

She was glad it was Phelps on the line. It had been pretty obvious that Jacobs wasn't keen on her being part of the surveillance team. Phelps struck Tia as a decent sort of guy, not to mention a solid cop. When he spoke, she heard frustration in his voice, the car door slamming in the background as he got in. "That was some bullshit."

Tia listened as he described the evening.

"A whole night and we didn't see so much as a hand-to-hand dope deal. That was the most legit strip club I've ever spent six hours in."

"Yeah. I'll bet it was just killing you guys to sit around with all those half-naked women all over the place, huh?"

"Half? Hell, girl, you need to get out more often. There ain't no half about it. But yeah. We definitely took one for the team."

Tia laughed. "I'm out of here. Same thing tomorrow night?" She glanced at the clock on the dashboard. It was one thirty in the morning and her first thought was that she had thirty minutes until the liquor stores closed. *You got it bad, Suarez.* She forced herself to focus on Phelps's voice.

"Yeah. We'll do it again. We'll brief at the same place. Be there by nineteen hundred hours." She heard his car start up while he kept talking. "I'm going to run by Tanner's place. Make sure he's not out and about. Little worried that he never showed up. Hope he ain't off on some road trip by himself."

"Tanner's place? The place we covered in briefing? The farm on the county line?"

"Yeah," Phelps said. "Would've been good to put someone out there tonight to keep an eye on him, but we figured he'd be at the Roadhouse as usual. If I can get some extra bodies, we'll add his place as a target location tomorrow."

"Jacobs going with you?"

"No. Says he got plans at two o'clock in the morning, if you can believe that shit." She could sense his irritation. "No sweat. I got this."

Tia knew what she had to do, cop to cop. "You want some cover? I can tag along."

"Nah. It's just a drive-by. I want to see if Tanner's van is there. Only thing is, it's fifteen miles in the wrong direction for me. My wife's gonna be all pissed off. Not only did I spend the entire evening in a strip club; I'm probably not going to get home until about daybreak."

Tia got the not-so-subtle hint. "I know where the place is at. It's pretty much on my way home. Let me handle it."

"You sure?" The voice held feigned surprise.

"No problem. Just a drive-by to check for his ride, right?" Tia started the truck. "He still driving that white van?"

"Yep. He usually parks it near the shed alongside the main house. I went out there once before to poke around. The place is a real shit hole."

Tia fastened her seat belt. "What's the best approach?"

"About a quarter mile west of the place there's a dirt road between the cornfields. Park and walk in from there. Once you get within about a hundred yards of the house, you should be able to eyeball the van."

Tia held the phone away from her face and stared at it. *Fricking deputies. Drive-by, my ass,* she thought. *Sounds like a fricking recon patrol.* She knew that county cops were used to working alone and had a tendency to take a lot of unnecessary chances. Not wanting to come off sounding like a city cop or a wuss, she decided not to object.

"Just text me if it's there or not," Phelps said. "It he flew the coop or some shit, we'll deal with it later."

"Sounds good. I'll take care of it. Go on and get home."

"Thanks, Suarez. I really appreciate it. These U/C vice details drive my wife nuts."

Tia thought about Connor and what he would say if he knew what she had just agreed to. "I get it, dude. No sweat."

"See you tonight." She could hear his engine rev through the phone just before the call clicked off. A few seconds later she saw his truck pull out of the lot.

Anxious to be home and already regretting her willingness to help out, Tia blew out a breath. *Hell, it's not even my case,* she thought. The rain had eased off, but this little errand was going to cost her some time. If she didn't get home before Connor came by, he might not wait.

She tapped out another message.

"quick roll by for a house check then home. see u in a few. wait for me."

Yeah, he's going to love that, she thought. "Jesus, Suarez," she said out loud. "The shit you get yourself into."

Tucking her phone into her jacket pocket, Tia started the truck. She turned onto the roadway and punched the accelerator. In that same instant a sense of someone else's anxiety began to mix in with her own.

TWENTY-THREE

Angelica stood in the sunlight looking out over the courtyard of the only home she'd ever known. She wore the brightly colored dress her grandmother had made for her *quinceañera* almost two years ago. Her feet were bare but clean and she could feel the warm, dry earth beneath them. The cuts and bruises that had covered her body were gone, along with the pain, but her memory of the awful place remained clear in her mind. It had been real, she was certain of that, but now it was over. She ran toward the red adobe house, flew into her mother's open arms, and pressed her cheek against the careworn skin of the old woman's face. She had escaped, but how? The journey to America had taken days. Now, in the blink of an eye, she had returned home.

It was a miracle. God had heard her prayers after all. She stepped back from her mother and twirled around, again and again until she dropped to the ground from dizziness, her head spinning and her long black hair falling across her face. She looked between the strands into the deep blue Mexican sky, which was streaked by white wisps of clouds that looked like long, delicate fingers. *The*

Virgin Mary's hands, Angelica thought, *protecting me.* She reached out as if to touch the sky and laughed out loud, overcome with joy.

A short-tailed hawk flew high above, circling over her. Angelica stared at the hawk, amazed by the grace and ease of his flight. She watched as he circled lower and lower, until he tucked back his wings and began to dive toward her, then opened his wings again and grew larger and larger until he blocked out the sun and darkened the sky.

The world went cold and black. The hawk plunged lower, the sound of his wings like the beat of a drum. His open beak grew into a maw that threatened to swallow her. His talons plucked her from the earth and Angelica woke with a start, surrounded by darkness. The muted sound of thunder replaced the wings of the bird.

TWENTY-FOUR

Damn, is this it?

Tia found the dirt road just where the deputy had said, but it looked more like a path between two cornfields than anything that would qualify as a road. She turned off the two-lane highway and drove in slowly, headlights off. Leaning over the top of the steering wheel, she stared hard through the windshield, though she couldn't see more than a foot past the hood. She used the sound of corn leaves brushing up against both sides of the truck to navigate the narrow passage. Knowing she would eventually have to back out, Tia stopped after about twenty yards. Surrounded on all sides by eight-foot-high summer corn, she felt swallowed whole.

She opened the driver's door, slipped out, and closed the door without making a sound. It began to rain and within seconds she was drenched from a full-on downpour with raindrops that could fill a shot glass. The rain sounded like hammer blows on the metal surface of the truck. Tia flipped up the hood of her jacket, shook her head, and spoke out loud, no longer worried about the noise. "You've got to be shitting me."

She braced herself against the truck for a moment, looking out over a sea of corn that was swaying wildly in the wind. A four-foot-high fence of rusty barbed wire on either side separated her from the field itself. She vaulted over the nearest fencepost easily, but the mud caused her to make a slippery, cartoon-like landing. Tia grabbed the post with both hands and righted herself, but the near fall only added to her growing irritation.

After just a few steps into the field, her sense of direction vanished. With no moon or stars and no man-made light to steer by, her vision was limited to a few inches in front of her face and she was no longer sure she was walking in a straight line. Even if she had one, using a flashlight would be way too risky. Then again, if she wandered too far into the field and became any more disoriented she might still be wandering around come daybreak. Tia pulled her cell phone from her pocket, cupped her hand over the screen, and pulled up the compass app. According to the deputy, the house should be about two hundred yards due east. She set the phone flat in her hand, got a bearing, and stepped off, thinking to herself, *Quick drive-by, my ass. Who am I? Vasco frickin' da Gama?*

A lightning bolt flashed across the black sky, immediately followed by a crack of thunder. The dark blue strobe of light gave Tia a flash glimpse of her surroundings.

Corn.

She risked another glance at her phone, making sure the letter *E* was directly in front of her, and kept walking. A minute passed and Tia figured she had to be at least halfway to the house, maybe more. A lightning bolt even stronger and brighter than the last arced low overhead, striking nearby. An instantaneous explosion of thunder shook the ground. Tia was pretty sure she felt a jolt of electricity through the soles of her boots. *Damn. That was close.*

The rain fell even harder and the mud sucked at her boots. Each step took her farther from the safety of her truck, not to mention her warm, dry house.

Connor was probably getting off work right about now. If he got to the farmhouse and she wasn't there, he'd worry. *Forget this shit,* she thought. *Tell the deputy the damn van was parked right where it belonged and be done with it.*

Not an option. Tia trudged on, once again admonishing herself for getting caught up in this bullshit assignment.

She made out the black outline of a structure another twenty yards out. She hunched down low and slipped closer. Three low-watt lampposts cast a dull, gray light over a clear space that barely had room for the buildings it held. As she took in the scene, there was no doubt in her mind that this was the home of the lowlife tweaker militia freak, ass bag Jessup Tanner.

The disorganized clearing looked like a poorly managed junk-yard. A ten-foot chain-link fence topped off with looping razor wire surrounded the entire area. A half-dozen rusted-out trucks and ancient relics of boxy sedans sat abandoned inside the enclosure, left to die in place. Kitchen appliances, busted-up furniture, and a dozen or so heaps of junk were scattered around, a couple of the piles several feet high. A mountain of wood chopped for a fireplace was tall enough to last several Wisconsin winters. In the middle of it all stood a two-story brick house that was only slightly distin-guishable from the trash and rubbish surrounding it. Most of the windows were boarded over and the stone steps leading to the front door appeared to be crumbling away. Dim shapes in the crawl space had her guessing that several large dogs were sleeping under the house. Lording over it all, a tall flagpole rose from the ground like a stubborn middle finger. In the hazy light of the compound Tia could see a soaked and tattered yellow flag tangled in rope and bound against the pole. She could barely make out enough of the image of a snake and a few letters to guess that it was the "Don't Tread on Me" banner. Away from the house, set off by itself, she saw the dark outline of a low-slung woodshed with a corru-gated metal roof.

Tia strained her eyes, staring into the darkness, trying to spot Tanner's van. Staying low to the ground, she moved closer—way closer than she wanted, but the rain was playing hell with her vision. She looked back at the house, telling herself that if Tanner did happen to glance out and get a glimpse of someone sneaking around his cornfield he was likely to shoot first and ask questions later . . . and not many Wisconsin farmers would blame him one bit.

A massive lightning bolt ignited the sky like an illumination grenade, giving Tia a short but thorough glimpse of the entire compound. *There.* Backed up against the entrance of the shed. A van, and it sure as hell looked like the one she remembered so clearly. It was white, gray, or something similar. She couldn't be sure, but it was good enough. She whispered to herself, "I'm calling it white, Deputy. You owe me big-time."

Mission accomplished, Tia fought the urge to turn and break into a run. She wanted distance between herself and Tanner's goddamned Bates Motel of a house. She oriented her compass due west and began retracing her path back to the truck. In her mind she was practically home, and each step brought a growing sense of relief. The sounds of the wind and rain surrounded her. And something else. A voice, quiet but firm, asked her to be calm and listen.

Ella aqui.

Stunned by the sudden presence of another, Tia answered in a frantic whisper, "What? Who? Who's here?"

Frozen in place, she waited, heart pounding. Nothing. She shook her head, telling herself this was no time to lose it, and took another step. The voice came again.

Escucharla.

Tia listened, holding her breath, concentrating hard, trying to break down each wave of sound into its components. Wind. Rain. Ten thousand rustling cornstalks. The whining engine of a big rig, ten miles away on the interstate. Mixed in with all that, barely discernable, were muffled voices. Then another sound. A clink of metal against metal, it came from the shed.

Damn it, what is that?

She heard it again. Definitely metallic and coming from inside Tanner's compound. A scraping sound. Another clink. Oddly familiar, but out of place here on this sorry excuse for a farm. Laughter. Men's voices. Hunched over at the waist, Tia took two steps back toward the fence line, staring at the faint light that came from inside the shed, already regretting what she was about to do.

TWENTY-FIVE

In the darkness she heard water seeping through the roof and walls above her head, making new puddles on the muddy floor. A cool breeze from somewhere above blew against her face. She closed her eyes, trying to return to her mother's arms. To see the adobe house again. *I saw it*, she thought. *I know I did.*

She felt a spirit of hope and a voice from somewhere inside.

No se rinden, Angelica. No se rinden.

I don't want to give up, she thought. *I want to go home.*

She heard muffled thunder and other noises. Voices. She couldn't make out the words, but she was certain the voices belonged to men. Then another voice. Different. The sounds grew louder. Shouts. The crack of a gun. A scream.

Angelica pulled herself to her knees and crawled into a corner, her heart pounding. She covered her mouth so as to not cry out loud. Looking into the blackness above her, she began to pray. Pray that the men would not come for her. That God would protect her from whatever was happening above. Terrified, Angelica pulled her knees against chest, doing her best to not make a sound.

TWENTY-SIX

Tia walked along the fence line, staying a few rows back in the cornfield for cover. Lightning flashed and for a millisecond the sky was lit up as if it were noontime, and Tia was able to see the shed, about twenty yards in front of her. From this angle she could that see the back doors of the van had been left open a few feet in front of the entrance.

The lightning subsided and the area went black, but Tia kept her eyes trained on where she'd seen the shed. She saw a wavering light, coming and going as the wind whipped through the fields. A lantern maybe?

Crouching, she approached the fence, her boots heavy with mud. She was close enough to be able to determine that there were at least four men inside the shed. Under their voices she heard another, more muffled sound. Something told Tia a woman was making that suppressed sound. *Could it be* her?

The fence that rose a good four feet overhead was topped with tight loops of concertina wire. No way to clear it by going over. She looked down and tested the mud, which easily gave way to her boot heel. She moved ten yards down the fence line, to a spot blocked from view by the van, then dropped to her knees and scooped mud away from the bottom of the fence. It was cold, heavy, and wet. Her hands and arms were immediately coated in thick mud.

Using all her strength, Tia pulled up hard on the bottom of the fence with both hands, slowly bending the wire. After several pulling sessions and more mud scooping, she'd made an opening she figured she could squeeze through. Preparing to do that, she stopped, full of doubt.

She knew better. At this point she was breaking the law and Tanner would have every right to shoot her full of holes. With one last admonishment mixed with self-loathing, she decided to go in headfirst and on her back.

Tia's heart hammered against her rib cage. With a shaking hand, she pulled her gun from the waistband of her jeans. She lay on her back, hands above her head, and began to shimmy under the fence, being careful to keep her weapon clear of the mud. In a matter of seconds she was mud covered and soaked through. Rocks, pebbles, and clumps of dirt mixed into her hair and fell into her ears. Muddy rainwater flowed like a stream down the collar of her jacket and she cursed herself for having such a stupid idea. The rain fell so heavily against her face she experienced the same sense of panic as she had during waterboard training.

Halfway through she got stuck—something sharp poked at her waist. She pushed hard against the mud but got nowhere. She tried to go back the way she came, no luck. The stabbing feeling continued and she knew her jeans were hung up on the fence. She dug in her boot heels but could gain no purchase. The voices of the men sounded closer and she suddenly remembered the sleeping dogs and wondered if they'd been awakened by the storm. Fear overtook her and she began to wildly scissor-kick her legs, splashing mud everywhere. Nothing.

You're stuck, dumb ass.

Tia transferred her pistol to her weak hand, then reached down to fumble at her jeans, feeling her way around the waistband until she found the problem and was able to unhook herself from the fence. Pushing off with both boots, she slid a good six inches. Elated to be moving, she gave one final shove and slid clear. Scrambling to her hands and knees, Tia quick-crawled to the van. Exhausted, she sat in the pelting rain, leaning against the wheel well. She took a moment to consider what she had just done and the predicament she was now in, all because of a voice in her head.

The jury is in, Suarez. You're nuts.

Once she'd caught her breath, she was again able to hear the metallic clinking sound, now clearly coming from the shed, which was no more than eight feet away from her. Below the men's voices Tia heard a higher-pitched voice that seemed to be moaning or crying or both.

Standing up, Tia stripped off her sopping windbreaker—at this point the wet fabric did little other than cling to her arms and chest and restrict her movement. Her short-sleeved T-shirt was soaked through but fit tight, like another layer of skin. Her detective shield, on the chain around her neck, was buried under a clump of mud. She brushed off enough of the muck to show the metal, then swiped her face with the palm of her hand, clearing mud away from her eyes, nose, and mouth.

Ready, she moved toward the entrance of the shed, her raised gun leading the way.

The wood planks of the shed's walls were riddled with gaps and knotholes that allowed beams of light to shine through. Tia spotted a gap in the rough siding that she hoped would provide her a sneak peak without being far enough apart to give away her position. She raised her gun up alongside her cheek and moved her eye to the seam and stole a look inside. A sudden surge of adrenaline flushed her skin and poured through her body.

Mother of God . . . this can't be.

A woman stood on a small raised wooden platform, her arms pulled above her head, cuffed by the wrists to a metal pipe that stretched from wall to wall, a foot beneath the low roof. Whenever the woman shifted, trying without success to find a comfortable position, the handcuffs clinked against the pole with the now-familiar sound. Skimpy clothing sat on the platform in a neatly folded pile, as if things had started out a bit more cordially. She was naked and her pale skin was near translucent in the low light. Blond hair spilled across her face and her bare but ample chest rose and fell in panic. The reason Tia hadn't heard her screaming was now obvious—a ball gag was stuffed into her mouth, held in place by a leather strap.

Clustered around the makeshift stage, four men sat in a half circle of theater-style chairs that looked out of place in the rough setting. It wasn't until he spoke that Tia even became aware of a fifth who stood alongside the woman on the stage: Jessup Tanner. He seemed to be in charge. Tia stood and listened.

"All right, boys, you got your look." Tanner scanned his audience as he went on. "A smoking-hot piece, no doubt. And like I said, she's been working under a strict no-touch policy. We're talking fresh meat."

Tanner moved in close to the captive and cupped his hand around her butt. "For the right price, she's yours. Gotta warn ya, though. She's used to being a bit pampered and she's got a bit of an uppity streak. You can either abide by that or knock her down a peg or two. That'll be up to you. But no marking her up. She's gotta come back in one piece, ready to get back on the pole."

Tanner looked at the young woman and moved his hand up her body. She pulled away from him and Tia again heard the now-identified sound of the cuffs scraping against the metal pipe. The woman gave a strong kick that caught Tanner off guard, landing on the seat of his pants. A round of catcalls rose from the men, praising the woman's feisty nature. Tia saw a look of embarrassment flash across Tanner's face. He grabbed a handful of blond hair and yanked back on the young woman's head. She glared at Tanner, her eyes full of hate and contempt. Another round of laughter came from the men, clearly entertained by the exchange.

His voice was harsh when he spoke. Tia knew he'd want to regain status with the audience and feared what he might do next. "Like I said, she's a handful. Transportation arrangements are your responsibility, but I've got a little something that will knock her out until you get her settled somewhere."

The watching men nodded in silent approval. Tanner released the woman's hair and stepped a pace to the side. He concluded, "Bidding opens at three thousand dollars."

The response was immediate.

"Three thousand." The man who had spoken stared at the woman onstage, practically salivating. In his mid- to late sixties, with badly dyed greasy black hair, he was big enough that his girth flowed over the sides of his chair. His heavy accent struck Tia as Asian, but she couldn't be sure beyond that.

"Thirty-five hundred." This offer came from a much younger man who wore dark glasses and a ball cap pulled down low on his head. He looked like the sort of guy you'd walk by in a Walmart and not think twice about.

"Four thousand." A third bid, from the tallest man in the group. Tia saw he carried a forty-five semi-auto in plain view on his hip.

"Five thousand." The fat man with the accent was back in the mix and there was an excitement in his voice.

"Five thousand is the bid." Tanner pointed to the man who was now working to loosen himself from the chair.

"Seventy-five hundred." The man with the sidearm.

The Asian countered with ten thousand and Tia saw Tanner's mouth sag open for an instant.

She did some quick calculations. Five of them, and at least one was armed. She had thirteen in the magazine and one in the chamber. She reached down to take the second clip from her boot and stick it in the waist of her jeans for easier access. *If I need that,* she thought, *things will have really gone to shit.*

Shifting to a two-hand grip, she brought the forty cal to a low ready. The door was three feet to her left. She moved as noiselessly as possible, knowing her shadow might be visible to the occupants but hoping they would remain preoccupied with the action onstage. She made it to the doorway undetected. She stood in front of the closed door and took two deep breaths. A small, familiar voice came from inside her.

Cuidado, Tia.

Tia reared back and kicked with all her strength, hitting the door just above the lock. Though she'd executed the kick perfectly, striking with the heel of her boot, a bone-deep pain shot up her leg as the wood splintered and the door swung wide. She stepped inside, the barrel of her gun leading the way. The sudden absence of rain felt like someone had turned off a spigot, but the noise against the metal roof seemed louder than ever. Every eyeball snapped her way and Tia knew she'd caught the group completely unaware. She had their undivided attention and she spoke with absolute confidence in her ability to control the situation. She shouted to be heard over the rain.

"If a hair on the head of any one of you sick bastards so much as twitches . . . !"

She figured the tall guy would go for it—he had that cowboy look. But she had to give credit where credit was due. He got to his feet and had his gun out of its holster in very short order. Tia was faster. She squeezed off a round and he fell to the ground as if all the bones had been removed from his body in a single instant. His right eye socket was a gaping red hole with a pool of bubbling blood.

The naked woman on the stage pulled hard at her bonds and

kicked out at Tanner, screaming into the ball gag. Not wanting the distraction, Tia called out, "Shut up and let me work." The victim continued to whimper, but the screaming stopped.

Tia turned back to the men, who at this point might as well have been mannequins propped up in their chairs. "Anyone else?" She paused as if actually waiting for an answer. The men remained stone still, so she moved on to giving instructions.

"You three. Off your asses and down on the floor. Flat on your stomach."

All three men scrambled to their feet, the fat Asian to her surprise the first one out and down. Tanner came out from behind the woman, moving as if he, too, was ready to surrender. Tia called out, "Not you, fuckwad. You stay right there."

Tia walked toward Tanner. She stepped over the body of the man who stared up with one eye, and jumped onto the wooden stage.

"You're Jessup Tanner?"

The only response was a nervous nod of his head.

Tia smiled. "We didn't get a chance to properly meet last time. You know, the parking lot in Milwaukee? You were in such a big hurry to leave. But we're going to get acquainted now. We most definitely are."

"Hang on," Tanner said, his voice conveying desperation. "You can't hurt me."

Tia looked at the woman cuffed to the pole, whose eyes remained wide with terror as if she wasn't sure yet if she was actually being rescued or just handed over to another insane captor.

Tia turned back to Tanner. "Hurt you?" She rested the barrel of her gun against the bone of his cheek, holding it there, gangster-style. "Dude, either you tell me where the other girl is or I'm seriously thinking about saving everybody a lot of trouble and executing your ass right here."

"No, let me explain—" Tanner raised his hands out in front of him.

"Shut up, Tanner." Tia closed in until she was shouting in his ear. "Now you've got five seconds or—"

"No. Don't. I need to make a phone call."

"You need to—" Tia couldn't believe what she was hearing. She yanked on the man's belt and shoved the barrel of her gun down inside his pants. His hands flew up and back, away from her. "Tanner, if the word 'lawyer' so much as crosses your lips, I swear I'll pull the trigger."

"Not a lawyer!" Tanner yelled. "I'm not calling a lawyer."

"Who then? Who do you want to call? Kane?"

"No. I'm not calling him. I need to call a cop."

Tia shook her head, irritated with Tanner's nonsense. "What the hell are you talking about? What cop?"

"The one I'm working for."

TWENTY-SEVEN

Ben pulled his unmarked Crown Vic in to the long driveway that was blocked by half a dozen SUVs and no shortage of black-and-whites from Waukesha County Sheriff Department. The SUVs and a couple of lifted pickup trucks had a federal feel and Ben could only wonder what would bring a bunch of G-men out to the middle of corn country at three o'clock in the morning.

He parked and stepped from the car. The rain had stopped; the damp breeze was cold against his face. He headed toward a cluster of people standing near a shed, then searched the crowd until he spotted Tia.

Her arms were folded across her chest, covering the detective shield that hung from a chain around her neck. Her hair was plastered against her head, soaking wet where it wasn't coated in mud. The stoic and grim expression on her face signaled Ben that Tia was feeling isolated but ready to fight. He picked up his pace, not sure if it was anticipation or dread he was feeling about what the night might have in store.

Less than half an hour earlier, a phone call from Tia had woken

Ben from a dead sleep. She'd launched into a story about federal agents, U.S. Attorneys, and some sort of sex auction in a cornfield. The first time she took a breath, Ben told her to stop talking and tell him where she was. It took him less than ten minutes to get dressed and drive to the farmhouse, ten miles outside Newberg city limits.

Ben saw that Tia was leaning against the rear door of a marked sheriff's Crown Vic. A couple of suits and a woman dressed in jeans and a stylish raincoat were standing around her in a semi-circle. Sheriff John Solo stood nearby, huddled in a quiet conference with a couple of long-haired men. Ben figured they had to be the U/C detectives he had been told about.

Ben intended to join Tia until a thin reed of a man stepped forward and blocked his path. The man's pale skin looked ghostlike against his black windbreaker, which was at least three sizes too big for his slight frame.

"Chief Sawyer? Special Agent Lester Stahl," the man said. "Unit chief out of D.C., on temporary assignment to the Milwaukee federal field office."

"Call me Ben." He accepted the man's handshake, which was weak and quickly withdrawn. "What agency did you say you're with?"

"I didn't." Stahl's smile was thin and forced looking. His sharp eyes looked out through rain-dotted, thick lenses of the wire-framed glasses that sat on his beak of a nose. Beads of rainwater had collected on his short dark hair, which was greased flat against his head.

"I'm glad you're here, Chief. We've had a bit of an issue with your detective," Stahl said, nodding toward Tia. "We need to get this issue resolved and clear out of here. We are jeopardizing a major federal investigation."

"What kind of issue? Whose operation is this?" Ben looked at Tia, who was studying him and Stahl. Her expression struck Ben as a challenge and he could practically hear her voice. *So how you going to play this, Chief?*

Stahl introduced a woman who had stepped up beside him. "This is Patricia Graham, assistant U.S. attorney. She's on temporary assignment to our team."

Graham put her hand out and Ben picked up on some uncertainty in her grip. He thought perhaps it was the tactical environment that was throwing her off, no doubt an unusual setting for an assistant U.S. attorney.

"Nice to meet you, Chief Sawyer," she said quietly.

The voice was familiar and, it then dawned on him, so was the name. Then he remembered. The prosecutor who cut the deal with Gunther Kane—he'd spoken to her on the phone several times. Confused, he tilted his head and asked, "U.S. Attorney's Office?"

As if on cue, Tia straightened up and said, "Can you believe that shit, Chief? She passed herself off as a deputy DA. She's a federal prosecutor. And Agent Stahl?" Tia pointed an accusing finger. "He was with her at the courthouse the day she punted the case against Kane. I saw him slinking off in the elevator."

Graham took a deep breath, blew it out, then smiled in a way that said she'd already had her fill of Tia Suarez. The attorney's annoyance was as obvious as Tia's anger. Graham didn't address the detective's comments, speaking to Ben in a voice dripping with self-importance.

"Apparently there's been some confusion, but now that you are here, Chief, I'm sure we can clear it up. Would you mind stepping over here with me for a minute? I'll explain everything."

Graham took Ben lightly by the elbow, intending to walk him away. He didn't move. Once Graham's hand slid off his arm, Ben turned to face Tia. He stepped close to her, looked directly into her eyes, and put his hand on her shoulder. She wasn't trembling, which was good, but he could feel the tightness in her muscles, which was not.

"Are you okay, Tia?"

Tia nodded tautly. "Yeah, Chief. Now I am." He could hear the anxiety in her voice and squeezed her shoulder slightly, trying to be reassuring without words. "Sorry to drag you out, but she's here somewhere. We need to wake up a judge and get a warrant. I know—"

"All right, Detective Suarez," Graham said, interrupting. Ben turned to face her, putting himself beside his detective. "Now that your Chief is here, let me tell you again. You need to release that man into federal custody."

A voice came from the backseat of the patrol car, muffled by the raised window. "Yeah, god damn it. Let me out of here. I'm working for you guys, for Christ sake."

Startled, Ben shined his flashlight into the car. The man sitting there turned his face from the light. By the awkwardness of his movements and position Ben knew the man was handcuffed. Tia smacked her open hand against the window and the man flinched away from her.

"Jessup Tanner is my prisoner and I'm booking him into county jail on charges of kidnapping and false imprisonment," Tia stated firmly. "And I'm searching this property tonight."

Stahl spoke up. "You can't do that, Detective. We are in the middle of a federal investigation."

"What investigation?" Tia looked back and forth between Stahl and Graham. "I was following up on a surveillance as part of a joint operation with the county sheriff and I've made an arrest. That's all I know."

Tia began to fill Ben in. "Tanner was in the middle of some sort of sex auction. It got a little ugly, Chief, but I took him into custody." Tia's voice turned contemptuous. "Tanner said he wanted to reach out to his very own special agent. I let him make his call, just to see who he was talking about."

Ben looked at Stahl, who opened his mouth, but Graham interjected before he could speak.

"A little ugly, Detective?" she said, her tone icy. "She shot a man. Killed him."

From the corner of his eye Ben saw Tia begin to move. He made a flat gesture with one hand and cut her off, his voice absolutely serious. "Hang on a second. Don't say a word, Detective."

To his frustration, Tia ignored her boss and leaned forward. "You and Stahl here, *Counselor,* appear to be associated with a man who was conducting a sex auction. A man who is also involved in the abduction of a still-missing girl."

It was Agent Stahl's turn. "We've already explained that, Suarez. We will not disclose the facts of a case involving national security."

Tia called out to Sheriff Solo, who still hung back, outside their little knot of confrontation. Her tone was more respectful as she said, "Sheriff Solo, I need to report an officer-involved shooting that occurred in your jurisdiction. Now that my boss is here, and seeing that I was working under the direction of a Waukesha county deputy, I'll cooperate with *your* department investigators in any way necessary. I waive my right to consult with legal counsel and I'm ready to give a statement."

Solo stared back but said nothing. Tia went on. "I recommend Jessup Tanner be booked into your county jail. After that we need to wake up a judge and get a search warrant for this property and for the Roadhouse Score. There is more than enough probable cause to believe at least one victim of a kidnapping is located somewhere out here or at the strip club."

The wind had kicked up; the rustling of the leaves of the nearby corn was the only sound as everyone waited for Solo's response. The county sheriff leaned over, listening to one of the undercovers, who was talking right into his ear. When Solo finally spoke, he sounded entirely overwhelmed by the circumstances.

"Well, it's my understanding, Detective Suarez, you were directed to do a house check. Nothing more. All things considered, at this point I think we need to cooperate with the federal authorities."

Tia shook her head, disappointed, as Graham said, "Thank you, Sheriff."

Solo said nothing, staring at his feet. The woman turned to face Tia. "There you are, Detective. Sheriff Solo agrees that it's appropriate for the federal government to assume jurisdiction on this incident." She paused and waited for Tia to meet her gaze. "If you choose not to cooperate and continue to interfere, I will have no choice but to have you taken into federal custody."

Tia threw her head back and laughed out loud. "Lady, I'd love to see you try."

"All right, knock it off!" Ben shouted. He made eye contact with each of the players before he went on. "Now, let's all just calm down."

He herded the group away from the car—except for Tia, who stayed put, jealously guarding her prisoner and glaring at her boss. He let his frustration show when he said, "Tia, just come over here. I don't want your prisoner listening to everything we say, all right?"

With obvious reluctance, Tia joined the gathering. Ben had carefully positioned them in the middle of the driveway, out of earshot of everyone else. Seconds went by with cold stares all around. Ben took a deep breath, then turned to Tia. "Detective Suarez, if you have been involved in an OIS, you need to stop talking until I say otherwise. Is that clear?"

Tia raised her hands in mock surrender, but her voice was serious. "Yes, sir."

Ben faced the attorney and her sidekick, his voice like ice. "This is Wisconsin, not D.C. Officer-involved shootings are investigated by the local jurisdiction."

He turned to the sheriff. "This is your jurisdiction, Sheriff. You ready to step up?"

All he got in reply was a blank stare. Ben tried again. "John?"

Solo's gaze darted toward Stahl, then back to Ben. "I . . . uh . . . I'm prepared to relinquish my jurisdictional authority to the federal government in this case."

Stunned, Ben shook his head, making no attempt to hide his disappointment and even a certain degree of contempt. But there was no time for argument. He knew he had to move fast. Once the feds got a foothold, there would be no stopping the onslaught of their power. He returned his attention to Graham.

"Fine. As much as I'd appreciate the cooperation of the agency with primary jurisdiction, I'm well within my authority to investigate the actions of one of my own, who was clearly acting within the course and scope of her duties as a Newberg Police Detective."

He turned to Stahl. "Now, either identify yourself, your agency, and your authority right now or I'll call out my people for an OIS investigation. I'll send Suarez back to the station with her prisoner."

Ben managed to conceal the satisfaction he felt at the look of shock mixed with anger that passed over both federal faces. He'd called their bluff and everyone knew it. The two sheriff's deputies appeared ready to jump ship and take direction from the man who had clearly decided to step up and take charge. Tia's smile and the look in her eyes told Ben she was glad he was here.

Stahl wasn't ready to give up. "You seem to be missing the point, Chief. This little operation you all cooked up? You have stepped on some very, very big toes."

Ben responded, making it clear he had no intentions of giving any ground, "Whose toes, Stahl? I mean, specifically, who are you talking about?"

Stahl kept up his game of hide the ball. "Let's just say if you choose not to cooperate, the ramifications will be significant."

Ben turned to Tia. "Get your prisoner and put him in the back of my car. Call the coroner's office and tell them to respond for the body. I'll contact Travis Jackson and tell him to bring out a team."

Tia spun on her heels and headed for the patrol car. Stahl reached out to stop her before she'd taken more than a step. "All right, just a minute."

Ben could tell that Stahl was disappointed that once again his bluster had failed to intimidate. He wasn't surprised when the man changed tactics. "Ms. Graham and I are currently assigned to the Special Investigations Division of the Office of the Director of National Intelligence."

Ben shook his head at that nonanswer. "Say that again?"

"We represent the direct interest of the executive branch of the federal government."

"Bullshit, Stahl," Tia said, and every head turned her way. "The ODNI is a coalition of federal agencies. Answer the Chief's question. Where do you call home?"

Stahl seemed annoyed by Tia's knowledge but remained evasive. "How about this, Chief? Let me tell you what I can about our operation. Get you up to speed on the investigation to date; then we'll go from there."

Ben looked at Tia, who shrugged as if she was growing bored with it all. Ben nodded to Stahl.

"Start talking."

"I take it you are familiar with Mr. Gunther Kane?" Ben was watching Tia as Stahl spoke; when Kane's name was mentioned, he saw her eyes grow wide, then narrow. She stared suspiciously at Stahl.

"What about him?" Ben asked.

"Kane is the target of a federal investigation going back several years. We have identified him as a member of a subversive political group that is considered a major threat to national security. They call themselves the North Aryan Front."

"Wait a damn minute," Tia said with a laugh. "You've got Gunther Kane and the graybeards of NAF listed as a threat to national security? Where the hell do you people come up with this shit? Chief, we should just—"

Ben cocked an eyebrow at Tia. Getting his unspoken message, she went silent. "Go on," Ben said to Stahl.

"As I was saying, we've been working Kane for a number of years and learned that he has stepped up into a leadership role in the NAF. He has made a number of illegal firearms transactions. Some of those purchases included weapons stolen from the U.S. military. Our sources have learned that for the past several months, Kane has been attempting to negotiate a major arms deal.

"He's trying to purchase a cache of automatic weapons and ammunition. If successful, he'd be able to go toe to toe with your department." Stahl paused, studying Tia. "He'd probably win."

Tia chimed in, "So we need Uncle Sam to come save the day?"

Now it was Ben's turn to ignore Tia's aggressive comment. He spoke to Stahl. "So you mean to tell me there's a man walking the streets of Waukesha County, buying up military weaponry, and no one bothered to tell local law enforcement?" Ben glanced at Sheriff Solo, hoping the other local lawman would speak up, but Solo remained impassive. When Stahl answered, Ben picked up on a trace of defensiveness.

"So far Kane's dealings have been low-level, single-gun transactions. We've maintained good intelligence on all Kane's associates and we've kept track of the weapons. When the time comes to round people up for possession of stolen property or whatever other charge we deem appropriate"—Stahl flipped his hand through the air—"we'll be more than happy to hand off much of that work to the locals.

"The headlines should look good for both your agencies. But Kane is ours."

Ben shook his head. "I'm not really interested in headlines. I'm still stuck on the fact that we've got stolen guns hitting the streets." Ben hooked a thumb at the sheriff but kept his eyes on Stahl. "*Our* streets."

Stahl waved off the comment. "This is a federal case and Kane is a major target. We believe he has every intention of purchasing a large number of automatic weapons and distributing those weapons among the membership of a known hate group operating out of your jurisdiction. I would think you'd appreciate our efforts here and see how this case needs to take precedence over what amounts to a prostitution ring being run out of a strip joint."

Tia stepped toward Stahl. "Prostitution ring? Is that what you call it? A woman being auctioned off to the highest bidder? Another woman, probably a teenager, kidnapped and tied up in the back of a van?"

"Chief, if I may interject." Graham sounded like she was in a courtroom. "Based on what has come to light this evening, it may very well be that we have underestimated the seriousness of Mr. Tanner's criminal association with Gunther Kane. It would appear the manner in which Mr. Kane has been financing his illegal weapons purchases has been a very serious crime in and of itself. But that is a discussion for another time. We need to get out of here."

Tia looked around the yard and dilapidated house. "I'm not going anywhere until we search this property."

Graham looked only at Ben. "There will be no search, Chief. There is a corpse inside that shed. A very important federal investigation is at risk of being derailed. We need your detective to start cooperating or face very serious consequences."

The challenge in Tia's voice was unmistakable. "Bring it, lady."

Graham rolled her eyes and finally looked at Tia. "Detective, can you try to understand the gravity of what we are dealing with? We have an opportunity to take down the entire network of a subversive organization."

"You had your shot at Kane and you let him walk on an abduction case. With his history, you could've locked him away for the next ten to twenty years. Instead you all get in bed with Tanner . . . and, big surprise, he pissed backward all over you. Well, that's too bad, because now he belongs to me."

The mention of the hooker detail reminded Ben about his conversation with Graham. "Ms. Graham, I remember something you said on the phone. Something about surveillance tape from the night Detective Suarez had her run-in with Kane. What exactly was that about?"

Tia's head swiveled between Graham and her boss. "What surveillance tape?"

Graham squirmed and looked at Stahl, who didn't try to hide his frustration with the lawyer, who had apparently said too much. Stahl took a deep breath and spoke up.

"Well, as I'm sure you've already figured out, Jessup Tanner is a registered federal informant. His activities that evening in Milwaukee were being monitored. That of course is absolutely confidential."

"You watched?" Tia said. "You watched those sons of bitches try to drag me into that van?"

Neither Stahl nor Graham said a word.

"You let him drive away? Did you hear the radio traffic? I broadcast an abduction in progress."

Stahl directed his attention to Ben. "Look, Chief, we monitored the situation. We stayed on point until the officers took Kane into custody. We have since reconnected with our informant. We admonished him for the activity."

Ben narrowed his eyes. "*Admonished* him?"

Stahl blew out a breath as if he was growing tired of explaining himself to the low level of local authority. "According to Tanner, Kane decided to finance the weapons purchases through prostitution. Apparently, Kane thinks it's less risky than dealing in dope. We've directed Tanner to do whatever he can to keep that activity to a minimum. But I can assure you we've debriefed Tanner thoroughly. All the players involved are strippers, prostitutes, or border-jumping illegals."

"So just a bunch of people not worth your effort." Tia fumed.

"Chief, we have significant security concerns," Stahl said. "We are highly exposed here. Kane is due to take delivery of the automatic weapons in less than twenty-four hours. We need to reinsert Tanner so he can orchestrate Kane's purchase of the weapons. Then we'll have him.

"That will be the act in furtherance of a major conspiracy. With that, plus the two years of intelligence we've collected, we can take down every major player in the NAF. We will cripple the organization in one fell swoop. Now please. Order your detective to turn Tanner over to us or, I guarantee, her actions this evening will be investigated by the federal government. I don't think she wants that; do you?"

Ben knew exactly what Stahl meant. If Tia had been involved in a fatal shooting that was the least bit controversial, she was already highly exposed. If the federal prosecutor got involved, anything was possible. He knew the shit storm that Tia might be walking into.

"If you want my detective to cooperate with federal authorities, there are conditions," he began.

Tia cut him off, "Hang on, Chief. I don't care what they threaten me with. I'm not letting them take him."

Ben ignored her and Stahl blew out a deep breath. "Such as?"

"First off, nothing that went on here tonight is subject to federal prosecution."

"Fine," Stahl said through gritted teeth.

"You get Tanner for twelve hours. After that, he will be turned back over to Newberg PD for prosecution on state charges and we will pursue the original abduction case."

Stahl and Graham exchanged a glance.

"And from this point forward, your investigation is a joint operation. I am assigning Detective Suarez as my liaison to your team." Ben looked at Sheriff Solo. "If the county doesn't want to play, that's their business, but Newberg PD is not sitting this out."

Stahl leaned toward Graham, but she put up her hand, stopping him. She spoke directly to Ben. "That's fine. I've got no interest in Suarez's actions here tonight becoming part of an official federal record and I really don't care what becomes of Jessup Tanner."

Ben focused on Tia. "Twelve hours, Tia. Then the feds get Kane and we take Tanner. You've got my word, we'll come back and search every square inch of this place."

Tia looked around the compound and surrounding cornfield. Ben could feel her angst and was tempted to tell the feds to get lost. At last she turned back and gave him a single nod.

"He's yours, Stahl," Ben said. "After that, he's ours. If you can't wrap this thing up by then, you'll have to do it without Tanner."

TWENTY-EIGHT

Kane awoke with a start at the sound of a key in the door. The wall clock with the picture of the PBR Bear read 7:02 A.M. He'd dozed off in his office several hours earlier. Moving quickly, Kane swung his feet off the desk, leaned forward, and pulled a forty-five from the center drawer. He raised the gun to eye level, squeezing off the slack, as the door opened. Jessup Tanner took a single step inside and froze in place, his ruddy complexion instantly draining to ghost white. Tanner lifted a hand in front of his face and turned away, as if somehow that would stop a bullet. His voice came out in a thin, high-pitched whine.

"Jesus, boss. It's just me."

Kane held the nickel-plated handgun steady as he looked at Tanner over the top sight. "Where the hell you been, Jessup?"

He risked a quick glance at the closed-circuit TV monitors and saw that the bar and parking lot were empty except for Tanner's vehicle. *Good.* In three hours they were scheduled to meet Curtis Bell to take possession of one hundred M4 machine guns and fifty thousand rounds of ammunition, and Kane didn't want any spectators.

With a thud, Jessup dropped a backpack onto the grimy floor of the office. He stammered, "L-l-listen, boss. It was a hell of a night, but we got it done. Just like you said. We're up twenty grand. It's all right here."

The barrel of the forty-five didn't twitch as Kane gazed at the bag. "Twenty grand, huh?" he said, staring at Tanner.

Tanner nodded, his eyes stuck on the gun like he was waiting for the lead to come out.

Kane watched him closely. "So you did all right then, huh, Jessup? Got us covered?"

Tanner swallowed—Kane could see his Adam's apple fall and rise in his throat—and nodded. "Yeah, boss. We're good."

"So what's the story?"

"The story, boss?" Tanner seemed mesmerized by the gun.

"Yeah. I want to hear it. Start talking."

"All right. All right. Relax, boss. Here's how it went.

"I did like you said. I put the word out to the high rollers. Set up a red-light auction. Just like you figured, Pepper blew it up. Couple of those old boys got into a full-on bidding war. We pulled down fifteen thousand. Hong Kong Pete took top prize. He kicked in another five g's for me to transport her down to his high-rise in Chi-town. I just got back."

"Twenty grand?" Kane said with mild surprise. "That's a high-dollar night."

Tanner nodded again, robotically, still staring at the gun. "Anyway. That's the story. We're good, boss. We're up twenty K."

"So you couldn't check in? Make a damn call?"

Tanner blinked a few times and went on the defense. "You told me never use the cell when we're holding product. I turned it off like just like you said. Pulled out the battery. You're the one who told me they track that shit."

Kane nodded, more impressed with Tanner than usual. "So we're good."

"We're fucking great. It went off without a hitch." Tanner nodded toward the end of the gun. "Boss? You mind?"

Kane held Tanner's gaze for a few seconds more, then dropped the gun to his side and eased his finger off the trigger. Tanner took a deep breath and blew it out in relief. Kane set the gun on the desk, keeping his hand on the grip, and watched as Tanner's eyes refocused on the weapon. Smiling to himself, Kane used one foot to push a chair toward his second in command and signaled the man to take a seat. He gave Tanner another moment to settle his nerves, then started back in.

"So, that's the story they gave you?"

"Yeah, boss." Tanner sounded like a whipped dog. "That's it."

"You ain't leaving nothing out, are you, Jessup?"

"Hell no, boss. That's it. That's all they gave me."

"All right then." Kane released the weapon and leaned back in his chair, not taking his eyes off the face of the man who sat before him. "Now. Forget all the federal bullshit. Tell me what really happened."

Tanner hung his head and spoke each word slowly, as if each syllable was causing great pain. "Things got pretty screwed up, boss."

"How so?"

"I was going to run the auction like you said, score as much as I could, capital-wise. Figured after that, I'd wait to hear from the feds so they could tell me when to set up the meet. Everything was going great. . . ." Jessup dropped his head and his voice drifted.

"What?" Kane's eyes flicked back to the monitors. Still clear.

Tanner shook his head as if he knew the next piece of information spelled trouble for him. "That damn Suarez showed up. Came blasting in. That fella from Chicago, she took his ass *out*. Shot him dead where he stood. I mean he dropped to the floor, DRT. He was dead right there, boss. She looked like Annie Oakley or some shit. Like she was on some kind of mission."

Suarez. Kane felt the slow boil of anger start in his chest. He'd had about all he could take of this small-town cop. From what he'd gotten out of Tanner, it didn't make any sense that Suarez would be mixed up in the investigation.

"What are you saying?" Kane couldn't keep the anxiety out of his voice. "Is she working with the feds?"

"No way, boss. That bitch was freelancing. The way they were all going at it, I'm sure of it. Yelling at each other and all. But I won't lie to you, she caught me flat-footed and I gave it up."

Kane sat forward, his voice louder. "What do you mean? Gave up what?"

"That I was working with the feds. I could tell that blew her mind. She didn't know nothing about it."

Kane leaned back, intrigued. "Then what?"

"Some calls got made. Feds started showing up along with a bunch of local cops. Next thing I know they put me on ice in the back of a squad car. That's when they all started arguing with each other. That Stahl, the one I told you about. The fed. He finally came around and took me out, gave me the story I was supposed to pass on to you."

Tanner nodded toward the bag on the floor. "Gave me twenty grand. Told me to bring it back and get this thing done. Said we need to close the deal on the long guns. No more dicking around, he said."

Kane nodded. "And once I take the hardware, the jig's up, right? They got me for conspiracy, possession, and intent to distribute. The whole damn thing."

"Yeah, boss. Seems like they're ready to pounce, that's for sure."

Gunther ignored him. "So they catch you red-handed, auctioning a woman off like cattle, but they let you walk so they can get to the promised land. Is that what you're telling me?"

Tanner shook his head, confused. "How's that?"

"Me, you dumb ass!" Kane shouted. "Me and the North Aryan Front."

When all he got was a blank stare, Kane went on. "Don't you get it? The feds don't care about anything but dismantling the North Aryan Front. They see you boys as some kind of major players. Threat to the country. Jesus, if they only knew."

Tanner shrugged. "All I know, boss, is they want to close this deal. Stahl don't seem to give two shits how we do it. And I can tell you. There ain't no love lost between Stahl and Suarez. He's got a real hard-on for her."

"So it would seem." Kane nodded, mentally laying out his options.

"Maybe we ought to rethink this," Tanner said in a pleading tone. "You know, sit down and do the math. Hell, between the club and working the fields, we're up almost a hundred grand. Shit, boss, even the feds kicked up twenty g's. That's a pretty good stake. We can just disappear. Head back out to Cali. Pick off some youngsters and turn them out for some big money. We could do the hotel circuit in Vegas. There's money in this trade. And the risk is nothing."

Kane said nothing, so Tanner kept going. "Think about it, Gunther. We don't need to be messing around buying guns and shit. The feds jump all over that sort of thing. Hell, we could be pimping out a dozen brown wets and nobody would give a shit."

Kane shot back, "Now you want to walk away?"

Tanner shook his head and actually began to cry. "I just can't take it anymore, boss. Trying to stay one step ahead of the feds is taking years off my life."

"I guess you should've given that some thought before you jumped in bed with the bastards and flipped over with your ass up in the air." Tanner sobbed and Kane kept piling on, his voice filled with disgust. "What did you think, Jessup? They were going to make you a junior G-man? Welcome you into the family?"

"They had me by the balls, Gunther." Tanner was pleading again and Kane rolled his eyes, already tired of it. "They were going to throw my ass in a federal prison for twenty years. Take every damn bit of land I have left. What the hell was I supposed to do?"

"Stand tall, god damn it! That's what you're supposed to do."

Tanner slumped in his chair and put his head in his hands.

Kane remembered how he'd discovered what was really going on. In a way, Suarez had done him a favor when she came to see him at the county jail. He'd already spent several nights thinking long and hard, trying to figure out how he was getting such a sweet deal. Suarez's visit had crystalized it for him.

She was right, he realized. Someone in the van that night must have had some high-level coverage, a powerful friend running blocker. Kane didn't figure it was the cargo they'd snatched up in San Diego and he sure as hell knew it wasn't him. That left one suspect.

It didn't take Kane long to get the truth out of Tanner. A lengthy and somewhat persuasive conversation, in the privacy of a well-stocked toolshed, convinced Tanner to give him the whole story. After that, it all fell into place. For the last two years, Tanner and the federal government had been playing Gunther Ulysses Kane for a fool. But now the worm had turned.

"So they're waiting for us to close the deal with Bell?"

"Hell yeah, boss," Tanner said, dragging his sleeve against the snot that bubbled from his nose. "That's all this Stahl guy talks about. Wants to know what the plans are for the guns. How you're planning to distribute the hardware. He keeps asking me about what the big operation is. Stuff like that."

"And what do you tell him?"

"I do just like you told me. I just act like I don't know much."

Kane felt disgust as he looked at the sniveling wretch opposite him. "I imagine they bought that easy enough."

Buster Cobb knocked once, then walked into the office. "He's here, boss."

"Good," Kane said. "You got it done, right, Buster?"

"Yeah, boss. Went real smooth."

"Any problems?"

"Nope. I did just like you said. Showed up in one of them really nice tricked-out black SUVs. Said her old man was hurt. She didn't ask no questions."

"Kids?" Kane asked.

"Told her to bring 'em. She was so upset she didn't think twice about it. Course, once it started getting ugly, she turned on us." Cobb held up a handful of Polaroids and tossed them down on the desk. "I got 'em nearby, but we best get them tucked away pretty soon."

Tanner sounded confused and desperate when he asked, "What's going on, Gunther? What's he talking about?" He leaned forward to look at the photographs.

"Atta boy, Buster." Kane nodded to the bouncer, ignoring Tanner. "You pick a girl tonight and tell her I said it's on the house."

"Thanks, boss." Cobb smiled.

"Put Bell at the bar and tell him to wait. But that's all you tell him. You hear me?"

"Got it, boss."

Cobb left, closing the door behind him. Tanner's face was etched in horrified confusion. "Who are these people?"

Kane reached out and slapped the man hard across the head. Tanner drew up his shoulders and cowered. "Jessup Tanner, it's like you really do have shit for brains. Have you not figured this out *yet*?"

When Tanner only stared back, Kane shook his head. "You're

just the middleman, you dumb ass. Right from the start, they've been playing you harder than they have me."

Tanner stared at the pictures and Kane thought somewhere deep in the man's limited intelligence the light finally started to flicker. He stood, grabbing Tanner by the scruff of the neck and pushing him toward the door. "Come with me, boy. It's showtime."

TWENTY-NINE

Tia drove around the last bend of the long driveway, surprised to see the beat-up yellow pickup truck parked in front of the house. The morning sun had cleared the horizon and the skies had gone to a brilliant blue. She stepped from the car into a world washed clean by the previous night's hard rain. She dodged the mud puddles and moved to the porch where Connor waited, drinking coffee from a mug and reading the *Milwaukee Journal* sports page. He spoke from behind the paper without looking up.

"Says here the Packers might actually reach out for some free agents this year." He shook his head. "Hope it's about shoring up the damn defense. A-Rod can't do it all."

She ignored the topic. "I figured you would have taken off by now. Either that or be asleep."

Connor looked at her over the top of his paper and shrugged. "You want me to leave? I can go."

"That's not what I'm saying." Tia had taken a quick shower at the PD and changed into clean clothes that she kept in her locker.

Now she climbed the steps and leaned back against the porch railing. When she saw Connor waiting for her, the weight of the night finally began to lift. "I'm glad you're here."

"I got your message. Thought I'd stick around. Make sure you were okay." He looked her up and down. "You seem to be all in one piece."

Once Tanner had identified himself as an informant, Tia had allowed him to make his phone call. A dozen federal agents descended on the field like something out of *Children of the Corn,* speedily followed by the sheriff's deputies. Quickly figuring out which way the wind was blowing, Tia had called her chief, then sent a brief text to Connor. She kept it purposely vague, saying something had come up and she'd be late.

She'd thought he'd go home, but he hadn't, and seeing him now gave her a sense of safety and belonging. She wanted to tell him about the night. She wanted to tell him everything. She didn't know how to begin. "Things got a little nuts."

"How so?"

Everything she had been told at the briefing was classified, but in Tia's mind that didn't preclude her telling Connor. First, the man had a top-level security clearance from the U.S. government, and second, Tia reminded herself, she had made a commitment: she was done keeping things from Connor Anderson. She took a deep breath and started in.

"Jessup Tanner never showed up at the club. The deputy in charge of the surveillance asked me to swing by his house, see if his van was there. You know, so we could be fairly sure he was tucked away."

"By yourself?"

She shrugged, trying to downplay it. "It was just supposed to be a drive-by." Connor looked at her, waiting.

Tia began by telling him about finding the men in the shed and the hideous, gut-wrenching discovery of the auction. Then she took him through the rest of the night, including how she had learned the feds had been involved in a U/C operation the night she was attacked by Kane and Tanner. Connor didn't say a word while she unrolled the entire story.

When she fnished, he sat quietly for so long Tia wondered if she'd sent him over the edge. Eventually he took a long, deep, lung-filling breath and shook his head.

"So the deputy DA is actually a federal prosecutor?" Connor asked, and Tia nodded. "The feds watched the whole thing in Milwaukee?"

"Yeah. She's as bitchy as a fed as she was when I thought she was a DA. And her lapdog is this guy named Lester Stahl out of D.C. He's a piece of work, too."

Connor looked out over the cornfield. "And now you've been in another shooting?"

"At least I was the one sending rounds downrange this time," Tia said, striving for lightness.

"You're making jokes about this?" His voice was no-nonsense. "Two shootings in less than a year? You know they're going to come after you, right? Call you trigger-happy?"

"I didn't have a choice, Connor. I was in the middle of a rescue operation. The guy pulled a gun on me. What else could I do?"

"How about not get yourself in that kind of predicament to begin with? How about you take a cover officer with you?" With each question his voice got a little sharper, a little louder. "How about you tell the damn deputy to step up?"

"The feds don't seem that concerned about it, and Sawyer's got my back. The feds are more worried about keeping their operation under wraps. The guy I shot? Feds had dope history with him, some state-level soliciting. They acted all butt hurt about it, but I don't think they'll have a hard time making him disappear."

"What about you?" Connor asked, sounding less angry, more worried.

There, she thought. *That's the man I know.* She smiled. "I'm fine. I really am."

He dismissed her response with a quick wave of his hand. "No. I don't mean 'are you okay physically?' I can see that. I mean, when they check—you're good, right?"

Tia understood what he was asking. Was it a clean shoot? Was *she* clean? All things considered, she knew she had no right to be offended, but she couldn't help it. She was.

"Yeah, Connor. My BAC will be zero and I haven't had any meds in two days."

Connor's relief showed clearly, but Tia could tell he was still angry. He sat up straight and kept asking questions—Tia felt like the conversation was halfway between a debrief and an interrogation. "What about this girl? She doesn't sound like the girl you saw in the van."

Despite her vow to not hold back with Connor, Tia couldn't help cutting her answers short, as if she were talking to IA. "A stripper from the Roadhouse. The feds tried debriefing her, but she couldn't give them much. Pretty much just a pole dancer. They plan on putting her in some sort of witness protection program. Tuck her away until we need her."

Tia turned her back to Connor and looked down the path; the metal of her family's trailer home gleamed in the morning sun. The sanctuary she'd felt when she'd realized he had waited for her had vanished. She couldn't wait for him to leave. He didn't really understand her, did he? She shuddered at the thought of how close she had come to telling him everything. To telling him about the voice that even now hummed somewhere quietly in her mind.

Without turning around, she spoke. Her voice was blank and revealed nothing other than a desire to be alone.

"Sorry to have kept you up. You didn't really need to wait for me. I'm going to grab a couple hours of sleep. Later, there's a briefing in Milwaukee about the planned takedown of Kane. I'm going."

"Tia, you've been in a shooting, not to mention awake for two days. You can't be serious. You are not working tonight."

"Sawyer already approved it," she said, turning back to him at last. "A few hours of sleep, something to eat, and I'll be fine." Her tone said, *Don't push me.*

She could see Connor process the information. He folded the paper and set it on the side table, then double-checked the tightness of both prostheses. When he stood, a quick blast of pain crossed his face. He walked past Tia without another word, went down the steps and to his truck. Before he'd reached the vehicle, Tia had gone into the house, the screen door slamming behind her. She gave some thought to running back outside. *Don't let him leave,* she thought. *Not like this. Tell him. Tell him everything.*

She heard Connor's pickup start and glanced up in time to see him back out of the driveway. Shaking her head, she turned toward her bedroom, the dog following close behind.

THIRTY

Kane tucked the forty-five in his waistband, making sure the grip was plainly visible, then walked into the bar to meet Curtis Bell. *One last time,* he thought. Kane had come to realize this particular relationship had pretty much run its course. Bell sat alone at the bar, projecting his usual air of smug arrogance. Kane strode forward, Tanner tagging along behind. The smaller man's head hung low; his pockmarked face was stunned with disbelief. It was obvious to Kane that the pressure was getting to Tanner. He couldn't take much more of the high-stakes gambling. It was a good thing that it would all be over soon.

When Kane approached the bar, he saw Bell's gaze shift briefly to his gun, then move away. Kane couldn't help but be impressed with how calmly the man accepted the fact that the only gun in the conversation belonged to someone else. He knew Cobb had made Bell turn over his weapon at the door.

"It's delivery time, Kane," Bell said by way of a greeting. "Your shipment is in the truck outside. How about my hundred grand? You got it?"

"Every dime of it." Kane stood in the well so the bar was between them. "Big day for us. We oughta celebrate. How about a shot for old times' sake? What're you drinking, Curtis?"

Bell gave Kane a smirk. "Little early for me. Let's just get this done."

"Aw, hell, Curtis. Couple of old bikers like us? It ain't never too early." Kane stared at Bell, wanting it to come to the man piece-meal. He pulled the bottle of Jack Daniel's from under the bar, never taking his eyes off the other man. Grabbing two glasses, Kane poured a couple of healthy shots, pushed one toward Bell, and raised the other to his lips. "Here's to old times, friend."

Kane held the shot in the air, waiting. He picked up on the slight-est twitch of doubt in the man's face, impressed that he stayed in character. After a moment, Bell picked up his glass. "Old times, Gunther."

Kane threw back his shot and Bell did the same. Both men gri-maced briefly. Kane moved to pour two more shots, but Bell put his hand over his glass. "I'm good. Like I said, let's get this thing done."

"God damn, boy. I've never known you to be in this big a hurry." Kane looked at Tanner and winked. "I mean, you're always a bit prickly, but what the hell? You got a date?"

Kane saw a flicker of worry in Bell's eyes. To his credit, the man again recovered quickly. "I'm just not crazy about having a stolen arsenal sitting in a parking lot. I say we make the deal, tuck the equipment away, and then we can throw a damn party."

Bell met Kane's gaze steadily, easily, looking like nothing other than a man ready to close a major arms deal. *Impressive.*

The head of the NAF poured himself another shot and threw it down, thinking, *Time to quit fucking around.* "Throw a party, huh? I guess we could do that, but tell me something, Curtis. Who would you invite? Some of your make-believe biker friends?"

The movement was small, but Kane was sure he saw Bell bite the inside of his cheek. Kane found himself enjoying the moment just as much as he had thought he would. The time had come to call the man out. "Or some of your real buddies in the federal government?"

As he said the last words, Kane pulled the forty-five from his waist and in one smooth motion centered the muzzle against Bell's forehead. Bell's mouth dropped open and Kane heard the air run out of the man and saw the life drain from his face. To his credit, Bell was able to muster real anger in his response.

"Jesus Christ, Kane. What are you talking about?" The man sat perfectly still.

Kane held the gun steady and shook his head. "Gig's up, *Delafield*. That is your real name, ain't it? Special Agent Curtis Delafield?"

"My name is Curtis Bell. You know that. Take that piece off my head. Jesus. What the hell is wrong with you?" Though Kane knew the man had to be scrambling for some kind of control, he had to admit Delafield was holding up a lot better than Tanner had under the same conditions. Tanner had nearly shit himself when Kane called him out.

"What's wrong with me?" Kane asked.

"Yeah, Kane. What the hell are you talking about? With what we've been through? You think I'm a cop? Get ahold of yourself for Christ sake."

"I don't think, Curtis; I know. You are Curtis Delafield. You live at 5123 Old Ranch Road, Cedar Rapids, Iowa. Now, who you with?" Kane pulled the gun away from his prisoner's forehead long enough to wave it at the door and cock the hammer, then returned the muzzle to Delafield's skin. "Who's out there right now?"

The supposed arms dealer swallowed hard and said nothing. Kane grinned and went on, nodding at Tanner, who still stood nearby. "If you're wondering, it was this dipshit right here who blew your cover. Once I figured out Tanner was a snitch, I thought back to our first meeting. I'm damn embarrassed to tell you how long it took for it to come to me. You remember? Sturgis?"

Kane shook his head. "Looking back on it now, I swear, if I could kick myself in my own nuts I'd do it, and don't you know I'd deserve it. Dumb-ass old me. Jessup carried on about how he'd never really been to a bike rally before. All about the party at Sturgis. How he wanted to go and tear it up. 'Come on, Gunther,' he said. 'It's on me,' he said. 'We'll kill it,' he said. Then I stumbled into a bar and happened to meet a man who changed my life. And dumb-ass old me, I bought it."

Curtis raised his hands as if trying to reach Kane's more reasonable side. "Look, Kane, I don't know how you got this all in your head. Maybe your dumb-ass friend is a snitch, I don't know, but that ain't got shit to do with me. Now, I'm telling you. Take that piece off my head."

Kane reached into the pocket of his denim vest. "And I'm telling you to save it. Game over, Delafield."

He tossed the Polaroid pictures onto the bar. Delafield looked down, grabbed the photographs, and screamed, "*Jesus and Mary! God damn, Kane. What have you done?*"

Delafield stood so quickly his barstool fell and smacked hard against the floor with a sound like a shot from a gun. He held the pictures in shaking hands. Kane rammed the forty-five harder against his head.

"Get hold of yourself. You want to see them again, you will settle your ass down."

Delafield fell to his knees, holding the pictures to his face as if he hadn't heard a word Kane said, his mouth hanging open in a silent scream. Kane knew he needed to reestablish control. He pulled a pair of handcuffs from his jeans pocket and threw them to Tanner.

"Get over here. Cuff him up. Move your ass."

Tanner vaulted the bar and reached out to grab Delafield by the arms. The bigger man pulled away and shot a look of aggression at Tanner. Suddenly he seemed ready to go on the offensive. Kane shouted, "I swear, boy, you go with the program or I'll skin one of your little ones alive while you watch!"

Delafield sagged in place and offered no resistance when Jessup moved again to handcuff him. He turned to Kane and asked weakly, "How?"

"How? Well, I guess that really is on you, Curtis. I mean, you get a few miles from Waukesha County and you take on a whole different personality, don't you?"

Delafield looked confused. Kane smiled and let him have it. "You fucked up. Got a little too comfortable. Last time we met, I followed you to your little rendezvous with Mrs. Delafield. After you left the hotel, I hung out for a while in the parking lot. She headed straight down to Cedar Rapids, picked up the boys from the neighbors, and went home. That teenage daughter of yours? She must give you fits, huh?"

Kane let it all sink in and watched as the man realized his cover was blown all to hell. "Don't blame the wife, Curtis. It really comes back on you. Involving civilians in this sort of bullshit. I figured you'd be trained to know better than that.

"Don't that gnaw at you fellas that work these lying-ass assignments? That somehow you might screw up? Put your family in the crosshairs?"

Kane pulled the handcuffed man to his feet and sat him roughly in a chair. He picked the pictures up and spread them out across the table. One had been taken at an odd angle, showing a pretty brunette about the same age as Delafield lying on a carpet. She was staring at the photographer, her eyes filled with terror and her mouth covered in thick gray duct tape. From the size and shape of the shadow that fell over her Kane knew that Buster Cobb had taken the pictures himself.

"Seems like she's gone a little pudgy over the years, probably from pushing out all those children for you. That does play hell on a woman's body. Bet there was a time she could stop a clock, huh?" Kane's tone was conversational and he tapped a fat finger against the Polaroid. "But let's give credit where it's due. That is still a very fuckable woman."

Delafield stared silently at the array of photographs, panting. Kane figured it best to give the man a few minutes. Cobb had done well. The entire Delafield family was laid out on the table.

Kane took a moment to study the images. The wife he'd already considered: she might be worth a go even though she was a bit on the old side for his taste. The teenage daughter, whose angry gaze shouted, *Put it anywhere near me and I'll bite it off*, was definitely one to spark a man's interest. But even Kane had to admit the picture of the twin boys was disturbing. They looked to be about four and the fear etched on their faces jumped out at him.

One of the blond boys stared straight into the camera, his face contorted in what could only be a mixture of a scream and a sob. The other sat with his tiny arm around the waist of his identical brother as if trying to comfort him or maybe seek comfort. But that boy's eyes haunted Kane. His gaze was focused somewhere off camera, reflecting a kind of emptiness. Kane figured all three children were already well beyond scarred for life.

"We've had a good run, you and me, Curtis. My understanding is, it was all supposed to end today. But I'm calling for a change of plans." Kane grabbed Delafield's chin and forced the man to look him in the eye. "We got some business between us yet, and if it don't go the way I say I guarantee each of these precious folks will be boxed up in a shipping crate and headed to one of the four corners of the earth."

Kane picked up the photo of the boys. "The market for little white boys in a few spots in Central America is off the hook. I'm just wondering how exciting it will be to offer a matched set. Damn, they're like bookends, huh?

"Now this one here," he said, tapping the picture of the teenage girl, "I'll bet she's a handful. She'll bring top dollar, but it won't be pretty for her."

He took the last photo, the woman, and stuck it an inch in front of Delafield's face. Kane's voice was dismissive. "Middle-aged housewives usually end up in domestic work. Mostly housecleaning and dick sucking."

Delafield finally broke. His voice was hollow. "Listen, Kane. You can't do this. I'm a federal agent. You know what they will do to you?"

"Well, there we go." Kane smacked Delafield with an open hand across the back of his head. "I'm glad we got that out in the open without having it get too ugly."

"Let my family go and I'll do whatever you want. We can make whatever deal you want," Delafield said. "Keep the money. The hardware, a hundred machine guns, is in the van. You can have all of it."

Kane laughed. "Think about that, Curtis. Every word you've ever spoken to me for damn near three years has been pure bullshit. *Every fucking word.* Why would I believe a damn thing you say now?"

"I swear, Kane. I'll do whatever you say. Just let them go." Delafield changed tactics. "You're HA, Kane. You don't do this. You don't involve civilians in this sort of thing."

"Normally that would hold true, but I don't think that sort of professional courtesy should apply in this particular situation. Just my feeling on it."

Delafield turned to the other man in the room. "Tanner, you're not involved in this shit. Do something before it's too late."

"You think his dumb ass is going to help you?" Kane waved the gun in Tanner's general direction. "Hell, Curtis. The boy didn't even know what he was doing. All this time, he's been in the damn dark. Apparently you fellas paid him five hundred bucks to get my ass to Sturgis and shit for brains didn't even ask why. I'm the one that had to tell him you were a goddamn fed. I'm telling you, Curtis, the scary thing is, as far as the NAF goes, Tanner here is the brains of the operation."

Delafield spoke, his voice full of defeat. "What do you want, Kane?"

Kane pulled up a chair and sat. "Are we there already, Curtis? Are we already to the point where we can discuss what I want?"

"Just tell me. Please. I don't want you to hurt them. I'll do whatever you say."

Kane put the chair up close to the defeated agent and leaned in. "I'm glad you feel that way, Curtis. I thought maybe it'd be harder to break one of you G-man types. No offense, boy, but I've had strippers hold out longer on giving a half-price blow job."

Kane clapped the man on the knee. "So tell me. What was the plan? How many of you boys are out there?"

Delafield hung his head. "I don't know. It's an arrest team. All tactical guys. Probably seven, eight guys. When you go out to the van and take possession of the weapons, you'll be arrested."

"Nice and simple, huh? After two years of jerking me off, building me up, you plan on taking me down in the parking lot of my own joint, huh?"

Delafield's gaze had gone back to the photos spread out on the table. His voice was soft. "Just tell me what you want me to do. Then let my family go. You can keep me, Kane. I don't care. Just let them go."

Kane got in closer and spoke. "I need you to hear me on this, Agent Delafield. We aren't anywhere in the vicinity of having that kind of conversation. Your family belongs to me and that fact ain't going to change anytime soon. You hear me?"

"Please, Kane. I'll do whatever you ask. Just let—"

Kane slapped the man hard across the face. "Did you hear me, boy? We ain't there yet. For now? Figure they are suffering beyond your imagination. But play your cards right and maybe, just maybe, somewhere down the line, we'll talk about a little family reunion. I imagine there might be a need for some pretty hard-core therapy, but hell, boy. It'll be a start."

"Tell me!" Delafield tried to stand, but Tanner kept him in his seat. "What do you want, Kane? I said I'll do it."

"Thatta boy." Kane patted the man's cheek. "That's where I need you, in that 'I'll do anything you say' place. Now, we got some things to go over. I'm not too concerned about you feds, but god damn, we gotta figure out how to deal with that pesky little bitch, Suarez."

THIRTY-ONE

Twenty minutes of wandering through the bowels of the Milwaukee federal building had Tia aggravated and ready to give up. She had decided to try to find her way back to the main entrance when she finally came across a check-in station behind a placard that read: "Federal Business Requiring Escort." A twentysomething man, built for rugby, sat hunched behind a gray metal desk, his face buried in a copy of *Guns & Ammo*. He wore standard junior G-man attire: an ill-fitted dark suit, white shirt, dark tie. Tia stood in front of him for several seconds and he didn't so much as look up. The pasty white skin of his face was pocked with acne red as a flame that looked to have been scrubbed off with a Brillo pad as recently as that morning. Her lingering frustration at the previous night's activities and the morning's conversation with Connor coupled with the desk jockey's obvious disinterest, brought out her irritable streak. She rapped her knuckles against the metal of the desk.

"Detective Suarez. Newberg PD."

He looked up, moving just his eyes as if to make sure Tia knew she was intruding, then looked back at his magazine. With a deep breath Tia knew was meant to signal obvious reluctance, he set *Guns & Ammo* aside and picked up a clipboard. He slowly moved his finger down a list of typewritten names, some of which had been checked off. When he found hers, as she knew he would, he tapped it with his finger, twice, then stared at her, eyes narrowed.

Setting down the clipboard, the agent handed Tia a large manila envelope. "Empty your pockets," he said in a thick New England accent. "Everything goes in. Cell phone, badge, ID. Jewelry. Everything."

"Lock your sidearm in one of the lockers," he added, gesturing with his head toward the opposite wall, where Tia saw several rows of small lockboxes. Key goes in the bag, too."

"My gun?" she asked.

"And all your ammo."

"You're serious?"

He nodded but said nothing more. Clearly, he'd heard the same complaint before. After a stare-off that lasted several seconds, Tia reluctantly disarmed herself. Figuring the guy was less than a year out of some federal training academy, she resisted the urge to ask him how long he expected to be stuck with such a shitty assignment. Instead, she followed his instructions and handed the full envelope over without further comment. The man dropped it into a safe, then came around from behind the desk, wand in hand.

"Arms straight out to your sides. Feet shoulder width apart."

"You're going to wand me?" Tia asked. She almost laughed but stopped herself.

He took a deep breath, gave an audible sigh, and tried again. "Arms straight out to your sides. Feet shoulder width apart."

Tia raised her arms while she shook her head, keeping her opinion over the process to herself. She did her best to strike up harmless conversation. "So what are you? FBI? ATF? DEA? What?"

He set the wand on the table, took a ring of keys from a desk drawer, and walked away, saying, "Come with me."

Tia followed her unamused escort to a nearby elevator where he summoned the car and used a key to open its doors. He waved her inside. Tia once again tried to make small talk as she stepped past him. "Sounds like you're from the East Coast. I'm guessing Maine, right?"

She turned to face the doors in time to see them close between her and the junior agent. Tia called out, "What the hell?" The whole cloak-and-dagger thing was getting old. "Hey, where am I supposed to go now?"

There was no reply. Tia scanned the inside of the elevator, realizing there were no floor buttons or indicator lights. A hint of panic came over her and she balled her fist, preparing to bang on the door. Before she moved, a TV screen built into the wall behind her came to life and she turned to watch. The words on the screen were read in a voice that was a too-perfect modular tone of disarming female.

"You have been granted limited access to the Sensitive Compartmented Information Facility of the Domestic Terrorist Assault Team. Prior to entry, you must acknowledge that all activity and conversations that occur in your presence, either intentionally or unintentionally, are classified. Any unauthorized disclosure of such information shall result in criminal prosecution under federal law governing the release of intelligence deemed vital to national security. Please acknowledge your understanding by pressing your right thumb firmly against the green box located in the bottom center of the screen."

Tia rolled her eyes but did as the voice commanded. When she pulled her thumb back from the screen an image of her fingerprint was revealed, the whorls and loops standing out in bright red lines. After several seconds the image faded and was replaced by her DMV photograph along with her full name, date of birth, and Social Security number. Two small buttons appeared, labeled Yes and No. The voice returned. *"Please confirm your identity by pressing yes."*

Tia pushed the button. Seconds later the elevator began a smooth descent. Tia paid close attention to the amount of time that passed before the cab came to a stop. Two levels down, she thought. Maybe three. The doors opened and Tia was met by yet another man in a suit. "Detective Suarez, you have been granted limited SCIF access requiring escort. Come with me."

Tia followed him down a tight concrete tunnel that reminded her of the bunkers in Baghdad abandoned by the Revolutionary Guard. Their boot heels echoed sharply in the confined space, which was bathed in a dim red light. Eventually they reached a heavy steel door that opened after the guard submitted to a retinal scan. Beyond the door lay an underground cement parking structure, with a low-slung ceiling and about the size of two basketball courts.

Tia paused when she came through the door, taking in the scene. A conga line of vehicles included two tactical trucks, an ambulance, and a fleet of matching dark-colored SUVs. A group of what looked like uniformed cops in black BDUs stood beside most of the vehicles; Tia noted that none of their combat fatigues bore any type of insignia. A dozen or so men in full SWAT gear, also absent any sort of organizational patch, had taken over a large corner of the cavernous space and were practicing what Tia recognized as mock entries. It was obvious an assault was imminent. *Maybe all the bullshit will be worth it,* she thought.

"This way, Detective," said her escort. He led her across the open area to a structure that looked like a sleek high-end shipping container. He opened the door and nodded that she was to enter. Once she did, he shut the door behind her, staying outside.

When the door closed, all the exterior noise vanished. The sudden silence made Tia feel like she had stepped into a vault. The windowless room was lit with a brilliant white light and dominated by a large wooden conference table littered with hardline phones and built-in computer monitors. Along one wall were a half-dozen flat screens, each displaying a different angle of the exterior of a building Tia recognized as the Roadhouse Score.

Nearby, a group of men were gathered around a whiteboard that took up most of one wall. Several wore blue windbreakers with the letters *DTAT* stenciled in yellow across the back. Tia remembered the computer voice saying, "*Domestic Terrorist Assault Team.*" Apparently Ben's suspicions were correct. Tia had never heard of DTAT, but she didn't doubt it was a post-9/11 agency and very well funded.

She recognized Lester Stahl as part of the group studying the board, which was covered with names and mug shots arranged in a link chart configuration with Kane and Tanner front and center. Tia took a step forward; the shift in position revealed a familiar figure sitting a little off to the side: Patricia Graham. With her legs crossed and her body pulled in on itself, she looked like she would rather be anywhere else.

Stahl and Graham, Tia thought. *Two of my very favorite people.*

"Hey, Stahl," Tia called out. When he looked her way Tia picked up on his disappointment that she had actually turned up. "I'm good to go. When are we briefing?"

"Not now, Suarez." Dismissal was clear in his voice. "I'll let you know if we need you."

Tia took a seat at the conference table, studying the whiteboard crowd. Towering over the comparatively tiny Stahl was a man who looked out of place. His hair was cropped close like the rest, but he was dressed down, in jeans and an untucked flannel shirt. His leather boots were more biker-style than tactical. An oversized leather wallet was connected to his belt with a good-sized chain. *Damn,* Tia thought to herself. *They not only got that ass-clown of a snitch Tanner in the mix but a U/C agent, too. Big-time shit,* she thought. Good to know the entire case against Kane wouldn't come down to the word of a crook working off his own beef. Tia moved in closer to try to hear what the conversation was about. The U/C agent addressed the group.

"He wants twenty crates of Hellhounds. Along with launchers. Says he has a mission for the NAF and this will put them at operational readiness. That's why I signaled to abort the arrest. If he makes this purchase, it really ups the ante."

"Rocket launchers?" Stahl asked. "What's he planning? Did he say?"

"Not yet," the agent replied. "But if we make delivery, I can probably get him to talk about it."

The agent tapped his finger against the picture of Gunther Kane that stared out from the whiteboard. "Whatever he's up to, it's big. I don't care what kind of gun nut he gets on his jury. He can't talk his way out of grenades and launchers."

Tia recognized the argument. Winning a conviction against anyone in Wisconsin for illegal gun possession was always an uphill fight, especially in federal court. These days, most any defense lawyer could poll potential jurors and find one or two Second Amendment zealots. Always men and usually white, these were the guys programmed to believe the government was determined to take away their weapons through laws and regulations. Federal juries almost always came back hung on charges of illegal possession of firearms. At the end, there'd be at least one juror wearing a red, white, and blue shit-eating grin, overcome with the thrill of being able to tell Uncle Sam to take a twelve gauge and blow it out his ass.

Stahl turned to Graham, in the corner. "This would really strengthen the prosecution. Grenade launchers?" He shook his head and Tia could hear the excitement in his voice. "Holy shit. He'd be screwed. This would be the biggest domestic arrest since the Nichols case."

Graham seemed hesitant to accept what Stahl was selling, but Tia could see she was beginning to waver. Tia couldn't help herself. "What's going on? I thought the plan was to take Kane down this morning."

Stahl turned her way. "Officer Suarez, this is a federal briefing. Need-to-know basis only. Please wait outside with the uniforms."

"It's Detective Suarez," Tia said firmly. "And you invited me, remember?"

"Yes, of course. And you will be apprised of what you need to know. Now, please, Detective, wait outside."

"Wait," the dressed-down agent said. "You're Suarez?"

"Yeah, I am."

The agent walked over and offered her his hand. "Curtis Delafield, DTAT. I'm covert on this op."

"Tia Suarez, Newberg PD." Tia accepted the handshake. There was an intensity in the man's eye that seemed missing from the rest of the crowd. His grip was strong. She figured he had to be wrapped pretty tight.

Delafield glanced at Stahl, then returned his attention to Tia. "So you're the one who's got Kane all bowed up. In two-plus years of dealing with this shithead, I've never seen him so wrapped around the axle."

"How's that?"

"Stahl briefed me on what went down in Milwaukee," Delafield said, and again she picked up on some tension in his demeanor. "So you know, I had nothing to do with that bullshit. But I played it off with Kane, let him think I'm hooked up with a source inside the jail. He told me all about your meeting. Like I said, you got him pretty worked up."

From the corner of her eye Tia saw that Graham was listening— and plenty annoyed. Tia couldn't resist. She smiled at Delafield and said, "Yeah. I figured why the hell not. He was getting a pass on the whole thing. Might as well try and mess with him a bit. Glad to know it got to him."

Delafield smiled back, but there was something odd about his expression, almost like she was getting played. "He was hot under the collar for a couple of days after that."

Tia studied the man's face as she answered. "It was about all I could do at the time. No one else gave a shit."

"Excuse me, Curtis?" Stahl interrupted. "Do you mind? Can we get on with it?"

Delafield winked at Tia. "Sorry, Lester. Sure. C'mon, Suarez." He turned back to the whiteboard. "Now, where was I?"

Tia took a step after him and Stahl frowned. "Like I said, Detective, this is need to know only."

Before Tia could say anything, Delafield said, "She's need to know, Lester."

Stahl's frown deepend. "Look, Curtis. This—"

"Look nothin'," Delafield said, cutting Stahl off. Tia watched as the deep-cover agent squared off with the desk jockey. "I mean, if nothing else, out of respect. The way I see it, Suarez and I are the only ones who got real skin in the game."

"Fine." Stahl's irritation was clear in his voice. "Suarez, you can stay. But let's get back on track. What's Kane expecting at this point?"

Tia could tell that Delafield had the others eating out of his hand. Tia had a long history with undercover operatives, dating back to her early days in the Marines. She'd known CIA agents who worked deep cover in foreign nations for years, never coming up for air. Since becoming a cop she'd met a few narcs who did some limited undercover work, going into hazardous locations like gang hangouts or dope houses. That kind of work required balls big enough to carry around in a wheelbarrow. Tia had done some low-level U/C street work, but nothing that involved the high risk of an extended swim in shark-invested waters. In law enforcement circles, when a covert speaks cops listen.

"He wants to take delivery of the Hellhounds tonight," Delafield said. "Says he'll put up another two hundred thousand."

There was a low murmur from the crowd; then Delafield went on. "I figured we'd be interested, so to keep Kane dialed in, I let him hang on to the guns and his hundred grand in good faith."

Tia could hear the nervous strain in Stahl's response. "That seems a bit risky, Curtis. Kane is sitting on a lot of government hardware, not to mention cash."

It was Delafield's turn to be dismissive. "I know this guy. He can be a real dick if he feels like he's being disrespected. Kane likes to be courted. So I say, we let him hold the guns and tell him we'll close out the finances on final delivery. If we're going to try and close a deal on something like Hellhounds, believe me, we want everyone as relaxed as possible."

Stahl turned to the attorney. "That would be a three-hundred-thousand-dollar federal seizure. Plus, we can take Tanner's property and the Roadhouse. We could clear almost a million in seized assets and completely gut the North Aryan Front. We'll probably end up with at least a dozen bodies for federal prosecution."

"Hang on a second, Stahl," Tia interrupted. "What about the girl?"

Everyone turned to look at Tia. She didn't explain, just waited for an answer.

"Who are you talking about, Suarez?" Stahl asked.

"You know exactly who I'm talking about. We agreed that Kane would be arrested today and we would enter into search and rescue mode."

"And now we're discussing other contingencies."

"There are no other contingencies." Tia moved closer. "We've already had that conversation. Last night they were holding a sex auction. God knows what's going on with the women inside that club. And we still have no idea where he's holding the kidnap victim. Seems to me we have a call of duty here."

"Oh, the sex auction?" Stahl's voice held a sarcastic tone. "Would you like to know about the *victim* you rescued?

"Her name is Allison 'Pepper' Coltrane. Alias Allison Connors. Alias Allison Capers. Alias Pepper Hill. She's wanted by Chicago PD for fraud. Bilked an old man out of his life savings, about two hundred K. On top of that, she has a criminal history that goes back seven years for drugs, theft, credit card fraud, and—oh, this will come as a real shock—prostitution."

None of that mattered to Tia. "She was chained to a pole, Stahl. Men were bidding on her."

"And now she's in protective custody, all right? But I'm not sure who got protected from whom, to be honest with you."

Tia shook her head in disgust but moved on to the bigger issue. "And the underage girl in the van?"

"I think we can pretty safely assume her circumstances aren't too much different than those of Miss Coltrane-Connors-Capers-Hill."

"What the hell is that supposed to mean?"

"We went over this, Suarez. We're talking about a federal operation with years of investment." Stahl held up his hand, thumb and forefinger an inch apart. "We're this close to decimating a militia organization with designs against the U.S. government. We're not going to risk this operation for a bunch of hookers and pole dancers. Why can't you understand that?"

"They're just not worth the government's time, right?" Tia said scornfully.

"You're damn right," Stahl practically yelled. "You got a problem with that, Suarez?"

The room fell silent until Delafield spoke up.

"I got a problem with it." Stahl and Tia both turned to the undercover, who went on. "What the hell, Stahl? Did you really just say that shit?"

Stahl tried to bring the man back on board. Tia noticed the attitude Stahl had displayed toward her was gone, replaced by respect and negotiation. "Look, Curtis. You've put a lot of blood, sweat, and tears into this case. I don't want that to go to waste."

Delafield shook his head. "Sounds like we got a lot of cleanup work to do. Maybe we should move now, take him down like we originally planned. I'll go back in, bring him out to the parking lot." Other men began nodding.

The dynamic between Delafield and Stahl was now clear to Tia. The operation might belong to Stahl on paper, but he needed Delafield to make it happen. The classic desk jockey and foot soldier combination. Stahl didn't want to alienate his U/C, which meant he had to play nice with Tia. She could see the disgust on his face as he turned to her, before his professional mask slipped back into place.

"Look, Detective, all I'm saying is, it turns out the woman from last night is a pretty righteous crook. But even though she's got a felony warrant hanging over her head, we took her into protective custody. Unfortunately for her, it's likely to be upgraded to criminal custody before too long." Stahl shrugged as if to say, *Not my problem,* then continued. "And, as I've said all along, I don't want to risk this high-stakes case on an unconfirmed kidnapping."

"Oh? Are we back to that now? You telling me I didn't see anything that night?"

"No, but I am telling you that whoever you saw is likely to be a prostitute or another stripper. That's the business Kane and Tanner are in. If she wasn't being treated like a lady, we can deal with that issue later. But whoever she is, *whatever she is,* she won't come off as a credible victim. Prosecution would be unlikely. The best chance we have to put Kane away for any real time is our federal sting."

He turned away to the assistant U.S. attorney. "Patricia, we need to rethink our strategy. This new development gives us a chance to significantly increase our asset seizure. Plus, we can really

strengthen our ability to prosecute. If Kane took possession of grenade launchers?" Stahl shook his head. "Stick a fork in him. He'd be
looking at life."

Tia jumped back in. "What are you talking about? You've already got plenty to prosecute this guy on. You can't be serious about
stringing this out any longer."

Delafield said, "Obviously, Hellhounds and grenade launchers
purchased by a white supremacist separatist organization? That's
a fricking 9/11 headline, for sure. And it would completely destroy
any possible defense. Hell, *I* could try that case."

He looked at Tia. Something flickered in his eyes—uncertainty?
Insincerity? "But Suarez is right; there are other considerations."

It occurred to Tia that Delafield wasn't playing to her. Graham
was his target. Looking at Graham, Tia saw an attorney who wanted
her case wrapped tight and sealed with a bow before she walked
into a courtroom or, more important, before she stood shoulder to
shoulder with the attorney general in front of TV cameras.

"We've already handed over a hundred automatic rifles," Graham said. "I will not put grenade launchers in this man's hands
unless it is under the most controlled circumstances."

Stahl was quick to answer. "We can use dummies. Or disabled
launchers. Either way, the intent will still be there and we never let
him leave the delivery site."

Graham threw out another concern. "And the guns? The ammunition? He's already holding all that."

"All the weapons are serialized," Stahl said. He gestured at the
bank of televisions, clearly annoyed with the lawyer's questions.
"We've got eyes on. He can't move the hardware without our
knowing."

Graham looked around the room, managing to avoid Tia's stare.

"All right," Graham said. "I want to know if he's serious about
this next move. If so, we can make a controlled delivery of grenade
launchers. But I want us to use dummies. I can work with that for

court purposes. Once he accepts delivery, Kane will be immediately taken into custody. No more delays. Is that clear, Agent Stahl?"

"Absolutely. I agree one hundred percent."

"I don't believe you people." Tia was on her feet and headed for the door.

Stahl called out, "Just a minute, Detective. Where are you going?"

She spun around. "Away from here, Stahl. I don't want to have anything to do with this operation of yours. Count me out."

"You do realize everything you heard was classified?"

"I get it, Stahl. You people, DTAT or whatever it is you call your-selves, work whatever case you want. But I'm working a kidnapping. If our paths cross, so be it. Get in my way, Stahl, and you won't like what happens."

Tia reached for the door and found it was locked. She refused to turn around or ask permission to leave. Stahl spoke in tones of ice. "You're going to need an escort."

"I'll walk her out," Delafield said.

"Fine," Stahl said, "but hurry up. I want to decide when and how we're going to deliver the launchers."

THIRTY-TWO

They walked back to the elevator without a word between them, Tia doing a slow burn. While Delafield produced a key and called the elevator, Tia finally spoke. "That little act back there? You played Graham like a violin."

It seemed to Tia that Delafield did his best to look confused. "I don't know what you're talking about."

"Save it, Delafield. I've navigated a few minefields with deep-cover types. I'll admit it. You got skills."

As she expected, the man stayed in character. "Really, Suarez. I'm not following you."

Tia smirked and turned to face the closed elevator doors. "Fine. Sorry for my mistake. But seriously, I've gone after a few high-value targets. I know how sometimes you need to make changes on the fly. But you guys? You're out of control. Stahl is winging this shit. I'm going back to Newberg."

The elevator doors opened and Tia stepped in. When she turned back, Delafield abruptly stuck out his hand. Caught off guard, she shook hands. "I'm still hoping we get a chance to work together, Suarez. And trust me on this—nothing you said today went un-noticed. Thanks for speaking your mind."

Delafield withdrew his hand, turned, and walked away. Tia balled her fists as the elevator doors closed and the cab moved slowly upward. Her gaze drifted up to the red light of the security camera in the upper corner. A moment later the doors opened and the same thick-necked boy-guard stood waiting to silently escort her back to his desk. She gave him the side-eye but said nothing.

He handed over the envelope with her badge and ID and Tia's first act was to pull out the locker key and retrieve her gun. She felt him scanning her body as she jammed in the magazine and pulled back the slide to chamber a round. She reholstered, giving him a hard look. "If you get tired of this gig and you want to do some police work, you should give us a call."

His expression turned sour. "Sure. I'll join up with Newberg PD. Great career move."

"Yeah, on second thought, maybe you're right. I hear elevator attendants are making a comeback."

After making her way back through the rabbit warren of the federal building basement, Tia hustled to the car. She couldn't resist glancing back over her shoulder, half-expecting to see she was being followed, but the lot was clear. Once she was in her GTO, she opened her fist and looked at the bit of paper Delafield had slipped into her hand during their farewell.

TODAY. NOON. CROSSROADS CAFÉ ON HWY 53.

Tia looked at her phone. It was coming up on 9:00 A.M. Delafield wanted to meet in three hours, and whatever it was he wanted to talk about, he had gone through a lot of trouble to be sure they weren't going to be overheard. *Nothing you said today went unnoticed.*

Yeah, I'll be there, she thought. *But before that, I got one other stop to make.* She dropped the goat into gear and lit out of the parking lot, headed back to Newberg.

THIRTY-THREE

Tia parked in front of the neat Victorian home and smiled at the sight of old friends. Alex Sawyer knelt in the grass, surrounded by a half a dozen potted plants, a bag of organic gardening soil, and an assortment of yard tools. A few strands of blond hair peeked out from under her broad-brimmed sun hat and her cotton tank top showed off the toned muscle of her arms. Tia watched Alex scan the ground, stop as if she had found just the right spot, then plunge a metal spade into the lawn, clawing a hole in the soft black dirt.

Tia's old boss, former Newberg Police Chief Lars Norgaard, sat nearby, leaning forward in a folding lawn chair, pointing his cane at a nearby patch of grass. He wore a Packer ball cap that looked to be about as old as the team, and Tia saw he had given up the tight crew cut he'd long favored. Wispy red hair had grown to his collar and even from a distance Tia could see a shine in his blue eyes.

When she got out of the car, Alex was saying, "No. That's no good, Dad. It's too close. Impatiens like to spread."

Tia heard Lars's mumbled response but couldn't make out the

words. Alex shook her head and replied, "Well, I don't want them to mound. I want them to spread. So if you want a mound of impatiens you can—"

Tia shut the car door and Alex looked up, giving Tia the full effect of her warm smile.

"Well, hey, Tia. Long time no see. How are you?"

"Hey, Alex. I'm great." Tia turned to her old boss. It had been over a year since his stroke, and recovery had been difficult. "Hey, Chief. How are you, sir?"

Lars beamed and he gave a vigorous thumbs-up. Alex stood and walked toward Tia. The two women embraced.

"Him?" Alex looked back at her father, hands on her hips. "He's bossy as ever and now he's an expert in gardening. I'm starting to think I liked it better when he couldn't talk."

Lars reached out with his cane and poked his daughter in the butt.

"Dad!"

Lars grinned and spoke to Alex lovingly. Again Tia couldn't make out the words, but clearly Alex did. She kissed him on the top of his head. "Oh, you know I'm joking. I love having you tell me how to plant, cook, and clean. Who wouldn't, right, Tia?"

"No way." Tia raised her hands. "I'm staying a hundred miles away from this one. But you do look great, sir."

As if to show off, Lars began to stand, raising a hand in protest when Alex moved to help. It took some time and effort, but he made it to his feet. The frail old man Tia had seen last spring had been replaced with a new figure. He was by no means the "Redheaded Norseman" who had once walked the halls of Newberg PD with the four stars on his collar, but his chest had filled out and his ruddy Nordic coloring had returned. Leaning heavily on his cane, he pumped one fist in victory.

"Nice job, Chief." Tia nodded in approval.

Alex smiled at her dad, hurrying over to help him back into his chair. When she turned back to Tia, the younger woman could see the concern on her friend's face. "How are you, really? I've missed seeing you at the coffeehouse. Are you just dropping by or can you stay for a while?"

"Sorry, Alex, it's business. I need to see the chief. I went by the office, but Caroline said he wouldn't be in until later. It's kind of important. Is he home?"

Tia and Alex turned at the sound of the screen door. Ben and the Sawyers' son, Jake, stepped out onto the porch. Both waved, but it was the boy who seemed most excited.

"Hey, Tia," Jake called out. Tia thought he'd grown a foot in height since she had last seen him. Jake used one hand to vault over the porch railing and dropped three feet to land lightly on the grass like a jungle cat, not a teenage boy. He jogged over and gave Tia a hug.

"Jake, you're like six feet tall." Tia looked up at the teenager who towered over her. "What are you? Eighteen now?"

Jake blushed. All the adults knew the boy had a monster of a crush on her.

"I'm almost fourteen," he said. "I'm only five eight, but I'll be six foot before I finish high school."

"Keep an eye on this one, Alex. He's going to be breaking hearts pretty soon."

"He already is," Alex answered. "Mine. He's growing up too fast."

As if on cue, a coo came from the nearby bassinet, which was sitting on a blanket in the shade of the massive maple tree that dominated the front yard. Alex swooped in fast.

"Oh, I know, Izzy. I've got you to dote on now, don't I?"

Tia looked at Ben, still standing on the porch. Arms folded across his chest, he leaned against a support post, his face practically glowing with satisfaction and affection. Family was everything to Ben, and Tia knew it.

"Hey, boss," she said. "How are you?"

Ben came down off the porch and walked over. They shook hands.

"Good, Tia. I was going to head to the office in a few minutes. What's going on? Is Kane in custody?"

"That's what I wanted to talk with you about, Chief. I need to catch you up on a few things."

"Tia, stay for lunch," Alex said, now cradling the baby in her arms.

Tia thought it sounded more like an order than an invitation but knew she couldn't accept. "I wish I could, Alex. But I've got some stuff to do." Picking up on Jake's look of disappointment, Tia added, "Soon, though. I'd really like that."

Ben led her around the back of the house so they could have more privacy.

"Is it too much to hope you came by to tell me we bagged Kane? Victim recovered, mission accomplished?"

Tia laughed sarcastically. "We're a long way from that. Stahl and his team want to postpone the arrest. Something about Kane wanting to step up his game. They went into the whole national security bullshit again." She took a deep breath. "I walked out. Sorry, Chief. I can't handle these guys. I just don't get where they're coming from."

Ben stared straight ahead and nodded in a way that told Tia he was holding something back.

"Don't tell me Graham called again?" she said. "What did she say about me this time?"

"No. Nothing like that."

"Then what, Ben? Tell me what's going on."

They reached the back patio and took seats around the fire pit, which was still full of hickory ash from the spring. "I paid a visit to Sheriff Solo."

"Really?" Tia said, her voice disdainful. "And how is old blood and gutless?"

"Pretty bloodied up and feeling pretty gutless," Ben said. "He's handed over all jurisdiction to Stahl's team. He said he's gotten some very clear direction from the state capital, basically orders to stay out of Stahl's way. He made it pretty clear to me that he wants nothing to do with Gunther Kane."

"I don't get that, Chief. The guy ran for office on an anti-fed campaign. Every chance he gets to slam the federal government, he calls a press conference."

"True, but you said it yourself. *He runs for office.* In the end, let's face it: he's a politician. He's got to stay in the club or, come the next election, he'll find out all his money has dried up.

"Fact is, Tia, I got a couple of calls myself. The mayor and also a guy pretty far up the food chain of Wisconsin DOJ."

"And?"

"We've been urged to cooperate with Stahl. Let him run his operation."

"What the—" Tia stopped, took a breath, then said, "I don't get it, Ben. Where does this guy get his juice?"

"I got hold of an old friend," Ben said. "We were beat partners in Oakland fifteen years ago. Sharp guy, went to school at night, finished up his degree, and hired on with ATF. He's an ASAC now out of Los Angeles. I gave him a call. Filled him in. He called me back in less than an hour."

"Yeah? What did he tell you?"

"To take a lesson from the sheriff. My old buddy made it clear we ought to stay a hundred miles away from Stahl and anything he touches. Told me if I had any cops working with Stahl, pull them the hell out."

"Did you tell him that they're sitting on a human-trafficking case?"

"I did. To be honest, I don't think he wanted to talk about it over the phone. He's a good friend and I think that's the only reason he even called me back. I'm telling you, Tia, he sounded like he was trying to warn me. "

"About what?"

"Like you said. Stahl's got some serious juice. We know that he falls under the Director of National Intelligence, and I'd be willing to bet he's not part of any of the major agencies. He's not CIA, NSA, or anything like that. All that is too old-school and traditional for him."

Tia thought back on her conversation with Delafield. "You're right there. They call themselves DTAT. Domestic Terrorist Assault Team. I don't know, but based on what I saw, my guess is they pretty much freelance it. Looks like they've got a nice budget for toys. They're living out of a SCIF in Milwaukee."

"A SCIF?" Ben asked.

"Stands for 'Sensitive Compartmented Information Facility.' The whole concept was just coming online when I discharged. Basically it's a bunker. An ultra-safe room. Built to be bug proof. Supersecure phone and computer lines. Hell of a way to spend a few billion in taxpayer money. Course nowadays, all the spook agencies compete with each other. Who can have the most whizbang, bitchin' SCIF." Tia shook her head. "Bunch of boys making up for some other inadequacy, if you ask me."

"Well, I don't know about that," Ben said, "but Stahl definitely has that post-9/11 feel to him. You must have dealt with a lot of guys like him."

Ben was referring to Tia's days in the Marines, when she was part of a black-bag operation out of Afghanistan. The Marine squad she served on had a CIA contingent and she became more than a little familiar with the ugly underbelly of intelligence collection. But that was then and ten thousand miles away in a foreign hostile country. *This is Wisconsin for Christ sake.*

"Yeah. Too many. And I don't care about any of that anymore. All I know is that we, local law enforcement, have information about a kidnapping victim. Milwaukee PD doesn't care and somebody seems to have cut the balls off our county sheriff and put them in a jar on the shelf. That leaves us, Chief."

"What are you suggesting, Tia?"

"You know damn well what I'm suggesting. That we do something. We're cops, Ben. We've got all the authority we need to follow up on this case. The hell with Stahl."

"Why this case, Tia? Why are you willing to risk everything for this one case? We've had to walk away before."

Tia paused, then answered, her voice low, "It's personal, Ben. I can't let it go."

"Tia. You're the one making it personal."

She started to speak, but he raised a hand and kept talking. "I know what you're going to say, and you're right. I'm not one to talk about not getting involved, but Tia, that was my wife. The mother of my son. Don't you think this is just a little bit different?"

A long moment passed between the two of them. Tia thought back to her conversation with Connor—a conversation she already regretted. Connie had every right to feel angry and left out. She didn't want to do the same thing again here. She looked at Ben and saw, not the chief of police, but a friend. Someone who cared about her. Someone she knew she could trust. She started in.

"When I was shot down in Danville, I was pretty sure that was it. I could feel that I was checking out. It wasn't a big deal, I just knew it was the end, and I was like, 'Okay, let's get on with it.' I just figured it was time to see what comes next.

"And then a girl came to me. A little girl. She spoke to me."

Ben didn't move and his gaze never left her, so Tia went on. "She told me, in Spanish, that it wasn't my time yet. She told me that I needed to come with her."

"Did you go?" Ben asked. He looked serious but Tia thought she heard some doubt in his voice.

"Yeah, I did. We walked away together, left the café. The whole time, I kept asking her who she was, where we were, all the stuff you'd probably ask a ghost given the chance, right? Maybe she told me, maybe not. I don't know. It's not like it's that clear. But it happened."

"Okay." He nodded. "I've heard about that sort of thing. People who, you know, almost die. They have dreams . . . images that really stick with them."

Tia shook her head and spoke patiently. "It wasn't a dream, Ben. *It happened.* I left this"—Tia motioned to her body—"and went somewhere else."

Tia could see him thinking over what she was saying. "Go on," he said.

"That was the end of it, or so I thought. I talked to Gage about it." Tia couldn't help but roll her eyes. "That was a mistake. He told me it happens to people all the time in situations like that. He called it an NDE. A near-death experience. He just blew it off."

"Kind of like I just tried to do?" Ben said quietly.

"Yeah. Kind of like that. Only he writes everything down."

"That's when he told me I needed more time off." She shrugged. "Okay with me, I thought. I headed down to Mexico, spent time with Mom and Dad. Everything was pretty normal for a while."

A few seconds went by while Tia remembered her time in Mexico.

Ben encouraged her to keep going, saying, "Then you came home."

"Yep." Tia regrouped and shifted in her seat. "I thought a lot about it, but the more time that went by, the more I figured maybe Gage was right. It was just about blood loss and shock."

"You don't think that now?"

She shook her head. "The thing in the courtroom, Ben? The

whole 'What the hell got into Suarez?' thing? She came back to me that day, right then."

"The girl from the café?" The doubt in his voice was thick enough to cut with a knife. "She came back?"

"Yeah. While I was testifying. She took me out of the courtroom to where the molestation victim was . . . where the son of a bitch . . ."

Tia wasn't sure she could say what came next, but Ben waited, his gaze warm and open, and at last she was able to go on.

"I was in the room. I was watching what he did to her. Then, it was like somebody flipped a switch and I was back in the courtroom." Her voice went low. "That scared the hell out of me. Let me tell you, it was the oddest experience of my life and it scared the living hell out of me."

Ben looked away and Tia wondered about the position she was putting him in. *He's the chief,* she reminded herself. *There are things he doesn't want to know.* But he was also her friend. She plowed ahead. "After that I didn't even know what to think. You sent me back to the shrink and I get that; I know you had to do it. But I talked way too much with that jerk-off, Gage. Next thing I know I'm on meds, labeled damaged goods."

"What does all that have to do with this?" He didn't sound angry but genuinely curious.

"She's been quiet for a while. The girl, that is. I think all the drinking has been my way of trying to keep her that way. I don't want this shit in my head. At least, I didn't."

"And now?"

"After the van, after that night, she came back. Told me the girl in the van needs me. That she's waiting for me."

"She told you all that?" Tia could hear disbelief in his voice. She couldn't blame him.

"Yeah, Ben, she did. I know how it sounds, but I don't care. I know I can't explain it and neither can you. But I'm not crazy."

"I'm not saying you're crazy, Tia. But don't you think maybe there might be some reasonable explanation? I don't know. Something that doesn't involve . . . time travel, ghosts, and the supernatural?"

Tia sat forward as if accepting his challenge. "Okay. Then explain this to me. She was in the field last night. She led me to the auction. I was in the middle of a cornfield I'd never seen before in my life. In the middle of one of the craziest thunderstorms of the last ten years. Believe me, all I wanted was to get the hell out of there, but it was like she pulled me into that shed."

Ben spent a moment and she could tell he really was thinking about it, but she knew he still wasn't convinced.

"All right then, explain this. You didn't find the girl from the van, Tia. Why not?"

Tia got his point and looked away. Ben wasn't about to let her off the hook.

"Sure, you found some other woman, who definitely needed finding, but weren't you expecting the girl you saw in Milwaukee?"

Tia shook her head. "I thought of that, yeah. And the truth is, I don't know. But I don't think it matters either. I heard a voice. I followed it and, well . . . You know the rest."

"I don't think you're taking enough credit, Suarez. Sounds to me pretty much like business as usual for you. It's not the first time you pulled a rabbit out of the hat."

Tia looked at him doubtfully. "Come on, Ben. You know this goes beyond anything like that."

"Okay, Tia. Fine. I get it. You had a crazy night. But—"

"She's real, Ben."

"The girl in the van?" he asked. "I know that, Tia. And I should never have doubted you."

"No. The girl in my head. She's real. Maybe not the way you and I are. She's not walking around, have a beer with you real.

But in some way. In some strange way we *can't* understand, she's real."

"Have you told anyone else about this?" His voice was hesitant.

"No." She got his meaning. "Don't worry; I'm not going to."

He sighed in relief. "Probably just as well."

"But I'm not going to ignore it anymore either. I'm not going to disrespect her like that."

Silence fell, but it was comfortable. Tia felt more at peace than she had in as long as she could remember. He must have felt it, too, she thought, because he squeezed her hand and smiled at her in a way that he hadn't in a long time. A smile free of worry.

"So what now?" Ben asked.

"I don't know, but I'm not waiting around for Stahl and his team. We've still got a kidnapping case. I say we work that."

To her surprise, Ben didn't immediately disagree. "You got a starting point?"

"Maybe," Tia said.

Ben huffed. "Let me guess. You're going to tell me not to ask any questions and you need to work alone."

"That's why you're the chief, smart guy."

"The answer is no."

"I don't remember asking you."

"Look, Tia—"

She cut him off. "Chief, the deal was I get to work this case, no restrictions. If you still want my resignation, fine. But hear me on this." Tia leaned forward and looked directly at her boss. "I've sat on my hands for damn near a week while some girl is going through who knows what. Why? Why haven't we done something about that?"

Tia waited for an answer and when none came she went on. "Exactly. There's no reason. A bunch of yahoos show up, stringing together some bullshit about national security, puffing their chests out, making phone calls, telling us they've got the authority of the federal government, and we sit back and do nothing? The hell with that and the hell with them. They can work whatever op they want. But I am going to go find that kid and get her out of there. If I have to do it as a private citizen, fine."

Ben said nothing and Tia stood. She looked down at him as she said, "Sir, effective immediately, I resign my position with the Newberg Police Department. I appreciate everything you've done for me, but I think this is where I step out."

She'd taken only a few steps back toward the street when he called out, "Resignation not accepted."

She turned back. "Excuse me?"

"I said, I don't accept your resignation." Ben stood. "Damn, Suarez, don't you know there's all kinds of paperwork I have to fill out when someone resigns? Personnel forms. Pension stuff. And you have to write a letter." He quickly closed the distance between them. "So whatever it is you've got planned, for now, you are a Newberg police detective and you've got all the authority that comes with it. You understand what I'm saying?"

Yeah, Tia thought. *You're saying you got my back.*

"I hear you, Chief," Tia said. "Thanks."

"Be careful, Tia."

"Will do, sir."

They walked around the house together, both lost in thought. The rest of the Sawyers were still clustered on the front lawn. Tia gave Jake one more hug and said it was time they took in a Brewers game. "Just the two of us, huh?"

His smile was so bright it was practically incandescent.

Tia took Chief Norgaard's hand in both of hers and shook it warmly. "Good seeing you, Chief. Keep fighting your way back, okay?"

The old man spoke, but Tia couldn't make it out.

Alex translated, "He says you look good, too."

When she pulled away, she glanced back to see their smiling faces. Except for Ben. His expression was somber and his message clear. He was there for her; she knew that. But the time had come. She was on her own and she needed to get this done.

ACT III

THIRTY-FOUR

Tia slipped up to the back entrance of the Crossroads Café, pulling open the battered screen door that led down a long, narrow hallway. The rusty spring on the door went off like an alarm and the door slammed shut behind her. Tia stopped and waited for some sort of reaction, but no one seemed to notice. She heard the sizzle of grilling meat, along with voices singing in Spanish to the Latin dance music, coming from what she assumed was the kitchen.

By the accents, Tia made them for Oaxacans. A white woman in a flowered muumuu lumbered toward her, filling the space from wall to wall. Feeling trapped, Tia was prepared to give ground, but the woman turned off, squeezing through the restroom door. Tia's anxiety level climbed as she continued down the hall to the dining area. Her heart raced and sweat beaded across her forehead. Everything served as a reminder of the diner in Danville. The linoleum tile on the floor was damn near identical. The stale odors of pike and walleye. Up ahead a stout waitress poured coffee, making small talk with a man at the counter.

No time for one of your ridiculous flashbacks, Suarez. There was something about meeting a cop she barely knew in an unfamiliar café that caused her to grip the four-shot derringer in her jacket pocket a little tighter and make sure the safety was off. Even that didn't give her much in the way of comfort. Faces from the not-so-distant past flashed across her mind. Paranoia kicked in. What if it was a setup? What if Stahl and Delafield were getting her off by herself? Where would two agents of a semi-legit spook agency draw the line when it came to protecting their case? She rested her trigger finger along the pistol's short barrel and walked into the crowded café.

Looking around at the signs advertising blue-plate specials and "kids eat free," the place struck her as the kind popular with locals. Delafield sat at a booth alone. The café's dozen or so other patrons—who appeared to be average citizens—were enjoying hearty breakfasts, but Delafield sat stiff backed, a single, untouched cup of coffee on the table. His gaze was fixed on the front entrance and Tia was able to make it all the way to the booth undetected. She clapped him on the back and heard him gulp with surprise.

"Hey, Delafield." Tia slid into the opposite side of the booth. "The clock's been ticking for a while on this, so I'm not here for long. What did you want to talk about?"

Delafield put his hands out and his gaze darted around the café. In an urgent whisper, he said, "Jesus, keep it down, Suarez."

Tia didn't lower her voice, but his reaction pretty much convinced her that Delafield was not in cahoots with anyone. Like Tia, Delafield was acting on his own. If that was the case, she wanted to be sure she was the one calling the shots. "I don't really care who hears. I'm done playing games."

Tia saw the apprehension in the man's face as he looked over his shoulder, in the direction Tia had come from. "Were you followed? Were you careful?"

"Jesus, Delafield," Tia said. "What are you so worried about? Who's going to follow either one of us?"

Delafield's voice was insistent. "Were you followed?"

"No. I wasn't. But it doesn't much matter if I was. Like I said, I'm done dealing with you people. This is just a courtesy visit. I've decided the best thing for me to do is head over to the Waukesha County Courthouse and swear out an arrest warrant against Tanner. While I'm at it, I'll get a search warrant for his place. I'll do my best not to step on your operation, but you should probably tell Stahl that if he wants Kane he'd better go ahead and pull the pin."

Delafield didn't exactly relax, but he was able to give a nervous laugh. "Trust me on this, Suarez. You won't be getting any warrants against Jessup Tanner or Gunther Kane."

"Are you kidding? After what I walked away from last night, I'm just worried the judge might have me arrested for dereliction of duty."

Delafield shook his head. "If anyone enters Tanner's or Kane's name into a courthouse database, Stahl will know it. You start swearing out warrants? Graham will shut that down with one phone call."

"Thanks for the warning, but I'm in pretty good with the presiding judge in Waukesha County. I'll give him a heads-up. I think he'll be a little harder to push around than a county sheriff."

"Really?" Delafield said. "Patricia Graham is a U.S. attorney attached to the Foreign Intelligence Surveillance Court. Unless your judge-buddy wants to end up hearing traffic cases in a Sheboygan night court for the rest of his career, he'll stay off her radar screen."

"She's FISA?" Tia couldn't keep the shock out of her voice.

Delafield ignored Tia's question. "All I'm saying is that Stahl and Graham are connected. Trust me, nothing good will come out of going straight at either one of those two."

254 ■ NEAL GRIFFIN

"Bring it," Tia said, accepting the challenge. "Like I already told you, Delafield, you guys are out of control."

"I don't disagree with you, but even if we're out of control, we have some heavy-duty backup. Now, do you want to hear my idea or not?"

The waitress approached the booth. Tia waved her off, then waved at Delafield, encouraging him to continue.

"Kane is financing his illegal purchases with money made through human trafficking."

There it is, she thought. Tia recalled the conversation in Sawyer's office, when Sheriff Solo revealed the intel his deputies had gained through the illegal tracker. No way she was giving that information to Delafield. The trust wasn't there yet. She looked at Delafield across the table, her face deadpan. "Go on. I'm listening."

"I'm not talking about the strip club stuff; forget about that. Kane's got a guy on the West Coast who identifies good targets for their little business. He calls Kane, and Kane and Tanner head out there to pick up the merchandise."

Tia played along, curious to see how much Delafield was willing to talk. How much he really knew about the crimes of Kane and Tanner. "The merchandise?"

"Women. Young. Just across the border and alone. The kind of girl nobody is going to report missing."

Even with what Solo had already provided, it was hard to hear. Tia sat in silence and allowed Delafield to go on.

"Kane and Tanner are hooked up with a coyote. After he IDs the target and notifies them, he hangs on to the girl until Kane and Tanner come out and close the deal."

Tia felt the anger building inside. She couldn't believe what she was hearing. That cops would sit by and allow such crimes to occur. Allow innocent girls to be kidnapped and raped. Treated as nothing more than slaves. Fighting for control, she could hear the tremor in her voice.

"How many times? I mean, how many girls have they brought back?"

"So far? At least four," Delafield said. "They got a regular circuit. Starts in LA. Then Vegas. From there they hit a dozen or so truck stops, a bunch of labor sites, roadside hotels. They were just getting back from the last run when you came across them. Kane surprised everyone when he tried to snatch you off the street."

The fury began to boil over and still Delafield had more to tell.

"Kane's got an arrangement with a pimp down in Chicago. Once Kane's done with 'em, he sells the girls off for a few hundred bucks. Then they walk the blade in Cicero. Bottom-rung shit." Delafield shrugged. "From the time Kane makes the snatch until he gets rid of them is usually about three months. I figure he's cleared about thirty or forty-K per girl."

"Jesus." Tia shouted in frustration, covering her face with her hands. She had never imagined that Stahl and his team could have been so complicit. So negligent.

Delafield reached out with both hands and grabbed Tia by the wrists, whispering. "Damn it, Suarez. Are you nuts? Keep your voice down."

Tia looked around the restaurant and saw several faces looking her way. Delafield was right. Prying ears could create big problems. She lowered her voice to a whisper, but the wrath remained.

"What the hell is wrong with you people? You know all this and you leave the guy out there walking around? I don't get it. Do him for kidnapping and lock his ass up."

"Seriously, Suarez? Are you really that naïve?"

Tia clenched her jaw and said nothing.

"Who's going to prosecute with an illegal immigrant prostitute as the victim? California? *Vegas?* Some circuit judge in a farming town in Kansas? I suppose you think the feds will take this on." He shook his head. "The human-trafficking angle is a nonstarter. The DTAT angle on this whole thing is domestic terrorism. Nothing else."

Tia leaned in. "What is this DTAT shit? Who are you guys?"

Delafield looked around the café before bending toward Tia and lowering his voice.

"Stahl is Colonel Lester Stahl. He's Army Special Forces and Intelligence, but strictly as an analyst. A real pencil neck. I doubt he's ever even seen the business end of an M4 and I sure as hell know he's never kitted up for a real mission. This is his first field assignment."

"And he's running the show?"

Delafield finally took a sip of his coffee, nodded, and went on. "Four years ago Stahl was tasked by the Director of National Intelligence to create the Domestic Terrorist Assault Team—DTAT for short. He's got about twenty-five agents, mostly military, Special Forces types, a few from old spook units. The agency budget is classified and most of the work is reported straight to DNI. But in four years, Stahl hasn't been able to break a single case. The guy belongs behind a desk. This whole thing with Gunther Kane is the closest Stahl has been able to get to making a real case on somebody."

"Real case?" Tia smirked. "Is that what you call this?"

Delafield shrugged. "What can I say? He's a fed. Different breed."

"Funny to hear you say that about one of your own," Tia said.

The big man snorted and briefly looked disgusted. "Not 'my own' at all. Believe it or not, I'm just like you, Suarez."

"Come again?"

"I was a detective working narcotics for the Cedar Rapids Police Department. I heard about a hotshot new spy agency, recruiting guys to go deep cover. Targeting high-level domestic terrorists. Sounded great. Getting on with a federal agency. Doing big-time covert ops. You know, the kind of thing you could tell your grandkids about." Delafield shook his head. "I wish to hell I'd stayed in Iowa. I'd go back to pushing a patrol car tomorrow."

"Why'd Stahl hire you?"

"Before I was a cop, I did four years regular Army. Ended up working a sting operation with army CID, targeting stolen weapons. We were pretty successful. Got a lot of stolen guns off the street and put some very bad soldiers in Leavenworth. Told Stahl about it when I interviewed and he was impressed. Must've thought I was a good fit for this op.

"I've been working Kane for more than two years. I've spent so much time with that fat-ass, racist prick that I've started to forget it's all a game." He shook his head. "And Tanner? Don't even get me started. That little tweak has been playing Stahl like you wouldn't believe."

"What do you mean?"

"Tanner was my original 'in' with the NAF. I worked him as an unwitting—he didn't know I was working for DTAT—and managed to get him to set up a meet with Kane. A few months after that, Tanner got nabbed by state police with a pound of meth in his trunk. Stahl went off and signed Tanner as his own personal informant."

"So wait." Tia stopped him with a hand up. "You mean your original intro to Kane is now working for Stahl?"

Delafield could only shrug as if admitting to the incompetence surrounding him.

Tia shook her head and she spoke with sincere "cop to cop" concern. "Dude, I'm no U/C expert, but that sounds risky as hell. You're cutting pretty close to the bone."

"Tell me about it. It was news to me until you had your run-in with Kane in Milwaukee. That's when Stahl let us in on his little secret. That Tanner was his bitch." Delafield's voice was more emotional than she had heard before. Angry, even. "But that's been Stahl's MO all along. He figures it's his op. His world, you know. The rest of us just live in it. Fuckin' guy."

Tia could feel her trust for Delafield growing, but she could also tell the man was under the gun. He was feeling the pressure. She sat quiet and let him talk, wondering what else he'd let slip.

"It's been slow going," Delafield said. "When we started on Kane, it was supposed to be a six-month assignment. Turns out Kane wasn't all that hooked up. We've really had to walk him down the aisle."

"You must be single," Tia said, shaking her head ruefully. "I mean, what woman in her right mind would put up with this kind of bullshit for two years?"

Delafield gave a quick shake of his head as if to dismiss the topic. "Look," he said, "are we going to talk about getting this case back on track or not?"

"You called the meeting. What do you have in mind?"

"You need to let this run its course."

Tia started to scoot out of the booth. "Not an option."

"Wait." Delafield grabbed her arm with an almost-bruising grip. Tia pulled back, wrenching free. He softened. "Just hear me out."

Tia sat still, letting her silence serve as a signal for him to go on.

"Just a few more hours. Stahl wants me to deliver Kane to a neutral location. Away from the Roadhouse. Away from Tanner's place. He figures that way, it'll be easier for us to control the takedown. Once Kane accepts delivery, we'll pounce. He'll never get a chance to even move the product."

"I told you, I'm done working with you guys."

"I need ten hours, Suarez. You need to give me that."

"Forget it." It was Tia's turn to lay things out. "I get it. Stahl and his buddies are like the New Avengers or some such shit. Frickin' untouchables. But that's got nothing to do with me. I'm local and I don't answer to your people. I told you, Delafield, I'm out."

"No. You're not." Delafield's gaze went to the entrance, then back to Tia. "You think you get to walk away? Or better yet, you think you get to tramp all over this op?"

Tia didn't reply. Delafield said, "I'm just telling you. Better yet, I'm *warning you,* beat cop to beat cop. Stay out of this. Stahl is already looking to take you down and he's far enough up the food chain to screw you over big-time."

"What the hell is that supposed to mean?"

"After you took off this morning, he huddled up with Graham. I overheard him talking about a mental breakdown, some kind of courtroom thing? How you needed to be taken out of the equation. I heard him telling Graham the shooting at the farm needed to be taken federal."

"The hell with all you people." Tia pushed her way out of the booth. "Go back to your bunker, Delafield. I've got police work to do."

"Do you want to get that girl away from Kane or not?"

Tia stopped. Delafield had said the one thing she could not resist. She sank back into her seat. "Tell me what you got in mind."

"Like I said, everything is set for tonight. I'm going to the Roadhouse at nine o'clock. My job is to get Kane to the meet location, twenty miles away and in the middle of nowhere. One way in and no way out. We've got it all pre-staged with a tactical team. He'll be bagged and tagged in no time. After that, I'll go with you to see your judge. I'll give him everything."

"What are you saying?"

"I'm saying, I'll spill it all. The trips west. Kane's attempt to kidnap you. Everything. Then, you and Stahl can argue over who has the better case. It won't matter to me, because I'm done with this shit."

Tia knew what the offer meant. If Delafield went on the record, she'd have no problem getting search warrants for the Roadhouse and Tanner's place. Hell, with Delafield's corroborating statement she could swear out arrest warrants for both Kane and Tanner for multiple counts of kidnapping. Not to mention felony assault on a cop.

260 ■ NEAL GRIFFIN

"You'll give it up? All of it?"

Delafield nodded. "I told you. I get it. We fucked up. It's time to get back to basics. But if you go it alone, Stahl is going to shut you down in a big way."

Tia thought it over.

"All right, Delafield, we'll do it your way. Twenty-one hundred hours. I'm following you guys to the takedown location. Soon as Kane's in custody, you and I hightail it back to Newberg. We have a late-night date with a judge I know. He'll give us what we need."

"Fine." His voice was anxious.

Tia got up to leave and gave Delafield a last look. She knew he needed to be brought in. He'd been out of his real world for too long. No one should go two years deep cover with a shit bag like Kane. The look in his eye felt more crook than cop. "You sure you're good, Delafield? You can handle this all right?"

"Don't worry about me." He shimmied out of the tight-fitting booth, stood, then pushed past her. As he walked away, he said, "Tonight, Suarez. We get this shit done tonight. After that, I don't really care what happens."

THIRTY-FIVE

Tia pulled the GTO in to the alley behind the Piggly Wiggly and found Connor sitting on the edge of the grocery store's raised loading dock, legs dangling over the side. The white apron his manager insisted he wear was wadded up on the cement floor beside him; his John Deere cap was pushed back on his head. He was reading a worn paperback of *The Life and Times of Hunter S. Thompson.*

Moving as quietly as possible, trying to catch him off guard, Tia had gotten to within a few feet of him when, without looking up, he spoke.

"Break time, Officer Suarez. I'm not inclined to spend it with the cops."

She smiled. "It's Detective."

His blue eyes turned a little green against the cap he pulled down tight to block the sun, which shined a bit more directly in his eyes when he turned to look at her. "Well then, that's different."

She hoisted herself onto the cement platform. "Why are you reading that communist crap again?"

"Say what you want, the man knew something about being free." He set the book aside. "What are you doing here?"

She hesitated, then answered, "I'm sorry for the way things ended. I wish you had stuck around. I don't think we were done talking."

He looked back. "Funny. I kind of got the impression you wanted to be done with me, period."

"No." She shook her head. "You're wrong. I wasn't thinking that at all. I doubt I'll ever think that."

Looking at Connor now, older and with many more miles on him, Tia couldn't help remembering their bus ride to Parris Island. Hope and energy had poured out of him then. He'd stayed awake the whole time from sheer excitement, even after she had finally fallen asleep, leaning on his shoulder, for the last hour of the trip. Even all these years later, with all they had been through, she could hear the boyish excitement in his voice as he'd whispered in her ear, *"Wake up, Tia. We're here."*

His real voice brought her back to the present.

"Then I should have stayed with you. I'm sorry."

"Next time."

"Next time?"

"Yeah." She moved in closer. "Next time you get all worked up and put out with me? Just stay. Okay?"

He nodded. "So now what?"

She took a deep breath. "I've got a way to wrap this up tonight. If things go right, Kane and Tanner will be in custody on both federal and state charges and I'll have search warrants for the girl. It's all legit. Low risk, too."

He looked at her, almost expressionless, assessing. "Sawyer know about it?"

"He knows enough."

"Low risk, my ass." He looked away, shaking his head. "Damn it, Suarez. Don't you have some burglary cases to work or something? Maybe get a cat out of a tree?"

"Firefighters get cats out of trees. Cops *shoot* cats out of trees."

He pretended to ignore her and reached for his book. "All right, then. Like you said. We'll talk later, I guess."

Tia put her hand on his, pinning it and the book to the cement. She got his meaning and she didn't blame him for being frustrated with her.

"Don't."

He looked steadily at her. "Don't what?"

"Don't shut me out."

He said nothing, but he didn't have to. Tia could practically read his mind. All she had to do was go back to the department, sit at her desk, and earn her paycheck. God knows she had plenty of her own issues to worry about. She didn't need to go looking for new ones.

"This is it, Connor. If I can't help her this time, then I'm done. But I have to do this."

"Let me guess," he said. "There's this voice. Am I right?"

When she only smiled in response he went further. "So? You going to fill me in or what?"

She shook her head. "I think you're going to want plausible deniability. Just in case."

"Well, that sure as hell puts my mind at ease."

Tia got to her feet but stayed in a squatting position so their eyes were at the same level, then leaned in and kissed him on the mouth. "I love you, Connor. I know we don't say things like that very often, but I want you to know it."

He started to stand, but she put her hands on his shoulders.

"No. Stay here. I'm going to do this one thing. I have to. Then after that, you and I are going to talk about how to live our lives together. Put all the craziness behind us once and for all."

He shook his head. "Okay, but I just want to point out, it's all *your* craziness. I stock shelves at the Pig. I don't do crazy."

She laughed. "Yeah, agreed. *My* craziness."

264 ■ NEAL GRIFFIN

She jumped down off the dock and stood looking up at him. She put her hands around his legs and leaned closer.

"When this is over we're going to sit down. Talk about some things I need to tell you. I want you in my life, Connor, but you have to know what you're getting into."

He reached out one hand and stroked her cheek. "It doesn't matter what you tell me. I am in your life for as long as you'll let me stay there."

"Yo, Anderson," the manager called from the doorway behind Connor. Neither he nor Tia looked around. "I need you for a cleanup on six. After that, stock toilet paper on aisle five."

He shook his head, smiling at his own reality. Tia laughed, just once.

"I guess duty calls for both of us, huh?"

"Want to switch?"

He stood. "Don't ask me twice—you might wind up grabbing a mop."

She pushed off his legs and walked backward for a few steps, watching Connor struggle to his feet. For an instant she saw pain in his eyes, saw how awkwardly he moved. In that moment she wanted to go to him, help him. Then he was on his feet and his composure returned. The flash of pity she felt faded when she saw his strength, the solid core of him that no one could take away.

He shot her a crooked grin, but his eyes were serious. "Don't worry about me. Go do what you have to do and be done with it. Remember. You said we were going to figure out a way to put all this behind us."

He bent over, grabbed the white apron and his book, and turned away. A moment later he disappeared into the grocery store, walking with the sort of quiet nobility reserved for those who had never once failed to answer when called.

THIRTY-SIX

The now-familiar scrape of chain against wood woke Angelica from a fitful sleep. *They're coming again*, she thought. *I won't go. I'll fight until they kill me. Today, I find a way to die.*

Overhead the door was flung back, and blinding light flooded the pit. Fresh air fell from above like rain, but Angelica found no joy in it. She retreated to the dark corner; her vision returned in time for her to see the ladder drop into the space.

She waited for the familiar, heavy sound of his boots. Of his cackling call, as if she were some sort of farm animal. Light footsteps against the wood froze her in place, fearing the break in what had become a terrifying routine. She saw a woman's bare feet and legs appear in her field of view, moving uncertainly down the ladder. Angelica pushed herself farther into the shadows, hoping for safety in concealment.

The woman, dressed in a bright-colored sundress, reached the bottom. With both feet firmly on the ground, she looked up through the opening. She called out, her voice strong but flooded with emotion, "See? I'm not making any trouble. Let me have them."

Angelica watched as another pair of feet became visible—the tiny feet of a child. A young boy descended into the pit, lowering himself down the ladder, both hands tightly gripping each wooden rung. He couldn't be more than three or four years old, his face covered in dirt. He stopped halfway, whimpering.

"I'm scared, Mommy," he said, looking down at the woman waiting below.

When she answered, Angelica heard fear in her voice. "It's okay, sweetie. You won't fall. Mommy is right here."

The woman was wrong—the boy slipped an instant later and fell—but his mother reached out and plucked him from the air. She held him close, pressing him to her body.

Seconds later another person descended the steps—this one a girl who looked to be about Angelica's age. She was wearing shorts and a jersey, like the soccer players Angelica had seen back in Mexico. Angelica could see her lean muscles—the girl must be strong, Angelica thought. She had honey-colored hair that fell to the middle of her back and her skin was the color of dark copper. She stared up at the hatchway even as she climbed lower and Angelica could see the spite in her eyes.

Partway down, she jumped off the ladder, then called up to whoever was above, "Pass him down to me. I'll catch him."

Angelica heard a voice she didn't recognize. "No. He stays with me. If you all start carrying on and stirring up a racket, you won't see him again."

The woman in the bright dress shrieked. She dropped the little boy to the ground and flung herself onto the ladder, climbing frantically. She was nearly halfway to the top when the ladder began to pitch back and forth. She held on but couldn't go higher or lower. After one particularly quick twist, she fell hard to the ground.

From above came the high-pitched, terrified scream of a child, so piercing it shook the dirt under Angelica's feet. The awful sound drew something out of Angelica she hadn't known was still there.

The image of the bold one filled her mind—the one who had fought for her. The one who had tried to pull her out of the darkness. Angelica ran to the ladder and bolted up. She was so quick she managed to almost reach the top. She grabbed one of the boy's feet. The ladder was being pushed and pulled in an attempt to dislodge her, but she managed to go up another rung. She wrapped one arm around his waist; with the other, she clung to the ladder. A white man, one she had never seen before, towered over her, holding the boy.

Angelica pulled hard on the now-screaming child, who had begun to flail at the man. She lost her grip on the ladder—but not her grip on the child. She sailed through the air and landed hard, with the boy on top of her. He scrambled to his feet and ran to his mother, who grabbed him and held him close.

In those moments that Angelica spent lying on the floor, dazed from the fall, a man jumped into the pit. She dragged herself to her feet and found herself face-to-face with a man as big as any she had ever seen. She didn't have time to move before he swatted her across the face, swinging his whole arm and open hand, knocking her onto the floor again. He looked at her for an instant, then turned to climb the ladder and leave. The fear that Angelica had carried inside her for so long turned to rage. It consumed her.

Angelica threw herself onto the big man's back. She was ready to fight him now. She would fight like the bold one. Angelica felt strength surge through her body. She felt the spirit of the bold one. She was ready to be free.

THIRTY-SEVEN

At half past eight, Tia drove the GTO into the parking lot of the Roadhouse Score and took up a spot in a distant corner. Right on time and true to his word, Delafield pulled in thirty minutes later. He wasted no time getting inside. Tia put the radio next to her ear and listened to the tactical channel, where a half-dozen voices called out locations and activity. The comings and goings from the club appeared ordinary; no one would suspect that a major federal sting was nearing its final act. Tia scanned the crowded parking lot and tried to pick out the close-in surveillance. To their credit, they blended in well.

She reviewed the plan Delafield had laid out for her. He was to take the crooks to a neutral location where, if things went badly, Kane wouldn't have a bar full of civilians to hide behind. Simple. Not great, but good enough. Tia just hoped it went off quick. She'd made a call to the district attorney—the real one, not a fake one like Graham—and let her know to expect a late-night request for a search warrant. She'd heard doubt in the woman's voice, but no matter. Tonight all the doubting would be done.

Stahl's voice came over the radio, higher pitched than usual and full of excitement, like a kid playing with a new toy. "Subjects are exiting the location. They're on the move. All units stand by."

Tia didn't have as good an angle on the doorway, but she could see the familiar white van pull into view. She risked the use of hand-held binoculars, cupping them with her palm to lessen the chance of detection by any countersurveillance. In the dark and from a good fifty yards away it wasn't easy to see details, but she made out Jessup Tanner behind the wheel. The hulking figure of Kane looked to be in the passenger seat. That put Delafield out of view in the backseat, the desired position of most any U/C cop when riding in a car with crooks. It didn't take more than one or two episodes of *The Sopranos* to know why.

The van hit the roadway and Stahl's voice came over the radio. "That's our package. Tanner's behind the wheel and U/C is pinging inside. Surveillance team, fall in. Arrest team, be advised we're on our way to your location. ETA twenty minutes."

Tia had no formal role in the takedown and she sure didn't want to be accused of burning the surveillance. She held back and watched as the van quickly reached full speed. Before it had gone far, two other vehicles pulled out of the parking lot, followed a few seconds later by a third. All the tail cars followed a little closer than she would have, but feds were like that. Tia waited until the entire caravan of U/C cars was well down the road and nearly out of sight before she started her engine.

Tia moved her hand to the floor-mounted stick shift, then stopped. A deep chill crawled across her skin and she stared at her hand, expecting to see an army of ten thousand fire ants marching there. Overwhelming dread took hold of her and a dark image filled her mind: Trapped. Alone. Terrified. Her heart began a familiar banging in her chest and the voice was as clear as it had ever been.

Ahora, Tia. Ve ahora.

"Go where?" Tia said out loud in a mix of anxiety and anger. *Not now*, she thought. She got nothing back but stone silence.

"Damn it," Tia continued her one-person argument, "I don't need this right now."

The follow cars had disappeared. Tia used a shaking hand to drop the goat into gear. She pulled out of the lot faster than she should, filled with fear and needing to escape. A face flashed in the darkness across her windshield and Tia slammed on the brakes with a mixture of shock and terror. The voice practically screamed.

Ir a su ahora.

On the verge of a full-on panic attack, Tia pulled air in through her nose, forced it out through her mouth, and closed her eyes. She rested her head against the steering wheel and forced herself to be calm. Turn right to follow the surveillance vehicles to the takedown location. Turn left and there was no doubt as to the destination. A minute passed. Then another. Tia picked her head up off the steering wheel and sat staring straight through the windshield at the dark landscape across the road. She loosened her grip and rocked her head on her shoulders to relieve the tension. She spoke out loud. "Go ahead. I'm listening."

The voice was calm and reassuring.

Ahora, Tia. Ella te necesita.

Tia nodded in acknowledgment. She jerked hard on the steering wheel and floored the accelerator. The tires fishtailed in the loose gravel of the lot before gaining traction on the blacktop. Her mind was clear, her decision made. She knew precisely what she had to do. It was ten minutes to the Tanner farm, eight if she drove it hard. She decided to make wise use of the time and plan the best approach into the field.

THIRTY-EIGHT

For the second time in twenty-four hours, Tia found herself on a dirt road bordered on both sides by row after row of eight-foot-tall corn. The spongy mud under the tires of the GTO bogged her down and she wished she were still driving the 4x4. She kept the car in first gear until she reached nearly the same spot where she'd parked the night before, judging by the bent cornstalks on either side of the roadway.

When she got out of the car, the summer wind was warm against her face. Conditions were much better than they'd been last night—the sky was full of stars and most of the mud had solidified. She reached the fence and vaulted it with ease. She reached for her phone, planning to once again use the compass, then stopped.

Just listen.

Tia kept walking, the dead stalks soggy under her feet. She felt safe enough, concealed in the darkness. The outline of the Tanner compound began to come into view, black and lifeless. When she was close enough to pick up any movement, she hunkered down and pulled her forty caliber from her shoulder holster. No movement. No light.

The compound appeared deserted. Tia stood and moved forward, holding her gun low, alongside her leg. The shed lay ahead of her, its gray, moonlit silhouette visible through rows of corn.

To her surprise, it was easy to find the spot in the fence where she'd forced her way through before. Mud had filled in the hollow she'd created, but the fencing was still pulled up and out of place. Dropping to her knees and setting her weapon aside but near to hand, Tia had no problem scooping out enough soft dirt to a new pathway. She slipped under, this time without the distractions of the rain and getting stuck on the fence.

The shed was dark and lifeless. After a quick sneak peak inside, between the seams of the wooden walls, she moved to the doorway. She turned the handle and pushed the door open, revealing a black space. Lifting her handgun, she decided to risk using the forward light.

She clicked it on and Delafield's bloodied face came into view.

He sat in a chair atop the same wooden stage where Pepper Hill had been on offer the night before. His arms were pulled behind his back and a rag was stuffed in his mouth. A rope went around his neck and upper body, pinning him against the chair. Tia couldn't be certain, but he looked unconscious, though she could see the rise and fall of his chest. As she stood in the doorway of the shed, highly exposed, with no cover or concealment available, her instincts screamed, *Leave! Abort the mission. Run back to the road and call for backup. Not just backup. The whole state. This is not a situation that can be handled alone.* But she knew better. She couldn't leave him here. With her weapon straight out at shoulder height, she stepped closer, hopped up on the stage.

"Delafield." She took him by the chin and shook his head. "Curtis." Delafield mumbled a response and she knelt beside him. This close, she could see that his face was a mask of bruises and blood. His shirt was torn and bloodied.

She needed to get him out of here. It was time to blow the lid off this thing and rain down on the area with some cops.

Adrenaline surged through Tia as she realized that if Delafield wasn't at the takedown location Kane probably wasn't either. In that same instant she heard the flip of a switch and the stage was flooded with light from overhead.

"You sure are a predictable bitch."

She recognized the voice that came from beyond the curtain of light, but for some reason she felt no fear. "Step up, Kane. Out here where I can see you."

With her forty cal still at the low ready, she stared across the space between them, trying to make out a shadow or a shape. She told herself, if she got a shot she'd take it. A moment later she heard the distinct sound of a suppressed round leaving a barrel, followed by the splat of a lead bullet hitting bone and flesh. Tia felt no pain and it was Delafield whose body jumped, jerking against the ropes. He came to life enough to scream into the gag, then trailed off into sobs and silence. His knee now looked like a bowl of cherry Jell-O.

"Three seconds to drop the piece or the next one's in his chest. One, two—"

Tia raised her left hand and bent her knees, lowering herself to the ground. She set her firearm on the dirt floor, then slowly stood back up.

Kane emerged into the light. She hadn't seen him since the jail visit. He hadn't improved.

"I figured you'd be showing up. You should have heeded my advice, Suarez. I told you to stay clear of me."

"I was thinking the same thing, Kane." Her voice brimmed with confidence. "Your window is closing."

Kane stole a look at his watch. "True enough. I do need to be heading out. But since you dropped by, maybe we should take a minute to settle our differences once and for all. Seal the deal, you might say."

Despite the dire circumstances, Tia found herself to be astonishingly calm.

"I'm guessing you made Delafield for a fed." Tia looked back at the wounded man. Blood still flowed from his knee. She thought, *Without attention he's gonna bleed out right here.* "You know, they'll pursue your ass to the end of the earth if he dies."

"You came for the girl, right, Suarez? I know she's got you all spun up." Kane held up two fingers separated by an inch of space. "You're this close, but it turns out that's as close as you'll get."

Kane stepped farther into the light. He carried a military-style AR-15, the barrel pointing somewhere between her shins and her heart.

"I'll give you this, Suarez: you are doggedly persistent. That is the damn truth." Kane cocked his head at Delafield. "I'd sooner have to deal with a dozen of these federal dicks than one of you. But in the end, it's like I told you. You'd have been better off staying home."

Tia stood straight. She put her hands out, palms up. "You do what you're going to do, Kane. But, one way or another, this will be the end of the line for you. I don't know how the feds will feel about it, but I can guarantee you'll have ten thousand cops from here to California hunting your ass. They'll make book on who gets to take you out."

Kane gestured at several wooden crates stacked nearby. "I've got bargaining power, Suarez. I can lay low with folks who will be more than happy to help me outrun the law."

"Like I told you from the beginning, Kane. It ain't going to go like that. It doesn't matter where you hide."

A hint of respect showed on Kane's face. He smiled and said, "I tell you, Suarez, what you lack in perception you more than make up for in gumption. But in case you missed it, this is where it ends for you."

Kane raised his rifle and in that instant, in a moment that caught both adversaries mid-breath, a red dot materialized on his forehead. The red laser light glinted as it streamed through the darkness beyond the bright circle cast by the bulb over Tia's head. Tia watched Kane turn cross-eyed, trying to track the source of the beam. Without turning to look, she could tell that it ran over her shoulder and out the open door, and probably on into the cornfield beyond.

The big man stood statue still. Tia smiled to herself, considering just how quickly the tables had turned. She understood exactly what was at stake and she figured she'd better explain things to Kane, who was probably desperately trying to find another option.

"Don't move, Kane." She raised her fist in a military signal to hold position. "If you so much as twitch that gun, you're dead."

"What the hell, Suarez?" Kane's voice was both enraged and laced with defeat. "Who's out there?"

"No matter." Her fist still in the air, Tia took a step away from the door, to provide an even clearer line of sight between shooter and target. "Just let the rifle fall. Whatever you do, don't lift it."

Kane opened his hands and the gun fell to the ground. Tia kept her fist raised and waited. The laser began to bob ever so slightly, but the red dot never left the kill zone. A minute passed before she sensed movement behind her. Outfitted head to toe in a brown ghillie suit, Connor Anderson stepped up to take a flanking position alongside her, sniper rifle poised and ready at his shoulder. She shot a quick glance at the weapon and saw that his finger was on the trigger. Once Connor stopped walking, she heard the click of his site aperture and the laser disappeared.

"I think I can hold on him with the iron sights from here," Connor said.

"Step away from the rifle," Tia said. "Get on the ground."

Kane glared at them both, then dropped to the dirt floor, spread-eagle. Connor looked at Tia and she saw that his face was entirely hidden behind camouflage and dark green paint. He said, "Help is on the way. Do what you gotta do. I got this."

Dazed but energized, Tia moved to the wooden stage. Pulling a knife from her pocket, she cut the ropes binding Delafield to the chair. His breathing was labored but steady. She hooked her arms under his and pulled him off the stage, laying him on his back on the dirt floor.

Without taking his eyes or his aim off their prisoner, Connor called out, "Top pouch, right side."

Moving quickly while making sure she never got between Connor and his target, Tia ripped the first-aid kit off the Velcro that attached it to his harness. There wasn't much she could do beyond packing the wound, but she did that and hoped the help Connor had mentioned would soon arrive.

In the silence that had fallen Tia could hear the faint whine of a siren in the distance. *Good,* she thought, listening harder. Then she heard something else. Something much closer.

Voices. Female voices. Coming from somewhere near the stage, somewhere . . . underneath?

Then another voice, with an entirely different sound, called out in a way Tia knew only she could hear.

Ella aqui.

THIRTY-NINE

Angelica was once again on the porch, her mother beside her shucking corn and singing a familiar song.

I came home once before, Angelica thought. Like before, the pain was gone. Her body felt alive and youthful. The world around her was full of color and the sounds of the country. She turned to her mother and implored her, "How do I stay this time, Mama? I don't want to leave again."

Her mother smiled, saying what a beautiful young woman she had grown into. How she had missed her sweet Angelica. How sorry she was to see her leave at such a young age.

"I don't want to leave, Mama. I will stay here. I won't go back." She looked up and saw the hawk, circling high above her head. Angelica watched, waiting for him to dive down and scoop her up, but instead he soared higher into the sky.

Voices came from above, but she blocked them out. One was a familiar voice. A strong voice.

"*Mija.* Come to me."

But no. She would stay here. The music of her mother's singing filled her ears. She would not leave. The hawk flew higher until he was a small speck in a wide, blue, cloudless sky. She closed her eyes and breathed in the smells of home, nestling close to the warmth of her mother. *This is where I will stay,* she thought. *This is where I belong forever.*

"*Mija. Ven a mi!*" The voice sounded as though it came from a far distant place. Another world.

Angelica looked up. The hawk had disappeared and her heart was still and filled with peace.

FORTY

Tia looked down and saw that the stage was really nothing more than a wooden box set flush against the dirt. She bent down, took hold of the corner of the stage, and lifted. As she suspected, it wasn't fastened to anything. It was heavy, but not too heavy to shift. She began dragging it backward, leaving ruts in the dirt floor. The box jerked in her grasp a couple of times, bumping over small obstacles of some kind, but continued to move.

As Tia cleared the stage out of the way, the trapdoor was revealed. When she saw it, she was shocked into immobility for a second, then pulled harder and faster to clear access to the wooden hatchway. Once she was certain there was room, she dropped the stage and rushed to the trapdoor, which was chained and padlocked. She could hear a woman shouting from below. A child was crying.

How many people are down there?

She exchanged a glance with Connor, who gave her a single nod, signaling the confidence he held in her. He kept his rifle trained on the prone figure of Kane. A dozen or more sirens wailed from the highway, growing closer by the second.

She dropped to her knees and shouted through the door, "Move as far back as you can!"

Tia pressed her ear to the wood and heard sounds of shuffling and hushed voices. She got to her feet and studied the lock, determining the safest angle from which to take a shot. She fired once, hitting the padlock dead center. Though damaged, the lock remained closed.

A second round did the trick; the metal exploded into pieces, scattering bits of shrapnel about the area. Tia rapidly pulled the chain through the hasp and threw back the trapdoor. She dropped to the ground, her head and torso projecting into the opening, and stretched one hand out in front of her, reaching into the darkness of the pit.

"*Mija*," she called. "Come to me."

When there was no answer, Tia yelled again. "*Mija. Ven a mi!*"

A woman called out in English, "Please. Help us."

Without hesitation Tia scrambled into a sitting position on the edge of the opening, feet dangling into the hole. She jumped into the blackness of the pit, landing hard on the dirt floor but staying on her feet, gun at the ready. A small child rushed toward her and encircled her legs in his arms. Tia heard the cries of the others and tried to sound reassuring.

"Calm down," she said, half-shouting. She scanned the area with her flashlight. "I'm Detective Suarez, Newberg PD. I'm here to help you."

The woman, her once-bright dress covered in dirt, began to cry. "Where is my husband? I need my husband."

Tia aimed her flashlight in the woman's direction. "Who are you?"

"I'm Elaine Delafield. My husband is Agent Curtis Delafield. Do you know where he is?"

The sirens were close. It sounded like every cop in Wisconsin was headed their way. "Your husband is going to be okay, ma'am. Please stay calm. Help is coming. I'll get you out of here."

Tia scanned the small enclosure. A storm shelter, not unlike the one on the farm where she'd grown up, less than ten miles away. Basically a featureless box in the earth. Tia turned to Mrs. Delafield.

"Ma'am," Tia said gently, more in control of her voice, "is there anyone else here? A young girl? About the same age as your daughter?"

When Mrs. Delafield spoke, her voice was hesitant. "In the corner." She gestured toward a dark corner of the pit. "But she—"

Tia spun, shining her light into the corner, revealing a figure under a blanket. She flew to it.

The familiar face was quiet and serene. Tia stroked her hair. *"Estoy aqui, mija. Estoy aqui."*

Tia pulled back the blanket and saw that the young woman's slender body was covered with bruises. She took the girl's cold hand in her own, noting how pale it was, how still the body was. A trail of blood ran from the young girl's ear; Tia could tell from the way it reflected the beam of the flashlight that it was still moist, not yet dry.

"She died about an hour ago," Mrs. Delafield said quietly, close behind. Tia glanced back and saw that the woman had drawn near, leaving her children on the other side of the space

In the same soft tones, she continued, "I'm a nurse. I did all I could, but . . ." She paused to stifle a cry. "She protected us. She fought one of them and he beat her terribly.

"I tried to stop him—" Her voice broke then and she turned away. Her daughter stepped forward and embraced her.

Tia sat still, stroking the dead girl's long black hair, pushing it away from her face. She heard a dozen voices overhead, men shouting. A ladder was dropped into the pit and a moment later the space was full of Waukesha deputies and officers of Newberg PD. One of them was Travis Jackson, who pushed through the group to Tia's side.

"Tia, are you all right? What the hell happened up there? We need to get everyone out of here. This is a major crime scene."

Tia looked at the girl's face and saw peacefulness. Serenity. Her skin was dirty but still smooth. Her mouth was shaped into a slight smile as if something had brought a happy thought to her mind.

"Tia, come on," Jackson said. "We've got to clear this area."

"Leave her alone, TJ." Ben Sawyer's voice, conveying both an order and concern. Tia did not look around.

"But Chief," Jackson said, "you saw what's up there. Some shit went down."

"I know, Travis. Just leave her," the chief said.

Tia could hear TJ continuing to protest as he climbed back up the ladder. The rest of the officers and deputies followed him up, escorting the other captives. Tia could tell, by the woman's scream, when Elaine Delafield first saw her husband. Her shouting was immediately mixed with the calming voices of paramedics who were undoubtedly already working on the injured agent.

The pit itself was silent and Tia thought she was alone until she heard Ben's voice, thick with sad emotion. "You did all you could, Tia. You did all *anyone* could. Take all the time you need."

Connor knelt beside Tia, still in his ghillie attire but with his face wiped mostly clean. He looked somber. He reached for her, but Tia leaned away and would not look at him. Expression unchanged, he waited for a long moment, then got to his feet and left. Tia felt nothing, not even regret that she had hurt him once again.

Tia stared into the quiet face of a dead girl whose name she would probably never know, whose brief life she would never fully understand. A girl who had begged for help . . . but no one had listened. Minutes passed and the voices above faded. Silence fell.

At last, the normal sounds of a peaceful night returned. Time went on.

Still Tia sat there, in the black pit, dimly lit by the beam of her flashlight. *What a lonely place it must have been to die.*

Tia pulled her knees up high under her chin, lowered her head, and cried.

FORTY-ONE

H ey, Tia. How you holding up?"
The familiar voice seemed to reach her from a thousand miles away and she was reluctant to even acknowledge it. She'd managed to drift away to a place where there were no consequences for failure. No shame or death. No unnamed bodies to bury. But she knew all those things mattered, so she allowed herself to be pulled back to the present.

She was sitting at her desk, facing a blank computer screen, just like she had been for almost an hour. No idea what to write, how to summarize recent events.

Beyond exhaustion, she gave just the slightest nod of her head when she turned to face the speaker. "Hey, TJ."

"Chief's asking for you. He's got that Stahl guy in his office. Along with the sheriff and some other guy I don't know."

Tia nodded. *Here it comes,* she thought. "Thanks, TJ."

"You sure you're okay?"

"Yeah. I'm fine. Tough couple of days, but I'll be all right. Thanks for asking."

"Sorry about the girl. I should have—"

"Not now, TJ." Tia shook her head and put her hand up, then realized she'd come across as harsh. "Sorry. I just mean, don't worry about it for now. There's a whole long list of people, me included, that are going to say something that starts with 'I should have.' Just not now."

"Yeah, okay," TJ said. She could tell he understood. "Well, be careful talking to those guys. I mean, don't go off on anybody. And, don't say any more than you need to."

She smiled. "Thanks, Counselor, but I'm good. Sawyer's got my back."

Tia took the familiar walk, thinking of the two days since her last summons to the chief's office. That time, she'd thought she was going there for the last time. She shook her head at herself. She'd survived that and everything else they had thrown at her. Now she thought, *Here we go again.*

Tia walked in to see Ben behind his desk and Sheriff Solo standing nearby, looking out the window. On the couch, Lester Stahl sat, staring at her with the sort of look he might give to a dog with mange. Next to Stahl was Elliot Gage practically glowing with self-righteous satisfaction.

When Tia entered the room, Ben stood up and the sheriff turned around. Both seemed at a loss for words. Stahl and Gage whispered to each other. Tia decided to set the tone. She did her best to mask her exhaustion as well as the overwhelming sadness that she had not been able to shake.

She addressed her boss.

"We've cleared the crime scene, Chief. Last I heard, Agent Delafield was conscious and responsive. He was headed into surgery, but his prognosis is good. I don't think we'll be talking to him until sometime late tomorrow."

Tia looked at Stahl, then back at the chief. "From what he was able to tell me, the case we have against Kane will be strong.

Multiple counts of kidnapping. Conspiracy to commit rape. And, of course, now we have him dead to rights for murder."

Stahl frowned slightly at Tia before turning to the chief. "Kane will be transferred to federal custody. I am here to initiate the process."

Tia didn't wait for Ben or the sheriff to respond. "No, he won't. He'll be charged in Waukesha County Courthouse on state charges. Kane is my prisoner. And you should know, your informant, Jessup Tanner? He's being taken into custody as we speak."

Stahl stood and closed the distance between them. "The federal government has more than three years invested in this case. It is a major case of domestic terrorism. National security dictates that—"

"Your case is shit," Tia said defiantly. "Hell, you don't even have a case. All you have are the rifles, which were recovered from Tanner's property. Kane is already claiming no knowledge."

"We'll charge him with conspiracy to purchase, along with the assault against Agent Delafield and the kidnapping of his family." Stahl faltered and his voice turned sheepish. "And of course, he'll be charged with the death of that girl."

Tia glared back. "He's in state custody. For murder. That's where he'll stay."

"Chief Sawyer," Stahl said, turning to the local authority, "this is obviously a situation that should be handled at an executive level. Perhaps we should dismiss the rank and file—"

"Shut up, Stahl," Ben said crisply.

Stahl went silent, his face taking on a look of shock and confusion. Tia was inwardly amused but kept her expression neutral. When Ben spoke again, she easily picked up on his anger, mixed with what sounded like disgust.

"You have screwed this case from the start," the chief said. "You've got nothing but a questionable firearms deal and an informant who will be shredded on the stand. As far as your undercover agent being nearly killed and a young woman being murdered, all of that is a direct result of your incompetence. The last thing in the world your case needs is a courtroom."

Clearly flustered, Stahl worked to hold his ground. "That isn't your decision."

"He's right, Ben," Sheriff Solo chimed in, stepping away from the window and staring at Tia. "It's my decision. Most all the crimes were committed in county jurisdiction."

Stahl lifted his chin with satisfaction and opened his mouth, but Solo put out a hand. "It's a county case and it will *stay* a county case. But obviously, we'll work hand in hand with Newberg PD."

Solo turned to Tia, his manner serious. "Detective Suarez, if you wouldn't mind coordinating the investigation from this point forward? Interviews, evidence collection, liaison with the district attorney? It would all be much appreciated."

"Of course, Sheriff." Tia nodded. This was a victory, but not one to take pride in. It was a chance to do the job right.

"Apparently you've both forgotten," Stahl said, "that Detective Suarez was involved in a shooting on Jessup Tanner's property a few days ago. A man was killed. The federal government still has an interest in that case."

Stahl turned to Ben and went on. "It is my understanding, Chief, that you had been told of Detective Suarez's instability, that she was not fit for duty. I believe this whole situation calls for some federal oversight."

"He's right, Chief," Gage piped in. "There is no way Detective Suarez should have been put in that situation. She was in no condition to be working in the field. I think I made that clear in my report."

"A report," Stahl said, "that I have read in its entirety." In a condescending tone, he said to Tia, "My, you have had a tough time of it, haven't you, Detective?"

288 ■ NEAL GRIFFIN

Ben shook his head as if annoyed with the games. "Well, until someone tells me different, this is still my department and it is sure as hell my office. Gage, you can leave."

"Chief Sawyer," the doctor said, "I think you—"

"Leave, Doctor," Ben repeated curtly. "Or I can have you escorted out." He reached for the phone on his desk

Gage got up from the couch. He brushed by Tia without looking at her as he headed out of the room.

"Just so you know, Stahl," Ben said conversationally, "I've already spoken to your assigned counsel, Ms. Graham. Based on the facts as they stand now, she has no interest in pursuing federal charges."

Tia saw Stahl's eyes widen fractionally in shock.

"Tell you what, Stahl," she said. "I've got a few crates of M4 machine guns and ammunition you can have. We've got no need for it."

Clearly furious but thwarted, Stahl walked to the door. "This is not over, not by a long stretch."

"That I agree with," Tia said. "But we'll do our best to keep your name out of it. I think we'll all be better off that way."

Stahl left, practically slamming the door behind him. Tia turned around to look at the sheriff and the chief. She knew they each realized that there would be no victory celebration at the end of this case.

No high fives. No gloating over showing up the feds. There would be no sense of vindication coming out of this. Tia nodded at the sheriff, then addressed her boss.

"I'll get back to my desk then, Chief. I've got a good bit of paperwork to get through."

Ben looked at her quietly for several seconds, then nodded. "Get to it, Detective. Let's wrap this up."

FORTY-TWO

With stomachs full from a dinner of roasted pork, refried beans, fresh tortillas, and jicama sprinkled with lime and chilies, Tia and Connor walked out onto the front porch of the farmhouse. There was a coolness in the air and Tia wondered if it was the first hint of an early fall. She looked up into the trees in the dying light of the sun and, sure enough, a half-dozen leaves were tinted with orange. Ringo came up the steps, back from some sort of adventure, his beet-red tongue hanging from his mouth. The dog pushed past Connor to put his head under Tia's hand. She dropped down and pulled at the loose skin around his head. He leaned into her, tail beating.

Connor patted his stomach. "That was amazing, Tia. I had no idea you could cook like that."

"Thanks," she said, giving the dog a final pat and standing up. "There are two things unmarried Mexican girls must be. Good cooks and verifiable virgins."

Connor smiled, rolling a toothpick to one side of his mouth. "Yeah? One outta two ain't bad."

He leaned against the porch railing and Tia leaned on him, her arms around his waist. The silence was long and comfortable, but there was a question Tia still wanted to know the answer to.

"What brought you to me that night, Connie? Did you listen like I told you to? Did you hear a voice?"

He kicked his head back and the sound of his laughter filled the quiet night. "You just aren't going to let it go, are you? The answer is no. I wasn't following any voices."

"Okay, what then?"

"Nothing as mysterious as that, I promise." Tia poked him, signaling without words that she was waiting for an answer. Connor shook his head and said, "You know, if you want to keep slinking around at night like some secret agent, you ought to disable the GPS on your phone."

The laugh burst out of her, completely unexpected. Tia rolled her eyes and smacked her own head. *Duh.*

"Sorry about all that, Connie. I should have told you. I thought Delafield was being straight with me and I didn't want to involve you. I had no idea it would get that crazy."

He turned within the circle of her arms and took her by the shoulders, pushing her slightly away. He looked her straight in the eyes. She saw no condemnation there, nothing but honesty and warmth. "You got nothing to apologize for. Nothing you tell me will make me regret what I did. That wasn't a hard call."

"So you're going to come out okay??"

"Well, both Sawyer and the sheriff made it pretty clear they'd rather not have civilians all kitted up and out on recon patrols, but they seem willing to make an exception this time."

Tia pulled him close for another hug, then took him by the hand. "Come on. I need to show you something."

She led him down the worn path, still holding his hand, convincing herself the time had come. She was really going to do this. Ringo followed them off the porch, then ran ahead.

"Remember all that time I spent down in Mexico after the shooting? Convalescing, they called it." She kept her tone light and he matched it.

"Course. You were there what, two months? Called me twice, I think."

"Yeah. Sorry, it was a . . ." Tia paused. "I had a lot on my mind."

"I think we've pretty much moved on," he said, sounding a little puzzled.

"Yeah, but I need to tell you some things. About me."

They arrived at the trailer. Tia took a deep breath, looking at her old home. Ringo sniffed at the green grass, turned around three times, then dropped like a lead weight. He held his head high as if enjoying the peace that had returned to their lives.

"I've never brought you down here before," Tia said, "but this is where I grew up. I lived here with my parents from the time I was five until I joined the marines."

Connor's face lit up with sentimentality. "No kidding? How come you've never showed me?"

Tia shrugged. "I don't know. Kind of embarrassing, I guess. Bunch of Mexicans living in a singlewide trailer behind the big house. I kept it pretty quiet growing up."

"Can we go inside?"

She sat on the grass and pulled him down next to her. "Sit here with me first." She looked at the trailer as she spoke, afraid that if she looked at him she wouldn't go through with it.

"My family has farmed blue agave in Jalisco for three generations. It's not a big operation, but it's quite a production. Some of the best tequila in the world comes from Rancho de Suarez. Not that I would know," she said with a wink. "I don't drink."

A smile crooked the corner of Connor's mouth, but she could see a growing unease in his eyes.

"There's a saying in Mexico that the only thing harder than life is the land. Some years, it doesn't matter how hard you work, the land gives you nothing. On most farms in Mexico, people don't *live;* they exist. They eke out a life of some sort and they're happy to have it.

"When my father was still a young man, he wanted to offer his family more. So he did what lots of oldest sons do. He took his new bride and went north. They crossed the border at Nogales. He found work in the fields of East Texas. My mom cleaned houses in town. It worked for them.

"They were able to send some money home to help their parents keep the farm and stay ahead even during the toughest seasons. My dad learned English. Even after I came along, we bounced around a lot. Texas. Oklahoma. I actually picked cotton one summer in Georgia. I was four. Eventually, Dad got permanent work right here." Tia patted the ground with satisfaction. "We settled in and I got to go to regular school. Mom made a bit on the side doing laundry and still cleaning houses. Life was good."

She could see she had Connor's full attention. She looked down at her hands and went on. "But before all that, a couple years after crossing over, while they were still in Texas, my mom got pregnant. She said it was her miracle baby. She had begun to think she'd never have children, and then finally it happened. When the time came, she made a midnight trip to the Brownsville Hospital Emergency Room, where she gave birth to Tia Juanita Solis-Suarez. The first bona fide American citizen of the Suarez clan."

Connor smiled. "That's you."

Tia squeezed his hand, looking at him now. "One winter, rubella went through the camp. My parents did what they could to protect their baby, but she got sick. A week later, Tia died. She was almost four. My mom still can't talk about it without grieving."

Connor's expression became a map of confusion and disbelief. He started to speak and Tia put her fingers against this lips.

"After Tia died, a young woman who also lived in the camp came to them. My mom said the girl was just a teenager, maybe fifteen or sixteen, a country girl from way down south. Her husband had been killed earlier that week in a thresher accident and she had decided to return to Mexico. She had no family to speak of, owned nothing of value. She was beyond poor and she knew the life that waited for her.

"When she and her husband had crossed the border on the way north, they had brought their little daughter with them. The girl was just a few months younger than Tia had been. The young widow knew that my parents' child had had an American birth certificate. She knew what that represented: the opportunity for the life of an American citizen."

Tia saw tears in Connor's eyes. She gently took his hand once more. "My parents took that woman's child and raised her as their own. As Tia Juanita Solis-Suarez. An American-born baby. A citizen of the United States. That's me, Connor."

Connor could barely speak. "So who are you . . . What is . . . ?"

She squeezed his hand. She understood his confusion. "You can still call me Tia."

"But you were a marine? You had a top-secret clearance. You're a cop."

His tone told Tia he wasn't ready to believe her. She understood. She had felt the same way for weeks after her father had sat down with her on the back porch of their adobe home in Jalisco.

"Yep, I am. And except for my parents and a woman I'll never know, no one knows the real story." She shrugged. "And now you."

He sat in stunned silence and Tia waited. Eventually he spoke in a halting voice.

"You okay with that?" He stopped and seemed to think more about it. "I mean, with everything? Are you okay?"

"When my dad first told me, it was as if someone had taken a shovel, shoved it into my chest, and scooped out everything inside me. Emptied me out and just left a bloody hole. I felt so betrayed. Deceived. By the people who loved me the most." Tia took a deep breath. "I'm not the person I thought I was. I've lived a lie my entire life.

"I felt ashamed, like I wasn't a real American, whatever that means."

She looked into his eyes, hoping to make him understand. "I thought about staying down there in Mexico."

"Why didn't you?" he asked, then seemed to regret the words in the next instant. He spread his hands. "I mean, I'm glad you didn't. I'm glad you came home."

Tia smiled, ready to admit it all. "Because of you. Because, yeah, I do think of this as home." She patted the soil. "At least, I want it to be. Then all the craziness happened. The courtroom, the booze, the pills."

Tia fell silent and drew a shuddering breath. Connor closed his hand over hers and stayed quiet, waiting. "I started doubting myself. Thinking maybe I was nuts.

"Maybe I didn't belong here." She looked at her lap, shaking her head.

"And now what?" he asked. "How do you feel about it now?"

"After everything that has gone on? I see it differently. I think of it differently."

Connor tilted his head and raised an eyebrow, encouraging her to go on.

"I think of my parents. I see them in that workers' camp, watching their child fighting for her life. I see them staying up night after night. I imagine my mother holding her baby as Tia takes her last breath."

Tia paused, lost in thought for a moment, her mind taking a new tack. "I think of that young mother who loved her baby so much, she gave her up so she might have a better life. Then I think of the girl in the van. What sort of life led her to that place?

"She and I, we come from the same place, the same circumstances, really, and things turn out so . . . so unfairly different. It's way too complicated for me. I just know that I've lived a fortunate life. And I have my parents, a young woman I'll never know, and the first Tia to thank for it."

She sighed and looked steadily at Connor. She knew she was throwing a lot at him, but she wasn't done. She hoped he could follow her the rest of the way.

"That voice I kept hearing? It was her, Connor. It was Tia."

"Come again?" She could hear the uncertainty in his voice, see the fear in his eyes. She plowed ahead.

"Ever since I got shot, she's been with me. She's been encouraging me, guiding me. At first, it really threw me off. I let it get to me. The shrinks made it sound like I must be a little nuts and I believed them. Then I started trying to shut her up with booze and meds."

"And now?" Worry clear in his voice.

"I don't fight it anymore. I accept it. I might not completely understand what's happening, but I don't need to."

Tia looked down. "In some strange way we came together, Tia and I. Together I think we have lived a life that matters. She got to live on, in a way. I got a life filled with opportunities I would never have had otherwise.

"Am I okay with it?" She shrugged. "I have to be. What choice do I have? But I'm glad to know the truth. It's a difficult truth, but I'm glad to know it."

She waited for his response. When he said nothing, she got to her feet and reached out a hand to pull him up. "Come on. I'll show you the inside."

He looked up at her then and said, "In a minute." He took her hand and pulled gently. She sat. Unshed tears glistened in his eyes.

"I just want to stay here for a while. With you." He wrapped an arm around her. "Thanks for telling me, Tia. It make sense to me."

"What makes sense?" she asked, perplexed.

"That you would have a story like that. That a woman as amazing as you would have an amazing story to tell."

He lay back on the ground and Tia settled down alongside him. She took a deep breath of air that smelled of evening and of Connor and felt the cool grass and earth beneath her body. She lay as quietly as she could, breathing and listening to the world, trying to keep her heart open.

There was no voice, no child calling for help. Her mind was still and filled with the peace that comes with knowing the satisfaction of a life well lived.

EPILOGUE

Like so many of the most important moments in her life, this one was private, almost intimate. The small gathering felt absolutely right to her. Tia hadn't wanted to draw a lot of attention to the day. It was something she needed to do without fanfare or outside attention.

Her parents had made the long journey from Jalisco, and for that she was grateful. The Sawyers had come and the Delafields, too—all five of them, Curtis still limping. Jake Sawyer and Ringo had teamed up to keep the Delafield twins entertained. Lars Norgaard sat in a wicker chair in the shade of an elm tree, holding his infant granddaughter, looking every bit the proud grandpa.

A few guests still lingered around the long table laden with pulled pork, carne asada, homemade tortillas, beans, fresh corn on the cob, and half a dozen varieties of peppers and salsa. Tia walked over to Ben and they embraced.

"You know how much I appreciate this," Tia said. "I could never have gotten it done without you. It means a lot to me."

He shrugged. "I wish I could do more."

She stood shoulder to shoulder with him outside the trailer where she'd been raised. They looked at the young grass, the new headstone. It was a simple, unornamented slab of dark marble. The single engraved word read simply: *Mija*. There were no dates.

Ben said, "The coroner tried really hard to identify her, but came up empty. Nothing in the national databases, nothing in Southern California, where Kane and Tanner picked her up. If she was from Mexico, she wasn't reported missing there." He sighed. "Eventually she would have been cremated and put in the county vault. It wasn't hard to arrange a private-property burial instead." He rested a hand on Tia's shoulder. "I think this is much better."

Tia remembered what the priest had said during the short, simple service. He had spoken of the tragic death of one so young and so alone. It seemed likely, he said, that somewhere a family would wonder what had become of their little girl. Someday the issues that cause such isolation and desperation must be resolved, the depravity that preys on the poorest and most vulnerable among us must be stopped. But for now, this young woman was at peace. He hoped that someday her family would find peace as well. "She's welcome here," Tia said. "She's part of my family now."

Together Tia and Ben walked toward the farmhouse. Ben asked, "Are you ready? I mean, for the case against Kane. Sounds like it will be quite the production."

"Yeah. He's not interested in a plea deal. Then again, the district attorney hasn't offered much. She's bound and determined to see that he spends the rest of his life in a Wisconsin prison. But yeah, I'm ready. They can come at me with whatever they want."

"I got a call from the office of the Director of National Security this week. Nice guy. Pretty high up the food chain. Assistant to the assistant director or something like that."

"And?" Tia sounded unfazed.

"Apparently DTAT has been disbanded. Stahl's been reassigned.

He's working for the U.S. Postal Inspector sorting suspicious mail in Nome."

Tia shook her head, feeling nothing, not even a mild sense of satisfaction. "So be it, I guess."

"Yeah, sounds like a good job for him. But anyway, the guy from ONDI. He just wanted to pass on that if there was anything we needed in the case against Kane we're welcome to it. He also said they're not the least bit interested in seeking jurisdiction over your shooting."

Tia wasn't impressed. "Big of them."

"You know, Tia. It'll be a little while before the trial. If you want to take some time off, I'd completely understand. You can have all the time you need."

Tia stopped and looked at him. "What do you mean? Like, to go see Gage or something?"

"No. Of course not." Ben sounded pained. "I'm not saying that at all. Just if you need to decompress, you know? Maybe you and Connor could take a vacation."

"Thanks, Ben. But I'm good. Really."

"All right." Ben nodded. "And, I gotta say, you do seem pretty much like the old Tia."

She laughed at the irony of his words and laughed even harder when he looked puzzled. "It's nothing, Chief, trust me. Some things are left best unsaid."

They'd reached Connor and Alex, eliminating any reason for Tia to explain further. It felt good to be surrounded by those she was closest to. Alex took Ben by the arm and said she wasn't getting seconds unless he came with her. He smiled and she dragged him in the direction of the food.

"I saw your dad," Connor said. "He said he thinks you should move back to the farm. In Mexico. Did he tell you that?"

"Oh yeah. That's my dad. He keeps saying it's time for us all to be a family, home in Mexico." Tia walked back toward the trailer, Connor at her side.

With a hint of anxiety in his voice, Connor said, "I thought we agreed. I thought you and I were—"

She put a finger on his lips, a gesture that was quickly becoming a playful habit. "Shhh. Take it easy, Connor."

He pulled her hand away and held it tight. "I don't want to take it easy. I thought we agreed that there was no reason for you to leave. Nothing's changed. Has it?"

Tia turned her head to look at him directly. "You ready to walk around with this secret for the next thirty or forty years, Connor? The cop who's a 'you know what'?"

Connor wasn't amused. "I already told you, I'm holding on to bigger secrets than that, Tia. Some of 'em would make pretty good bargaining chips if need be. But yeah. I say it's nobody's business what happened twenty-some years ago. I say we look forward. To the future, Tia. Not the past."

Tia took a knee by the gravestone, thinking of a little girl dying in a Texas labor camp. A mother, somewhere in Mexico, praying for a daughter she had given up. Another, praying for the return of one who had somehow lost her way. A young marine holding on to life in a foreign desert, ten thousand miles from home.

There was no undoing all the twists and turns that had brought any of them to this time and place, but Tia was certain of one thing.

This is where I belong.

Connor reached down and touched her cheek. "I don't want you to leave, Tia. We can have a life together. You and me."

"My dad said I should come home, Connor." She stood, reached up, and took him by the back of the neck, pulling his head down so she could whisper in his ear.

"I told him, *I am home.*"